THE ONE FACING US

THE ONE FACING US

A Novel

Ronit Matalon

Translation by Marsha Weinstein

METROPOLITAN BOOKS

Henry Holt and Company • New York

Metropolitan Books
Henry Holt and Company, Inc.
Publishers since 1866
115 West 18th Street
New York, New York 10011

Metropolitan Books is an imprint of
Henry Holt and Company, Inc.

Library of Congress Cataloging-in-Publication Data
Matalon, Ronit.
[Zeh 'im ha-panim elenu. English]
The one facing us : a novel / Ronit Matalon ; translation
by Marsha Weinstein. — 1st American ed.
    p.   cm.
ISBN 0-8050-4880-4 (alk. paper)
I. Weinstein, Marsha. II. Title.
PJ5054.M3274Z3413 1998   97-32303
892.4'36—dc21   CIP

Henry Holt books are available for special promotions
and premiums. For details contact: Director, Special Markets.

First American Edition 1998

DESIGN BY BETTY LEW

Printed in the United States of America
All first editions are printed on acid-free paper. ∞

1   3   5   7   9   10   8   6   4   2

My thanks to the painter Yitzhak Livne for permitting me to reproduce his
work *Pool View* (oil on canvas, 98 × 90 cm) on pp. 229 and 279 (photograph
by Meidad Suchowolski). I am grateful to Irit Segoli for introducing me to
Livne's work and for her insight. My thanks to Aharon Amir for allowing me
to reprint Jacqueline Kahanoff's essay "A Childhood in Egypt," from *The Sun
Rises in the East* (Tel Aviv: Hadar, 1978). My sincere thanks to the Berman,
Glusman, Hazan, Laniado, and Matalon families, who permitted me to use
photographs from their collections.

To Aimée and to Felix

THE ONE FACING US

Photograph: Uncle Sicourelle and Workers, the Port of Douala, Cameroon

That's my uncle, not exactly in the center but a bit to the right, the one with the hunched shoulders and thick waist, his back to the camera: his is the most important back, the back in white, the back that speaks.

The other figures do not speak: they are caught up in the routine movements of their bodies. Mute, they turn their backs to us, bending or striding toward the plastic tubs brimming with fish and the stench of fish.

Whom are their gestures for? If for anyone, they are for my uncle, who stands there like a camera on a tripod, behind which a second camera has captured his unwavering gaze.

The camera could just as easily have captured a different arrangement of bodies: the man bending over could just as easily have been standing next to the tub; the one with the bare black chest could just as easily have been something else entirely, a shadow gliding over the smooth paving stones, if by chance he had shifted slightly, moved outside the frame. Chance has erased the faces of these people, melding them into one mass, forging the multiplicity of their diffuse desires into one will, one intent, one response to the dominion of my uncle who stands there with his arms crossed, all eyes and observation.

Just off to the left stand several large objects, a yawning space between them; the photograph abandons all but the three inhabitants who seem to hover there, at the edge of the plaza. To their left is a wooden cabinet with doors of square glass panes. It is a little odd and out of place in the cement plaza, reminiscent of a dim, sheltered room. Instead of making the empty plaza homey, it only seems incongruous.

The covered plaza, paved with large cement slabs, is flooded. Light breaks on the stagnant, fetid water that spills from the plastic tubs, shimmering on the hard cement. The crisp, bright reflection lends everything, even the human activity, the air of a mirage.

· · ·

When does a photograph come into being? At the moment when real and imaginary meet? A photograph offers evidence of what is remembered, but it also intimates what might have been.

I use photographs to span the years, to picture myself wobbling across the plaza on high-heeled winter boots; I nod at my past self as if I were someone else. In the end, I admit that this could be me, and my lineage could supply a possible identity: Look, it's Monsieur Sicourelle's niece, who's come from Tel Aviv via Paris.

I watch the niece hobble across the plaza. I watch her and Madame Sicourelle, Erouan, and Richard cross the stinking wet plaza: Onward! Forward, comrades! On toward the slippery concrete stairs up to an office, *the* office, and to Monsieur Sicourelle, my uncle.

First, leading the way, is Monsieur Richard, Monsieur Sicourelle's secretary and man Friday. He is myopic, rotund, and—despite his intentions—dressed in poor taste.

Three hours earlier, at Douala Airport, the dim eyes behind his thick glasses had watched me walk the half kilometer of dingy gray windowless corridor choked with the sour stench of sweat, debris, and chicken shit: hordes of people were carrying roosters and hens crammed into bamboo cages.

"*Vous êtes la nièce,*" Richard determines in his soft, stickysweet accent, orange and mealy as the flesh of the ripe mango he offers me. "Does Mademoiselle like mango?" he inquires solicitously. Later, waiting in line at passport control, Richard regales me with Monsieur Sicourelle's digestive troubles. It seems Monsieur Sicourelle loves mango better than anything else in the world. Well, actually, mango takes second place. First place goes to chocolate and chocolate alone, at all times and under all circumstances. When Monsieur Sicourelle eats mango, his arms and face break out in a red rash, some kind of allergy. Monsieur Sicourelle is allergic to mango but still insists on eating it, despite Richard's entreaties. It is not good for you, Monsieur, Richard warns, but Monsieur protests. "You only live once, my friend." "That is the kind of stubborn man he is, Mademoiselle." As he talks, Richard fans out bills with his fingers and stuffs them between the pages of my Israeli passport. "This, Mademoiselle, is to smooth your passage," Richard explains. "Every wheel needs some grease, otherwise it gets stuck or makes an awful noise. A good machine requires careful maintenance, and that includes adding grease at regular intervals."

I examine his large face, framed by folds of skin. He looks serious, even severe, but also a bit weary.

Large fans swirl above us, making a monotonous whirring sound, a vacuous counterpoint to the anarchy of the line. What a line! Stretching ahead endlessly, full of children and headless, footless bundles of chickens. The heavy, stagnant air presses down on my two wool sweaters and my swollen feet, which are crammed into high boots. Richard has moved on to another topic: one by one, he flogs them to death.

"Correct administrative procedure," Richard explains. (The clerk vigorously flips through the passport of Sylvie, the young woman in a candy-pink suit who sat beside me on the plane, whimpering and snuffling the whole way like a dog that has been left locked up for so long it has given up hope of being freed and whimpers for the sake of whimpering.)

"Things are different here than in Israel," he continues. (Stocky, armed police in black uniforms appear from the right and pull someone out of line, some VIP in a pale suit.)

"There are a few honest people here and there, but most are corrupt. They only understand the language of power or money." Richard nods toward the money in my passport. (A curly blond head pokes out from around one side of the control booth; behind it, a hand adorned with rings waves at the crowd.)

"*Tiens, c'est l'Afrique, Mademoiselle.*" Richard shrugs. (With his odd accent Richard stresses the "de" in "Mademoiselle," elongating the word and giving it reverence, or at least seeming to—it's hard to tell with him.)

Richard has worked for Uncle Sicourelle for close to fifteen years, first as junior clerk and then as personal secretary, friend, and right-hand man—the one who gets him out of some troubles and into others. According to Marie-Ange, my aunt, Uncle Sicourelle made a man out of Richard, made him what he is. He didn't know a thing when he met my uncle, except how to read and write. My uncle is practically illiterate. He knows four languages, but none of them well. No one has ever seen a letter in his handwriting, in thirty years of business. Richard writes for him, or Aunt Marie-Ange. Uncle Sicourelle prefers Richard, who writes just what he is told to, over Madame, who changes what he wants to say, pouring his shapeless syntax into the molds of her stock phrases. He argues with her over this, among other things. Every letter ends in a blowup. "Go write it yourself, then," Aunt Sicourelle says, pretending to be insulted to mask her relief. "What do you want from me? Write to your family yourself," she says, retiring to her room at the end of the house, her long housecoat trailing behind her. She leaves him to gnaw his nails and stare at the blank page, finally scrawling a few sentences in his tangled hand, then erasing them and doodling the only doodle he knows in the margins: vertical lines, horizontal lines, a hail of diagonal lines above and inside the uneven spaces between them, and curvy lines like wrought-iron *S*s.

Out of the blue he sends photographs, one every few months, without a date, without a word of explanation. "Idiot!" my mother says, her eyes damp and her head shaking as if she doesn't believe her own pronouncement, as if her heart weren't breaking into a million pieces out of longing for him.

I am raised on these photographs. My grandmother, Nona Fortuna, raises me. She cannot see a thing. I hold up five fingers and say, "How many fingers, Nona, can you guess?" But she does not want to guess. She tells me what is in the photographs. "That is your Uncle Jacquo. He is a very rich man in Africa. He owns the whole port. Here you can see his ships at sea—he has five ships!—all of them nothing but trouble. They sail away, they don't come back, he has worries. Here his mouth looks just like it did when he was little, except that now he has no teeth. He lost them from eating too many sweets. Didn't take care of himself, just like everyone else in this family. Slovenly, the lot of you."

"*Mal tenu,*" she says in French scornfully, her lips taut, like when she teaches me the vowels: *a, e, i, o, u.* "Say it again, *sit al-banaat: a, e, i, o, u.*"

She calls me *sit al-banaat,* princess, lady, mistress of all the girls. "Stop, Maman! Stop swelling that child's head," my mother scolds, but Nona does not stop. "Tell him, *sit al-banaat,* tell your uncle his face is always in my heart. Will you tell him?" she asks before I leave.

"I'll tell him, I'll tell him."

"Tell him my heart is with him, and all my thoughts."

"Okay."

"Tell him that when he feels pain, I say 'Ay!' Understand?"

Her empty gaze follows me to the taxi. I see her standing at the edge of the path, immune to the noonday glare, smoking without inhaling. Feathers, withered leaves, and pollen from a nearby tree fall on her gray hair, wound in a bun. Oblivious, she crosses herself. She was an honor student at St. Anne's, a Catholic girls' school in Cairo.

At the last minute she shoves two gold-plated lead Chanukah menorahs into my bag, for the uncle and his family, a small "souvenir from Maman." When Monsieur Richard takes the bag from my hands he blanches, his dark cheeks turning a pallid gray. "This is heavy, Mademoiselle," he notes.

Outside the airport it is humid, cloudy, and still. The earth on the other side of the narrow road where the limousines and taxis are parked is burned, black. Some distance away stand strange, flimsy structures, shacks or makeshift houses, built of crooked plywood boards. Beside them, immense scorched barrels give off smoke. The place looks like an ancient wound: the scarred, afflicted earth and the unsightly attempt at a miserable, dubious urbanity. My heart sinks.

"*La nièce,*" says an unfamiliar female voice, very near, as the shiny doors of a black Bentley open, releasing a chill, fragrant draft of air-conditioning. Aunt Sicourelle is the first to peck my cheeks. "It took you a long time in there," she complains, fanning herself with a thin sheet of paper bearing my flight information. Richard straightens his tie, clears his throat, and prepares to make a speech: "*Vous savez, Madame, que—*" But Madame has no patience for him. "It is very hot today," Aunt Sicourelle mumbles absently, pushing me gently toward a man with dark glasses who is leaning on the car fender, watching.

"This is your cousin Erouan."

Erouan is twirling a key chain around his finger. He offers his sleek, freckled cheek. "Exactly two hours and twenty-three minutes," he says.

We sit, Richard and I in the back, my aunt in front next to Erouan, the driver.

"Twenty-three minutes?" my aunt asks, powdering her nose in the rearview mirror.

"Two hours and twenty-three minutes," Erouan corrects, turning the key in the ignition. "That's how long it took them to come out."

Richard tries again. "*Vous savez, Monsieur, que—*" but immediately leans back against the seat, grasping the handle in the roof. Erouan is intent on his steering wheel, pressing the gas pedal to the floor. It feels like he is tearing up the broken roads with their potholes and roadside stands and peddlers' carts dragged by three-wheeled mopeds or four-legged beasts. Black children throng the stalls, hanging off them or jumping heedlessly, joyously between the wheels of the cars.

"This is the main street of Douala," Aunt Sicourelle explains in a monotone, her eyes closed. I can tell that her eyes are closed by the way her head is thrown back and by the perfumed handkerchief that covers her forehead down to her eyebrows. "At this hour of the day this place is a catastrophe, a catastrophe."

"Don't exaggerate, Maman," Erouan protests. "You always exaggerate. Don't alarm her for nothing."

"Am I exaggerating?" Madame Sicourelle asks, insulted. "I am not exaggerating, young man, I am being realistic, unlike some of us."

"Don't start with that again, Maman," he says, annoyed, lighting a cigarette and waving his arms in exasperation, letting go of the steering wheel until the car veers sideways.

Behind the two of them, Richard and I have practically become friends. A pact of fear and apprehension, the solidarity of passengers, rivets us to the back of our seat as the car weaves down the road. Ours is a purely functional pact, like that of poor people waiting for food: it will last only until we get out of this all right.

We do get out of it, about an hour later according to Erouan and his ugly beeping watch. To our right is the ocean, shrouded in a vast twilight, dotted with ships cluttered with masts, rags, and plastic tubs; to the left is the port, its deserted, flooded plaza illuminated by a weak spotlight that brightens one corner, relegating the rest to oblivion.

Menacing objects are strewn about the wet, shadowy plaza: empty crates stinking of fish, one crate on its side, another upended, draped with fraying fishing nets, a plank studded with bent, rusty nails jutting out here and there.

This is the ultimate desertion, the exit of meaning; this is all that is left when the day is over and the people who gave life to these things are gone. This is what remains after the photograph has been taken.

"Careful, careful!" Madame Sicourelle says to no one in particular; she gathers the hem of her skirt and places one foot in a puddle with an expression of disgust and daintiness. Richard passes on her right, stomping like an old horse in water, holding his brown briefcase on his head. "Careful, mesdames, careful," he says, tossing aside a spurned crate as he reaches the foot of the stairs.

Yellow light bursts from the windows of the office above. Uncle Sicourelle is dragging out his meeting with the Lebanese buyers who want their seafood at a good price.

Uncle Sicourelle has the bearing of a pasha. He sits for hours with the portly Lebanese buyers, who are festooned with glittery ornaments. From time to time one tears off a piece of pistachio-studded Turkish delight or pecks at the cracked Syrian olives and the gooey, salty cheese, clinking the ice cubes in his tall glass of pastis or Ricard.

So they sit, Uncle Sicourelle and the sly, corpulent buyers, lovingly prolonging their negotiations under a cloud of cigar smoke and the pungent smells of mold, sea, and fish, gliding on tiptoe around and around, hinting and not hinting at that unmentionable thing in their midst that tugs at their semblance of camaraderie, goodwill, and pleasant conversation: money.

Madame Sicourelle can contain herself no longer: "Chouchou," she says in a small, tentative voice, "Chouchou, this is your niece who has just arrived."

Missing Photograph: Uncle Sicourelle in His Office, the Port of Douala, Cameroon

There is a space of some ten centimeters between the right-hand edge of the enormous desk and the office wall. Through that space Uncle Sicourelle squeezes every day, several times a day, to reach his executive's chair: he stands on tiptoe, bends forward slightly, and rests his large belly on the desk as he presses himself past.

Richard looks pained whenever Uncle Sicourelle does this. He sits at his own small desk opposite the uncle's and peers from behind high piles of yellow and white paper. "Perhaps we should shorten your desk, Monsieur. We could cut a bit off one side," Richard suggests.

The uncle, who has already maneuvered halfway through the

space, is caustic. "Why don't we shorten you, Richard, chop you up very fine and make a *kookla* patty out of you," he says.

He falls into his seat, his thin legs splayed under the table and his bent toes massaging the soles of his slippers. He consents to the camera. He leans his body to one side, throwing the bulk of his weight onto his arm; the curtain behind him hangs loosely from its hooks; its folds rest on his bald head, which pokes from beneath the length of cloth as if from under the hem of a fat lady's long skirt.

The vast brown surface of the desk forms a dark mass in the middle of the photograph. It takes up only half the room, but seems to fill it entirely.

Behind the desk and the man leaning over it, behind the sagging curtain, large glass windows open onto the port. They are covered with a thick layer of dust and grease and old fingerprints. Beyond is the sea, bright lights dotting it like clusters of water lilies. I glimpse the sea for an instant when the uncle rises, irritably tossing the curtain aside and looking up for the first time, high over the heads of the Lebanese buyers, blinking.

"*La nièce,*" says Uncle Sicourelle to the room, spreading his arms wide. "*Ma nièce,*" he explains to the buyers, who nod their heads at me.

At fifty-five, Uncle Sicourelle has survived ten bankruptcies, many moves across the African continent from one struggling factory to the next, and every illness the place has to offer. Toothless and hairless—but with a voice like Tino Rossi's that makes women melt—he seems now more than ever to have been branded by the tyrannical mark of family likeness shared by Nona Fortuna, my mother, and Uncle Moise: the sensual lips tempered by severe, deep creases at either side of the mouth, the sunken cheeks, the prominent aristocratic bones seemingly unrelated to the heavy, indolent body, covered carelessly by the cloth of some shirt.

For thirty years he lived a life apart, roaming Africa like a tyrant, until the sentimentality of old age—the vibrato of emotion—seized him. Suddenly he had to see *quelqu'un de la famille,* had to have someone from the family come stay with him in his enormous house. Why not? There's plenty of room, and Madame Sicourelle would be happy to have someone to talk to, go shopping with, *une compagne,* he wrote.

• • •

From inside her deep cynicism, which grows deeper by the year and gathers evidence the way a stone in the bend of a river gathers flotsam and jetsam, Nona Fortuna doesn't believe him. "This is not like my son, this letter; it's that woman's doing—that woman," Nona says, her fingers skimming the plate, pressing cake crumbs into balls and, without looking, stuffing them into her mouth.

She drives Mother nearly out of her mind with her sharp words, jabbed like a burning torch up the ass. The two of them have a way of latching onto each other, digging into each other's flesh like rabid dogs, froth and blood and all, not letting go until overcome by fatigue or domesticity: an armoire that needs moving, a pot that needs stirring, the troubles of others, the body's failing.

Mother paces the room in her sleeveless summer shift, her pudgy white arms swinging in the air and furiously, imploringly punching out pleas that fall flat at the feet of the implacable old woman listening politely from her chair with the bemused curiosity of a modern-day missile confronting the bows and arrows of yore.

They send me to Africa, to the magnificent uncle, maybe he'll screw my head on straight, get me to settle down, if not here then there, what does it matter as long as something—if not the beef, at least the broth—the merest smudge of a notion of the patriarchal *famiglia* rubs off on me.

Uncle Sicourelle knows this; he comes from that family. He walks toward me, crossing the room as if no one else were present, his purposeful step leaving the others behind, putting the foreigners where they belong, in the void of not-family.

"*Anestina, ya bint al-uhti*"—You have delighted us, my sister's daughter—he says in Arabic, blinking his moist, narrow eyes and placing his large palms on my head, leaving them there a long moment, blessing me.

· · ·

Behind us, Madame Sicourelle dabs her nose. "It is so moving, Chouchou, your niece, after all these years," she sniffles. In an outburst of goodwill, heart overflowing, she turns to the others, explaining: "Monsieur Sicourelle has not seen anyone from his family for years, simply ages, *imaginez-vous!*"

Madame is not what she seems. I pondered this long and hard. I had plenty of time to think: the two hundred days I spent fishing yellowing mango leaves out of the swimming pool, wielding a long pole with a basket at its tip. Each eye-opening mango leaf spawned a new thought. It's not that she's malicious, she's merely impervious, absolutely indifferent to words and their nuances. She is sewed up tight all around; her impenetrability has taken on a life of its own, become an empire with cities and bridges, neighborhoods and villages, laws, traffic lights, alley cats. She is a world of errors and falterings, awkwardnesses of deed and word, a universe of faux pas waiting to happen.

Uncle Sicourelle shuts his eyes forcefully in the rank office, willing himself to stoicism with each passing second, waiting for Madame's battery to run down as if she were a mechanical toy making noisy turns about the room.

He clasps my elbow, his eyes searching out an empty chair, at last seating me in his executive's swivel chair and himself on the edge of the desk opposite, rotating the chair with his foot. "Your father," he asks, lowering his voice, "what's become of your father?" He speaks in Arabic, forcing on me an intimacy with a world that has never been mine: the derelict alleys of his life and memory, the empty streets prowled by gallant men in their twenties with dim, despair-filled futures, surviving on honor from one day to the next—shrewd cads with perfectly manicured fingernails, Levantine types like him and my father, bosom buddies in the Cairo of the 1930s.

"It's your uncle that brought him—your father—home to us; they were great friends, *ruh b'ruh,* soul mates," Mother said, swishing her filthy, blistered feet in a bowl of warm water in the roofless kitchen, which was open to the night sky. Stars fell all about us, and planes in flight tore the skies apart. For four months, all winter and into early spring, the kitchen had been undergoing a thorough remodeling that came to a halt when the money ran out.

"Every night he would bring your father home with three, four, five other friends. They all came, one sleeping on the porch, another on the floor, two in the attic—they slept everywhere. In the morning men would emerge from every corner of the house. Your father always appeared without a wrinkle in his suit, not a single crease; he would wake like a prince who had just washed and dressed," Mother said, clinging to the mist clouding her eyes. This mist of compassion and longing oils the story, easing it along, diluting the venom spit out with the words "your father"; it clears a space around the source of infection— the wound of memory—for reality, for an existence whose warmth and vitality shield the place where the blow falls.

She bore no grudge against Uncle Sicourelle, at least not when she cursed the dark, cramped office in the photograph. "How on earth can someone from our family sit in such a dump?" she cried, poring over the photograph as if torn between an urge to understand the meaning of the dismal office, to find an aesthetic principle behind its neglect, and her acute pragmatic instinct to grab a hammer, screwdriver, and broom and barge straight into the photograph, airing, expanding, dismantling, moving, tearing up, and turning the whole place inside out, as she said.

But Uncle Sicourelle dislikes having his things touched. Gently he pushes aside my elbow, which is resting on the back of a black appointment book, and furrows his brow. "*Ton père*," he asks again, "what has become of him?"

"I really don't know, Monsieur. I haven't a clue."

Photograph: Left to right: *Uncle Sicourelle, Erouan, and Father, Gabon, 1956*

They met (of course they met) in Gabon, when Uncle Sicourelle was running a leather factory there. It was during his third wealthy period. My father knew nothing, not about leather or anything else manual. He could barely change a lightbulb. The factory made a big impression on him, and he of all people knew how to be impressed. Anyway, the point is they did indeed meet, despite what my father said.

The fact of the meeting came between them—body facing body, words confronting words, glasses clinking. A wedge came between them that precluded communion, halted the ascent of their shared aspirations, which had long ago taken flight, leaving them behind.

My father came with all his friends in tow: Jacques Taieb, a Tunisian-French anthropologist and journalist who organized the trip and paid for it; the photographer Pierre Boucherat; Florence Goldman, an American studying in Geneva; and Salomon, a friend and gofer who followed my father like a shadow.

They were on their way to central Africa, to the depths of the jungle, and Father would not return for two years, until the year before I was born, bringing back slides and stories that he had published in five European papers. He and the others were in quest of the three kingdoms that burned in his brain like a mantra: the kingdom of diamonds, the kingdom of gorillas, and the kingdom of the pygmies.

In the dark of night they and their gear arrived at the house in Gabon. Uncle Sicourelle slept. He had fallen asleep fully clothed and slack-jawed in front of the television, a brown trail of chocolate saliva inching from the corner of his mouth toward his chin. He prepared a midnight snack of fried eggs and salami (he did not want to wake the boy) and took out a wheel of Edam cheese and jars and jars of things he had pickled himself—turnips, cucumbers, cabbage, cauliflower, carrots sliced in thin slivers, lemons. Father did not eat. A thin man, he picked at this and that, gulping down cup after cup of black Turkish coffee and smoking without cease. Later, after Uncle Sicourelle had made beds for the others— he put Florence Goldman, whom they called "la petite Florence," in his study—he and Father sat up in the kitchen until dawn.

Father talked and Uncle Sicourelle listened, from time to time shooing away the cat, which insisted on nestling in his lap and purring insatiably.

They had not seen each other for eight years. Uncle Sicourelle had left Cairo first, "to make a fortune in Africa." When he'd said that, Nona had hurled a vase at him. He'd ducked. The vase had shattered the colored glass partition.

Father had encouraged Uncle Sicourelle, had pushed him to leave and get away from the "Zionist scourge"—from Ha-shomer Hatzair, *le mouvement,* and all that—which had taken hold of Mother's two other brothers.

Moise, the eldest brother, the one who brought Zionism home, would talk to Uncle Sicourelle for hours, heart to heart. *Le mouvement* had given him experience in talking. He had a square, confident jaw and a natural instinct for authority; Uncle Moise never raised his voice, not once.

He was like the leader of a cult, with his thong sandals, his incessant furtive wheeling and dealing, and the punching bag and rings for strengthening his muscles that hung from his ceiling, cracking it and bringing a hail of plaster onto the lace sheets. He had a mythic capacity for food. He was the one with the strong nerves in a family of weak, jittery types who could drown in half a glass of water.

One by one he would trot out his arguments, each in its turn. First, he would talk to Uncle Sicourelle about the decline of decadent Egyptian society, which had contracted every imaginable social ill. Then he would describe the unique yet tenuous, even dangerous place held by the Jewish bourgeoisie in that society. "There's no way out," he would conclude, "not individually and not collectively. The choices are very clear. You'd have to be blind not to see them: you can be a Zionist or a Communist. Those are the only options," he would say.

They would spend hours in the living room, which was padded with heavy carpets that muffled Uncle Moise's steps as he paced back and forth. Everyone would listen from behind the door, peeking around it to see Uncle Sicourelle's black-and-white shoe tapping.

In his immaculate three-piece suit, Uncle Sicourelle would slouch in the armchair, his legs splayed. "What about just being a person?" he would ask, inspecting his fingernails. "Isn't that an option?"

Uncle Moise seemed never to respond, instead mopping his brow with a checked cotton handkerchief in the dark room thick with decisions long since made and words whose time had passed. Everything had gone awry: each uncle had been kicked into his own corner, left to determine his own life, unique as the initials embroidered, thread by thread, on his baby blanket and good sheets.

The room would stay dark after these conversations, after the uncles had gone out into the street to mingle with the throngs in the heavy heat; dark behind the blue velvet curtains that were removed in summer, aired out in fall, and then rehung in every new apartment. Each fall the curtains would move along with the nanny, the laundress, the cook, the gardener, an immense grandmother from each side, and vats of date cookies hidden from greedy children beneath monogrammed sheets. Always just one step ahead of a legion of irate landlords who demanded the cost of repairs, they moved twenty times or more—from neighborhood to neighborhood or within the same neighborhood in Cairo, from one side of the street to the other, from an apartment that faced the yard to one that faced the street. During summer vacations they went to my grandfather's summer house in Hilwan, in the hills.

That's where Uncle Sicourelle saw her—saw Nadine—for the first time. She was sixteen, too tall, too thin, too stooped, and Father's younger sister. Uncle Sicourelle called her "*harisa*": a dry, brown, shriveled cake. When she wasn't reading a book or playing an instrument or wandering in the Japanese gardens she would torment everyone, pricking them bloodlessly with the sharp pins of her words.

She had a way of moving, of crossing a space silently, of standing close to the walls, making her way under cover of heavy furniture and dark hallways, avoiding mirrors and appearing suddenly, like an apparition materializing out of nowhere.

She weighed heavily on Uncle Sicourelle's heart. There was something troubling about her, like an itch or a chore left undone. When he tried to conjure her face months and years later, he drew a blank, saw only a blur, as if she were an idea, an abstraction.

He would ask about her from time to time, although there really was no one in Africa who would have known anything. The few whites he befriended had, like himself, left the past where it belonged. But on that same long night, suffering heartburn from too many cigarettes and pickled lemons, he did ask Father. "Your sister Nadine," he said. "What's become of her?"

By then it was morning. Throughout the house, doors slammed, taps spewed water noisily into bathtubs, and the yellow cabs beyond the palm trees that lined the street sought someone to run down with a scandalous screech of tires.

Augustin—the boy—arrived, moving languidly through the kitchen, wiping the dust from the furniture with a cloth and clearing away the remains of their midnight meal. He whistled to the dogs in the yard to come and enjoy the leftovers. Madame Sicourelle, in her orange robe, was surprised. She had heard nothing, she knew nothing, he told her nothing. "Chouchou," she admonished, wagging her finger at Uncle Sicourelle. Father leaned over the back of her hand and kissed it. He had heard about her and had longed to meet her.

Uncle Sicourelle left for the bathroom when she began asking about the family, about Maman and Inès, Simeon and Dalia, Moise and his little ones, Sarah and her daughter Smadar, Marcelle and Nissim and Iris, Toto, Edouard and Haya and the girls, and the one with the funny hat in the picture—what was his name? Berto.

Uncle left in midlist, one hand over his face. He could not bear her pronunciation of the Hebrew names, which on his frequent journeys, in the loneliness of the car, he would gnash like gravel between his teeth in awe and rage.

When he came back, washed and shaven, with Erouan, then six, hanging about his neck, he hurried Father along. Father stood up in the middle of his story about King Farouk's falling in love with one Laila, a poor Jewess and a close friend of his mother's. Madame Sicourelle's large blue eyes were opened wide. From a family of poor Breton farmers, she had barely seen the world, and Father's casual shuffling of the hierarchy—royal families, wealthy noblemen, Jewish merchants, peasants—his dismantling it, then reassembling its parts like colorful building blocks, worked its magic on her.

Before noon they went into town to the bank, to arrange the loans Father had asked for. Pierre Boucherat went along and photographed them sitting at an outdoor café waiting for the menu, or perhaps it was after everything had been cleared away, the tall glasses and Erouan's dish of ice cream that had dripped and dripped, staining Uncle Sicourelle's off-white safari suit.

Back then Uncle Sicourelle still cared about his appearance. Suits that fit properly, custom-made shoes, and a thin comb that he took from his jacket pocket several times a day. In the foreground of the picture is the empty cane chair where Pierre Boucherat had been sitting only moments before he stood to photograph them. He commanded their attention, especially that of the child, who had long since gotten bored and now grasped the end of the table as if he wanted to escape. The hand that rested on him imposed its authority, holding him still like a tangible sign of the photographer's or the camera's will.

Uncle Sicourelle sits stiffly at some distance from the table. He is ceremonious, not happy but polite, acquiescent, chilling.

Beside him Father is a bit disheveled, with his narrow, sunken chest and his elbows on the table. He is turning slightly to the side, a cigarette held limply, absently between his fingers. He escapes the scene through the dialogue he has with what is most immediate: the photographer behind the camera, beyond the photograph. Father's lips droop. He is wrecked from the long night, which squeezed the life out of him, and from his plans, which—for a moment, for the duration of this photograph—he has shunted aside like an inconvenient bill that has come due.

The noon light shines on them, the emptiness of the street, and the front of the building behind them, with its row of air conditioners on the second floor, above the liquor store whose awning says SHO; a pedestrian pauses there aimlessly.

The pedestrian is stuck there between Uncle Sicourelle's shoulders and the cheek of the child, who is making a face, twisting his mouth and sticking the tip of his tongue out over his lip, his little leg resting on Uncle Sicourelle's thigh, his sockless foot fastened into a two-toned sandal.

His light bangs, cut carelessly, are barely discernible above his pale face, weak beside the dark, energetic face of my uncle. Most striking is my uncle's forehead, with its deep depression between the eyebrows and the eyes: a marked forehead.

The child was four when he met Uncle Sicourelle. He would not utter a word. Marie-Ange, then a young widow in Brazzaville without a penny to her name, had dragged him from one doctor to the next. Uncle Sicourelle had put a stop to that. He loathed doctors, male or female, along with waiting rooms, sick beds, and hospitals—anything that hinted at the weakening of the body or mind or that, as he thought, ultimately brought it about. He took the child in hand: *gymnastique* morning and night, heavy meat meals, an occasional glass of sherry, and a daily dose of the "man's world" of his factory.

The individual components of Uncle Sicourelle's recovery regimen vanished one by one before they had a chance to become a burden; the only continued semblance of a routine was Erouan's daily factory visits. For hours the child would sit on the floor in a corner of the factory office, crushing ants between his fingers, scribbling on old letters that Richard gave him, staring into space, or sinking into slumber, curled up with his blanket, wet and filthy with dust, stuffed into his mouth. All who came into the office—laborers, foremen, buyers, and guests—would cautiously step over the little body, hushing themselves with a long "Ssshhhhhh" at the door.

In the evenings, after work, Uncle Sicourelle would carry the boy out and place him on the backseat of the car among brightly wrapped packages large and small—furry rabbits, electric trains, chocolates, police cars and fire trucks and marzipan shaped like animals, trains, cars, flowers, fruit.

A few meters from the house he would turn off the engine, move to the backseat, and begin to unwrap the packages, flinging the torn paper to the car floor. "*Mange!*" he would order the child, his own mouth full of chocolate and marzipan. "*Mange!*" They would stay in the darkness of the car for a long while, tearing at the stiff cellophane wrappers, swallowing chocolates filled with cognac and sour cherries. Then they'd step into the chill air, bend over, and vomit—first the child and then Uncle Sicourelle—until Augustin appeared with his oil lamp at the entrance to his shack and rent the night's silence with a shrill cry: "Who's there? Who's there?"

Uncle Sicourelle loved this story. He told it over and over with a radiant face and liberal inaccuracy, changing the details every time, erasing and inventing them anew. One time it was trains and another tractors, one time it was the darkness of the car and another the bathroom or under the mango tree in the yard, one time Erouan was four and others he was five or six or seven, and it would be Madame who discovered them while Augustin napped in the yard. As for the sweets, on any given day they might be chocolate bonbons or marzipan or cherry cordials, depending on his feelings toward one or the other.

He always told the story in front of Erouan, who picked at his teeth with a toothpick in disinterest, his cheeks flushed with a web of thin capillaries that made him look both sickly and clownish. He would repeat the story as if in Erouan's honor, as if the story conveyed something warm and good about the boy's life, their life; as if the very words were warm and good, a glowing piece of tinder they clasped at either end, both warmed and scorched by it.

Uncle Sicourelle had all sorts of amorphous desires and vague plans for the boy who became his son at the age of four. There were no other children. There was only this one reticent, self-contained boy, every blink of whose watery eyes as he pored over the sports pages of the paper for hours each morning reminded Uncle Sicourelle of the inescapable role of heredity. Daily Erouan confronted Uncle Sicourelle with this fact, as if raining down blows on someone who has done nothing to deserve them.

I was one of the plans Uncle Sicourelle devised for his son. Like all the others, it came to him spontaneously and had something tragic and doomed about it. He brought me to Africa because he was driven by an oppressive need to fix things, to put back together what had been broken somewhere else, at some other time, by people who were not him, or not only him.

"*Quelqu'un de la famille,*" he had written to Mother euphemistically, his real meaning as easy to spring as a jack-in-the-box. After all, she spoke his language, the language of their childhood experience, real and imagined. It was rich in names, descriptions, and smells, code words for that experience, which photographs proved or disproved. Or did neither, instead representing an obscure third world where misapprehension grew, like a culture in a petri dish, into error and illusion.

I was five when I first saw the photograph of my uncle, Father, and Erouan. There is a photograph of me looking at it. In it, I am sitting on the striped rug in Mother's bedroom, leaning against the bed. I am wearing a bulky dark sweater and pedal pushers that reveal my socks, sagging above my high winter shoes. Wild thick hair hides nearly half my face, covering my eyes like a wide black thatch. The broad tree in the window behind me casts a shadow and darkens the room. In fact, it nearly blackens this photograph of me, which looks like a play of light and dark splotches in whose center is Mother's brown bedspread. It was Uncle Moise who took the picture: I did not look up. I hid the stolen photograph behind my back.

"What do you have there? Come, let me see," Mother said. I showed her. "That's from Africa, that is," she said. I fell in love with the angel child in the photograph, with his two-toned shoes. That spring I led Nona Fortuna to the shoe store. I forced my feet into similar shoes, two sizes too small.

The photograph of Erouan became worn; buried among broken pencils, beetles in matchboxes, and crumbs it lay forgotten at the bottoms of drawers. When Father returned once more, Nona kept him with her at first to prevent war between him and Mother. "This is your father," Nona Fortuna said, presenting him to me. I showed Father the photograph. "Oh, but I never saw your uncle there," he said. "That's your Uncle Edouard in the picture, your mother's brother. He visited the uncle in Gabon; he was looking for work."

Photograph: Father in a Room

Father sits in a room, the time and place unknown: it could be any time within a twenty-year period, any of twenty different places or circumstances.

All that information might be on the back of the photograph; none of it appears in it. But what is the back of a photograph? A word or two offering a meager explanation, like the jungle of television wires where we hope to find, hiding, the little man who appears on the screen.

This photograph is not of "Father" but of "*the* father," the universal archetype, the immutable image of "father," divorced from time, place, circumstance. His slim signature of a moustache, his Omar Sharif smile, his shiny shoes vanquish the fleeting capriciousness of the moment.

The photograph is in perfect condition, smoothed by the gentle movement of a palm like the sheet over a corpse. There are no greasy fingerprints to indicate the passage of time; there is nothing to indicate the place.

He hated the specifics of place and portrait. In Israel he was constrained to only one place and one portrait. But not in Cairo. In Cairo there were a thousand possible places. He never missed Cairo, though; he just kept inventing new places, preserving his illusion that there would always be a thousand places for him to go, a thousand shimmering possibilities of place. And where did he not go, seeking glory and then fleeing it; where did he not write that he had been, pretend that he had been?

Something about the floor of the room is deceptive. To the left of the bed, under the small, squat table is a bare patch of floor, with what looks like either parquet or old-fashioned terra-cotta tiles. This detail rivets my attention: if the floor is parquet, then the place is not Israel; if the floor is tile, then the place is Israel.

Overlapping rugs have been placed near the bare patch of floor. The larger one has a maroon and beige pattern. The section of it under Father's feet is fading so badly that it barely looks like part of the same rug. The other, seemingly smaller rug, a shade of pink, is hidden under the larger rug, as if it had been placed there for camouflage, not decoration.

In the lower left corner of the photograph is another pattern, another bit of information, another rug or a robe, blue and red check. The cloth overlaps the two rugs, hinting at the space outside the frame, at a chair perhaps that the robe was tossed onto or at someone wearing a robe, sitting in the chair.

Father's black shoes are polished; he is wearing purple socks. The socks look tight; they seem to hug his ankles. A yellowish sheen on the left ankle troubles me; it might indicate the socks' silkiness, their superior quality, or that the fabric is wearing thinner with each washing.

He washed his socks, his immaculate white shirts, and his underwear by himself. He trusted no one with them.

"I don't know how to do laundry, is that what you're telling me?" Mother would say, annoyed.

"I didn't say that," he'd protest. "I'd rather to do it myself, that's all."

He would soak his socks in the little bathroom sink, dreaming, his arms floating in the water, making bubbles. "What are you dreaming about, there are only two socks in there," Mother would say. Stuck in the corner of his mouth, spilling ash into the soapy water, his cigarette would burn down to the end, to the yellow filter he'd suck for hours.

He lived on cigarettes and coffee, coffee and cigarettes. It was a kind of nervous asceticism. His way of taking a break from the demands of the daily routine. Increasingly the breaks overtook the demands, until the demands became brief intervals, themselves a respite from his interminable restlessness.

Even on Yom Kippur he was like that. Coffee and cigarettes, lazing around on the porch in an undershirt, listening to the Arabic radio station.

"God will punish you, Father," I said as a child, worried. In dusty patent-leather shoes I'd come in from loitering in the central courtyard shared by the synagogues, all nine of them. I'd wander from the Adeni to the Yemenite, from the Yemenite to the Lithuanian, from the Lithuanian to the Tripolitanian, and from the Tripolitanian to the Turkish, with its strong scent of smelling salts and old ladies' lavender.

Father smiled his thin, sad smile. "God does not pay attention to these things, Esther. He has no time for such foolishness."

"He does, he does, he pays attention to everything," I insisted. Father closed his eyes, Umm Kulthum wailing in her frail, wan voice.

"God does not have a corner store, Esther. He does not keep a ledger."

This mention of corner stores and ledgers reminded Mother of our family's debts. "In the house of the hanged man it is best not to speak of the rope," she mumbled, trailing into the kitchen in her nightgown, opening the refrigerator, peering in for a long moment, and then closing it. She fasted. "It's not faith or anything," she explained, "just habit."

"Habits are faith," Father replied, his eyes still closed, ashes falling on his dark pants.

"A habit is not faith," Mother objected. "Faith is faith and habits are habits. I don't believe in it, but I'm used to it. I've been fasting since I was twelve. Should I stop now?"

"So don't stop, Inès. Who told you to stop? Everybody does what's best for them."

Mother was silent a minute, brooding. "What do you mean, everybody does what's best for them?" she asked, tearing rough dead skin from her toes.

"Nothing, Inès. What do I mean? *Vivre et laissez vivre,* live and let live, that's all."

"Yes, but you meant something by it. I know when you're trying to say something."

He sat up and stuffed his undershirt into his pants, his slim, bony shoulders drooping toward his chest. "I swear I don't know what you want, Inès."

He wandered off down the path to sit a while with Nona Fortuna. Nona had an agreement with God: At precisely one in the afternoon, she sipped soup. "Even half a day is something. It's better than nothing," she'd say.

Standing in Nona's kitchen, he heated his coffee, transfixed by the bubbling brown turbulence until it boiled over, flooding the stovetop. Slowly he mopped it up with a rag, sucking on the finger that had brushed the white-hot burner. By the time he was finished, the coffee had cooled in the cup. He poured it into the sink and started over, this time tense, his hand resting on the gas knob.

Mother followed him and crumpled into an armchair with her legs spread, one nervous knee swinging from side to side. Her body seemed massive and leaden: her thighs thick, the palms of her hands flat against the armrests, her head bobbing heavily from side to side, obeying the inner swirl of dismal thoughts, her heavy breasts rising and falling under the thin material of her nightgown.

• • •

Nona Fortuna began. "It's a hot one, this Yom Kippur."

"It is," said Mother, her voice choked.

"Do you want some coffee, Inès?" Father offered timidly. She shook her thighs, her head. Her eyes were fixed on Nona Fortuna's armoire, on its curved, chubby legs, each one tilting in a different direction. She got up, went over to the armoire, leaned her shoulder against it, and pushed. "What do you need these legs for?" she asked.

Not waiting for an answer, she disappeared for a few minutes and returned with a hammer. She lay down on the floor and began to strike at them. Four heavy blows and the closet landed squarely on the floor, legless.

Father mopped his brow with a handkerchief. "Really, it's much better like that," he concluded.

She smoothed her nightgown as she rose, turning toward the door. "Robert, your things are outside," she said. "I packed for you."

He turned gray. "What things, Inès?"

"Your things, I packed them for you. Everybody does what's best for them. Isn't that what you said? Everybody does what's best for them."

He stood up. Hands shaking, he lit another cigarette from Nona Fortuna's pack, curling his mouth in disgust at the awful tobacco. "How can you smoke these?" he asked.

Mother waited, shrinking as he passed.

"Where's he going to go on Yom Kippur?" Nona Fortuna dared ask. "There isn't even a cat out there! You could have waited a little."

Mother destroyed her with a glance that said, Shut up.

Fierce yellow noonday light scorched the dark asphalt of the road, burning through the thin cloth shoes of the supplicants returning home from synagogue for the afternoon break. Little white knots of people worked their way ceremoniously down the center of the empty street as if floating on the shimmering waves of light.

Father was swallowed up by them, a dark stripe in the white mass, as he trudged toward the corner bus stop, a small suitcase in one hand and a few things wrapped in brown paper in the other, dragging the lazy, skinny legs that in summer stuck out crookedly from his shorts like the legs of a cripple.

Mother watched until he reached the bus stop, until the dark stripe wilted onto the bench and was still. Her back slid down the door frame to the floor, her legs crossing in front of her and her short, thick neck rocking back and forth, slamming her head against the white frame until flakes of paint fell.

Nona Fortuna groped toward the door, reaching out, thrusting her arms forward, and following the steady sound of the banging. "Why did you send him away if you're sorry, tell me?"

"I'm not sorry."

"Go, *sit al-banaat.*" Nona Fortuna turned to me. "Go tell him to come back, at least until there is a bus."

He was lying on the bench, sucking on a cigarette, his head resting on the suitcase. "She said you should come back," I reported.

"Who said?"

"Nona."

He took a small comb out of his jacket pocket and combed his hair.

"Will you come?" I asked.

"Forget it, Esther, forget it. Come sit here a while."

The road had emptied; it was barren, entirely gray and brown: the gray of the asphalt and the dusty brown of the large trash bins, the tree trunks, and the buckled fences around each yard. From time to time someone passed, looked, and nodded in greeting—or didn't. Father smoked with his eyes closed, concealing the cigarette in the palm of his hand and blowing the smoke to the side, to the bushes. "These Jews and their holidays," he said dully.

He was overcome by a sudden fit of coughing, clearing his throat and spitting out a thick greenish liquid. I covered the greenish puddle with sand. "Do you believe there is a God, Father?"

"I do not believe there is a God the way most people conceive him."

"In another way?"

"In another way, perhaps. You have to believe in something."

"I believe there's a God."

"That's fine. It's good that you believe."

"And if I said I didn't, what would you say?"

"That's fine, too. It's fine either way."

"How can it be fine either way? Either there is or there isn't."

He sat up and rested his head against the pole that supported the bus stop's corrugated tin awning. He screwed up his face in a gesture of pain. "You tax the brain. Go, do something to amuse yourself."

"Like what? I have nothing to do."

"Think nice, interesting thoughts—that will amuse you."

"What thoughts? What's nice and interesting?"

"Think for yourself. If I tell you, they won't be your thoughts, they'll be mine."

I remember that his face had the same intense concentration as in the photograph, that sharp focus of the features on some object—the book he clasps in his pale hands—as if his attention is fixed on something. But it isn't really. He is always aware of the presence of his own likeness; he is absorbed by it. He keeps a framed portrait of himself on his night table.

"Look how much he loves himself, that father of yours," Mother notes bitterly.

I try to see what she sees. "Where?" I ask, narrowing my eyes and staring hard.

She takes the photograph from me and turns it over, hiding its face in the orange Formica of the table.

Missing Photograph: La Terrasse, *Douala, 1967*

A colonnade of towering white pillars set at evenly spaced intervals easily supports a huge white structure that stretches the length of the facade high above the dense green of the garden, about half a kilometer from the front gate.

The niece looks at it through the windshield. Streams of warm rain have begun to fall, and it is alternately revealed and obscured as the wipers whip vigorously back and forth, back and forth. "What is that white thing over there?" she asks.

"*La terrasse*," Madame Sicourelle explains curtly. Bending toward the driver's seat, practically lying across Erouan's knees, she leans hard on the horn. In the brief pause between blasts she shouts hoarsely: "Augustin! Augustin!"

Augustin has fallen asleep. Fallen asleep sitting up, the fool, collapsed over a book with the kerosene lamp still lit, reports Erouan, who has gone to examine the situation and come back dripping wet.

With a faint buzz the gate opens reverently. Wrapped in a blanket, a dreadfully gaunt figure hobbles after the car, holding on to the trunk all the way to the front door. Madame opens the window a crack. "Go bring an umbrella, Augustin, go." He brings two: a large black one for Madame and a flowered folding one with a broken mechanism for the visitor.

"This is Mademoiselle Esther, Monsieur Sicourelle's niece," Madame announces dryly, wiping her muddy heels on the doormat. The niece extends a wet hand: "Pleased to meet you, Augustin." Augustin does not know what to do with the hand. He stares for a moment, then touches the tips of the fingers limply. *"Enchanté, Mademoiselle."*

They stand in the dark hall with its wood-paneled ceiling. Spears, lances, and harpoons are hung at angles on the walls, tip to tip. Erouan passes, stepping over the three suitcases that block the hallway. He wants a drink. "I'm parched," he complains, feeling the wall for the light switch. Three low crystal chandeliers light up at once, spreading a dazzling light. "Hurry," pleads Madame Sicourelle, "hurry and have your drink, Fufu. Hélène and Gabriel are already eating dessert, if they have waited for us at all."

She disappears down one of the dark hallways, removing her shoes as she goes. A moment later her voice can be heard, high and impatient. "Show Mademoiselle her room, Augustin." Augustin drags the suitcases down the hall, leaving a wet, winding trail that the niece follows. At its end, before a window cloaked by blue brocade curtains, the hall splits off to the right and to the left. Augustin stops. The niece stops too, studying his toothpick legs lost inside wide khaki army pants. Erouan watches from the end of the hallway, his drink in his hands. "What are you looking for, Augustin? Go on, show her her room." Augustin does not know where her room is.

"Madame did not say which is her room," says Augustin.

Erouan does not hear well. "What?" he asks, approaching. "What are you mumbling about?"

"Madame never said which is her room," Augustin repeats firmly. Madame suddenly appears in a black dress with a million pleats, crossing the hall in a flurry, diffusing a mist of the perfume that envelops her like a cloud of mosquitoes.

"Come with me," she says, grabbing the niece's wrist and leading her to the right, to a small oblong room that looks onto the pool. "This is your room, Esther," says Madame Sicourelle as she struggles with the clasp on her bracelet. "Do you like it?"

"Very much," says the niece, pushing the curtain aside a little and peering out. She whistles softly. "That's quite a pool."

"Can you help me with this awful thing?" Madame Sicourelle asks, thrusting her arm forward. The niece bends over the bronzed arm that has been rubbed with lotion and fastens the clasp. "This bracelet is beautiful, Madame," she says.

"Not Madame," Madame Sicourelle corrects. "*Tante,* or Marie-Ange, or *Tante* Marie-Ange. Okay?"

Erouan is waiting back in the car, lighting one cigarette with another and nervously changing radio stations. "Stop that, Erouan," Madame says. "My head is splitting and Esther has not had an easy day, isn't that right?" She turns on the tiny light above the mirror and glances at the backseat. "Isn't that right?" Her eyes are pale blue and steady, not malicious, just hard.

"Not too bad," says the niece, undoing the top button of her pants in the darkness, under her wide shirt. "On the flight I sat between two women who clinked glasses and chattered over my head the whole time. The black one, Sylvie, was from Cameroon. She'd been studying in France and was coming back for the first time in years to see her brother, who has just gotten out of jail. She was telling this to the other woman, the older one, who kept going to the bathroom—she went about ten times—and every time, she stepped on my feet, dragging all these makeup cases and hatboxes. I wanted to kill her."

Erouan snickers. "I know those types."

"What types?" Madame Sicourelle asks suspiciously. "What types do you know, Erouan?"

"The ones Esther is talking about, all that pain-in-the-neck stuff on airplanes."

"It wasn't really a pain in the neck," says the niece, awed by the huge villas with the vast spaces between them, by the empty sidewalks where not even a cat passes, by the row of tall palms that seem to be arching toward some destination. "Actually, it was interesting. I felt like I was learning something about life in Africa, about the people and all. That girl, Sylvie, you should have seen her, she was very well dressed, her makeup was perfect, but she cried the whole way. For six hours she sipped champagne and cried."

"Where in Cameroon was she from?" Erouan asks flatly, bored.

"I don't know. From one of the cities, I think. I didn't quite catch the name."

"What do you care what city she was from?" says Madame. "Why are you pestering Esther with all these questions? 'Which city? Which village?' Are you drawing a map, Fufu?"

"I just wanted to know," Erouan explains. "Maybe I know her."

"You don't," states Madame Sicourelle. "And even if you do, it's better that you don't."

Erouan pulls the heavy bell at the gate twice, three times. "Their boy is probably busy inside. Let's go around the back," Madame suggests, her sharp heels tapping on the shingled path to the kitchen. They step onto the damp lawn to the left of milky French doors behind which shadows move slowly, in a swirl of clinking glass and silverware and scents of cleanliness, baking, perfume, lemons, and freshly mowed grass.

The kitchen door is ajar and Madame pushes it slightly, startling the boy, who jumps up at once, spilling a ladle of boiling pink liquid on his apron. She sails past him and the huge pots and baskets of potatoes, radishes, and washed lettuce and bursts into the living room. "Marie!" A young woman in a white dress and a ponytail hurries toward her.

"We had begun to think you would not come!" Having just finished dessert, the dinner guests have pushed their chairs back from the table and stretched out their legs in fatigue and pleasure.

"This is Esther, *la nièce,* who has just come from Israel," announces the mistress of the house, whom everyone calls "la belle Hélène." The niece takes off her glasses, wiping them on her shirttail and replacing them, nodding in every direction. One by one the guests approach, kissing her cheeks and offering little sandwiches of caviar and pâté, an aperitif, a chair, a napkin with an embroidered border, comments on the weather.

La belle Hélène is coquettish and flustered. Her heart-shaped, red-smeared lips are fixed in an O shape, as if holding a bubble of chewing gum; she looks alternately seductive and surprised as she floats about like a dancer, defying the force of gravity, gliding from kitchen to living room, commanding and cajoling, cajoling and commanding in a lilting voice that keeps its listeners poised for some great excitement that awaits them like a wrapped gift. She introduces the guests with nonchalant charm, easily sliding from one to another, swallowing her words: "Claude and Justine de Karini—Claude works with your uncle, Monsieur Sicourelle—Alexandre de Vilalville and Lucette de Vilalville and their daughter Emilie, my husband, Gabriel, and Jean-Luc Bellonnie, who arrived not long ago, like you, *ma chérie.*"

"Not long ago is a year," says Jean-Luc, who sits at Esther's right and continually fills her glass.

"A year is not very long around here," says Gabriel, who seems transfixed by the niece's white neck rising from her white button-down shirt. Esther places a hand on her neck and leaves it there, filling her fork with one hand.

"Do you feel unwell?" Jean-Luc asks, bending toward her.

"No, of course not," she says, startled.

"I thought maybe . . . you have your hand on your neck as if something hurts."

"No, nothing hurts. I'm just a bit tired, that's all."

"Those flights are murderous," Monsieur de Vilalville chimes in, having heard the end of the sentence. "I hate to fly. If I could I would sail from place to place."

"So sail, Alexandre," suggests Madame Sicourelle. "Sail. What's keeping you from taking a boat?"

"He has a tendency to get seasick, Marie. He goes all yellow and green when he's on the water," explains Madame de Vilalville.

The niece eats a lot, drinks a lot. Her cheeks are burning.

"Does this interest you?" Jean-Luc asks in a whisper. "Does this conversation interest you?"

"Not very much."

"I didn't think so. Me neither."

"So why are you here?"

"You have to keep up some contact. This is who there is. I work with some of these people. I can't act like a stranger."

"What do you actually do here?"

"I'm a bridge engineer. I'm working on a project up north."

The guests move from the dining room to soft, wide off-white couches sunk deep in a shaggy off-white carpet. They drink liqueurs, herb tea, lemonade. La belle Hélène serves petits fours of mango and kumquat. Erouan is attached to large earphones, checking out the sound of Gabriel's new stereo. His eyes are closed; he moves his head from side to side.

"So tell us something about yourself, Esther," Alexandre de Vilalville says in a fatherly tone. "How old are you?"

"Sixteen and a half, nearly seventeen."

"Like our Emilie. Emilie will be seventeen in December. Are you in school?"

"I finished eleventh grade a week ago."

"Emilie would be happy to show you around. What do you like to do?"

"I don't know. Read, mostly. Listen to music. I like to study, too, I think."

"Very clever," explains Madame Sicourelle, turning to her. "Nevertheless, you must clear your head from time to time, Esther, have a little fun. This is the age."

"I don't agree at all, Marie," Justine de Karini interrupts. "I say as long as there is the will to learn you must take advantage of it. That is the only way to succeed."

Jean-Luc cracks a pecan, offers Esther its peeled meat. "These nuts are wonderful. Taste one."

"I can't. I've never eaten so many courses in my life."

"You'll get used to it. You eat a little bit of each one, that's the idea."

"I can't get used to the 'boy' standing behind me. I feel like he's looking into my mouth. It's very tiring to eat politely all the time."

"Another week and you won't even see him."

"What do you mean?"

"You'll acquire the white people's gaze. You'll simply look past him."

"I hope not. That sounds terrible."

"Terrible or not, that's the way it is. Each side sticks with its own."

"Why? Does it have to?"

Gabriel suggests trying the plum liqueur he made himself. "It's quite good. It's my specialty, Esther." She tastes it cautiously. "I've eaten too much," she says in a strangled voice. Suddenly a stream of vomit spurts from her mouth and onto the carpet, staining the edge of the couch and the glass sides of the coffee table. The guests avert their eyes, shrinking in politeness or disgust. "It's nothing," says la belle Hélène, "they'll clean it all up in a minute."

The niece washes her face and neck in the bathroom. In the fluorescent light her white face stares from the huge, three-sided mirror. She goes out to the coolness of the garden. Jean-Luc is smoking in the dark, lying on one of the benches that is piled with pillows.

"I guess it really was too much for you, the food and the alcohol and the flight."

"I suppose so. I'm really sorry. It came out all of a sudden, just like that."

"It happens."

"Yes." Silence.

"So, are you the bride?" he begins again.

"What bride?"

Jean-Luc clears his throat. "Did I say something I shouldn't have?"

"I don't know what you're talking about."

"Really?"

"Really."

"Then maybe it's better if I say nothing."

"What do you mean?"

"I understood, like everyone else here, that they sent for you from Israel to marry Fufu."

"Fufu?"

"That's what they call Erouan."

"That's ridiculous. I can't just suddenly get married."

"Many people do, you know."

"But not me."

"Why not you, if I may ask? Just out of curiosity."

"Because it doesn't suit me. I will never marry."

"Never say never," sings Jean-Luc.

The niece turns her back on him, tearing leaves off a nearby bush. "You seem pretty smart," she says, "but I have the feeling there's not much competition around here."

"Are you angry at me? I'm sorry, I didn't mean to insult you, Esther. I was just joking. Will you forgive me?"

Madame Sicourelle comes out, throwing a silk shawl over her shoulders against the chilly night air. Jean-Luc sits up, runs his fingers through his disheveled hair. "Please sit down. There's plenty of room."

Madame takes Esther's chin in her hands. "How do you feel now?"

"Better. It's nothing. I just ate and drank too much."

Hélène and Gabriel walk them to the car. "Tomorrow the pair of talking parrots I ordered for Hélène's birthday will arrive," says Gabriel, sticking his hands in the pockets of his jacket.

"That's what I wanted," giggles Hélène, "so I'll have some company when he's away on business."

"What language do they speak?" Madame Sicourelle asks, gathering the hem of her dress at the car door.

"Whatever language you teach them—even Hebrew." Gabriel tousles the niece's hair. "What do you say to that, Esther?"

"Let them speak Hebrew."

"Come see the birds tomorrow," Hélène says. "And bring Jacques with you—we haven't seen him in ages." The couple stand there a while longer, arms entwined, brightly waving good-bye as they watch the car bump off over the bad road.

"Did you have a good time, Esther?" asks Madame Sicourelle, masking a large yawn with her hand. "I'm dead."

"It was fine."

"We have to drag your uncle to these parties from time to time. He never comes."

"You know he works hard, Maman," notes Erouan.

"Life is not just work and more work. Your father doesn't like to go out, that's all."

Uncle Sicourelle is sitting in his blue pajamas on the large, well-lit terrace. The whole house is lit up—all six windows in the bedrooms on the top floor, the kitchen, the living room, the rows and rows of round garden lamps, the two lamps at the gate, a veritable celebration. "What took you so long?" he complains, wiping his greasy lips with the palm of his hand. Three buttons are missing on the pajama top; the pants are held closed by a large diaper pin.

Madame sinks into a chair beside him, rubbing her bare feet, holding back for three minutes before protesting. "Chouchou, what is all this light for? Il faut économiser at least a little."

"I like there to be light," he says, draining his beer.

"But you are here, outside. Turn on the lights where you are—I'm not saying you shouldn't."

"This is how I like it, Madame. Now stop. How was it?" He turns to the niece, who is crouched on the floor, burrowing into the fur of the Irish setter.

"It was nice."

"Esther did not feel too well," Madame Sicourelle reports. "She threw up everything she ate."

The uncle turns pale. "Did you call Philippe?"

"Why should we bother the doctor, Chouchou? She threw up, but now she's all right."

"I will call him now," he says, dragging feet that are stuffed into house slippers crushed at the heel.

"There's no need, *mon oncle,*" the niece calls after him. "I swear I'm fine. It's over and I'm absolutely fine now."

He studies her, furrowing his brow. "You look very pale to me."

"I am always pale, *mon oncle,* that's my coloring. I am a little bit anemic."

"Since when?" he asks suspiciously.

"As long as I can remember. I was always getting injections of iron. I still take iron pills sometimes."

"Where are these pills?"

"In my bag."

"Go take one of these iron pills you are talking about."

"But I'm fine."

"Take one."

When she returns, he holds out a glass of water to her, watching her swallow the pill. "Do you feel better now?" Behind him Madame Sicourelle nods her head in a big yes.

"Yes, I feel better."

He is appeased. He stretches his legs out onto the railing, smoking and staring at the garden. For a long while they sit there in silence, surrounded by the heavy, sweet smell of moths being immolated in the lamps. "I am going to sleep, *mes enfants*," says Madame. "You go, too, in a little while." She wakes Erouan, who has fallen asleep in his chair. She takes his arm and walks him to his room.

"*Viens, Titus, viens.*" Uncle Sicourelle clicks his tongue at the dog, who is slapping his large tail against the tiles, leaning his head on Esther's knees.

"He likes you."

"He likes anyone who pets him."

"No, he doesn't. Dogs can tell who likes them." The niece says nothing, searching for fleas in the dog's erect ears.

"Why did you invite me here?"

"What do you mean, why did I invite you? I wanted to see you."

"But you could have invited someone else from the family."

"Who, for instance?"

"I don't know, there are plenty of cousins you could have invited. Uncle Moise's kids or Aunt Marcelle's. Anybody."

"Did you not want to come, Esther?"

"Sure, I wanted to. I was curious. That's not the point."

"If you wanted to, that's enough. You're here and that's that."

"Yes, but why me of all people?"

"Because I liked you from the photograph that your mother sent when you were very small. I wanted to see how you turned out."

"That's all?"

"That's all. For years the family has been asking me for things. They ask me for all sorts of things. You never asked for anything. I like people who don't ask."

"I once asked for an African doll, when I was ten. Nona Fortuna spelled the letter for me."

"Really?"

"Really."

She turns to gaze at the dim corner of the long terrace, which stretches out into the infinite, indistinct darkness, out into the dense garden and beyond the large gate, spreading across the street to another white house with its own terrace. Esther trembles slightly.

"You're cold. Perhaps you should go in," says the uncle.

"Actually, it's nice out here."

Uncle Sicourelle bought the house in 1967 from a German leather merchant who moved to the Ivory Coast. He took pains to wipe out all traces of "that German." The old garden was dug up and a new one planted in its place; the bathrooms, the tiles, the wooden beams on the high ceilings, the fireplaces in every room, the goldfish pond in the yard with its cupid shooting water arrows—everything was destroyed and rebuilt. Except for the terrace. It was the terrace that had first caught his eye from the gate, white, immaculate, almost mysterious in its dignity. This was the first house he had bought since leaving Cairo, after staying in a succession of rented homes, friends' apartments, huts and hovels in the factories or mines where he'd worked— any place to lay his head.

He photographed the renovated house from every angle, drawing black arrows on the pictures: "the back," "the pool," "the window of the study by the pool," "the bathroom," "another bathroom," "the entrance," "the kitchen," "the bathroom seen from the garden," "the living room." Then, blurry in the bright light, a white spot like a puddle of spilled milk, with a bit of black frame and barely discernible pale trees: "*la terrasse.*"

Photograph: Left to right: *Grandpapa Jacquo and Uncle Sicourelle, Cairo Train Station, 1946*

That's Grandpapa Jacquo, to the left of the uncle: tall, slightly stooped, smirking like the best man at a wedding. *"Ta'al hena, ya walad"*—Come here, boy—he probably said to the character who took their photograph, one of those men who hang around train stations and fancy cafés snapping pictures for a few pennies: "Come here, boy. Take our picture." Then he'll get involved with the photographer, who might or might not be starving, who might or might not have a place to sleep, who might be a loner, a foreigner, or the sole support of a family of fifteen; in any case, he is *un orphelin*. They are all orphans. When Grandpapa Jacquo looks at the world, what he sees are *des orphelins,* legions upon legions of orphans, stripped of the trappings of social class, of profession, gender, and race, stripped to the bone, to the very core of their wretched orphanhood.

"*Ta'al hena, ya walad.*" He motions to the photographer, making the shape of a lens with his fingers and winking. Uncle Sicourelle retires to a nearby bench, rustling a newspaper until Grandpapa Jacquo finishes his business. "*Ta'al hena, ya walad*" can take half an hour, half a day, half a year, half a life, a whole life, all of Grandpapa Jacquo's life, which brims over, spills over into the peripheral, encompassing the most marginal, trivial, pointless of things, pointless conversations, pointless people with this name or that—he never remembers their names. This one is called Mustafa. "Mustafa the photographer," he says, introducing him to Uncle Sicourelle, an arm around the man's shoulder. The uncle nods his head coldly. "The train leaves in fifteen minutes, Papa," he reminds him. Grandpapa Jacquo doesn't like being reminded of the time. "What's your hurry?" he complains. "Why's everyone in such a hurry all the time? They're always hurrying." He turns to the photographer. "All of them. What's happened to people, I ask you?"

The photographer, held in Jacquo's powerful grip, steals a sideways glance toward the end of the track, toward a big group of travelers that has just arrived. He, too, is in a hurry. "Why not sit here, right where you are," he suggests meekly, "and I'll take your picture, *hawaja,* honorable gentlemen." Grandpapa Jacquo needs to think about this. He steps back, examines the bench, squints. "You won't be able to see our faces if we're sitting down." They try standing. "Wait," Grandpapa Jacquo signals, "wait a minute." He pulls Uncle Sicourelle's beret back, exposing his forehead. "I don't like it like that," Uncle Sicourelle protests, taking the beret off and putting it on again, angling it to one side. "Don't move," the photographer says, shrouding himself in the black cloth behind the camera.

Both of them have their arms crossed—one over his belly, the other behind his back—as if to keep themselves from each other. They are a little embarrassed before the photographer who will capture their embarrassment for posterity.

The photograph presages the future, the parting that will take place in a matter of minutes. It seems to wait for it to happen. But in fact, the dispersion has already taken place; Grandpapa Jacquo and the son who is his namesake parted long ago. They strike a formal pose as is fitting, as if hiding their feelings from the camera; really they hide them from each other. They struggle to control their feelings, to control the photograph, bargaining with the third presence, that of time and place, which extends greedy hands from all sides, reminding them of what they want to forget: the city, for example, their city, whose insistent buildings can be seen above the train that waits behind them; the man on the left in a white djellaba who fearfully descends the steps of the train; the woman in black on the right, her back to them, who peers into the train, looking for something—perhaps she's already found it and only wants to look at it a bit longer; the abandoned newsstand behind them, unattended; the strange long shadow on the asphalt that shows the sun's position in the sky, the time of day; and the white patch on the pole behind the two men, some paint perhaps. They turn their backs on it all—and rightly so. These routine, quotidian details can be taken for granted; it is only the photograph that elevates them to immortality.

Grandpapa Jacquo knows nothing about all this, he does not want to know, he accepts everything—even blue demons. "So what if he's a blue demon, he's still my son," he says to Nona Fortuna. Yet Grandpapa Jacquo is afraid of demons, blue or green. At night he shuffles home from the Cairo Opera House, where he works as the chief accountant. He talks to himself, his fez tilted over his left eyebrow, the hem of his coat trailing behind him. He stalks his own shadow, stopping from time to time to search out the darkness for what is hidden from the eye, for what harbors evil. Defenseless, he peers ahead, studying the outline of a garbage bin and the cat's tail that pokes from it, sizing up a gaping, toothed tin can and the indifferent face of the moon. He pushes open the front door with his cane, then wanders from bed to bed, falling heavily on his knees and rummaging with the cane under the beds, looking for thieves, demons, strangers. Once Uncle Sicourelle and Moise hung a rag doll in the window; they dressed it in a suit, tied a tie around its neck, and put a hat on its head, which flopped forward. He saw it swinging in the window, lit from behind by a lamp, and froze. "My very soul fled in fright," he whined later, mopping his brow, laughing and crying in turn at the sideshow to which the whole neighborhood had been invited.

Nona Fortuna thinks the boys torment Jacquo. She nags him to be stricter so Uncle Sicourelle doesn't have him under his thumb, won't think he can get away with such things. "Let him be, Ota. What do you care?" he says. "Ota," he calls her, "pussycat." She is not appeased. Bent over her embroidery, she purses her full lips. "You're ruining them, Jacquo, spoiling them. They shit on your head, those children, and you say 'thank you.' " He dips cotton balls in strong tea and places them on his eyelids, dripping dark drops everywhere. "What do you want me to do, Ota? Just tell me what you want."

"Convince him not to go to Africa, to those *sauvages;* don't give that son of yours one piastre!

"I didn't give him anything. I don't have a thing to give."

"But if you did, you would."

"If I did, yes, I would."

"So don't, that's all I ask."

"I won't, Ota, I won't. Besides, he'll do as he pleases anyway."

． ． ．

But Grandpapa Jacquo does give him money; he sells his mother's jewelry. "Just until you get on your feet," he says.

"I'll pay it all back," Uncle Sicourelle says, shrinking from the sweeping gesture Grandpapa Jacquo makes with his hand, waving away his son's promise.

． ． ．

He is the second of five children, Uncle Sicourelle. The eldest is Moise, but everyone calls Nona Fortuna Umm Jacquo, mother of Jacques, Jacquo for short. All day long Umm Jacquo this and Umm Jacquo that, from one end of the street to the other. Nona Fortuna hears people calling for Umm Jacquo and immediately feels ill. "That child will be the death of me," she says, donning her white lace nightgown, loosing the pale braids that reach to her backside, and taking to her bed, surrounded by pails of water, smelling salts, tablets, and servants who mumble, "*Ya habibti, ya siti,*" my dear Madam.

One by one or all at once they file into the room with the drawn curtains: the glassblowers and carpenters, merchants and neighbors, and a few curious strangers along for the ride. "How much do I owe you," she asks weakly, clutching her purse to her breast.

"Five piastres, *ya* Madam. He broke a window."

"And you—how much?"

"Three, just three, *fi al-nabi, ya siti,* I swear on the name of the prophet."

. . .

She is from a good family, Nona Fortuna, not one of those "hichic-hichic" families, as she calls the nouveau riche. In many ways, Grandpapa Jacquo's family is hichic-hichic: money, money, money, loud mouths, and those aunts—"every one of their shoes a steamship," says Nona Fortuna, spreading her arms wide to show the size. "Maybe you exaggerate a little, Ota," says Grandpapa Jacquo, who listens patiently, amused by her scorn, from time to time adding a small, guileless question: "Really, Ota, is that what you think?" Yes, that is what she thinks, and if only he'd open his eyes a little he'd see what's right under his nose.

"My eyes are open, Ota. But Sophie of all people, Aunt Sophie—she's a good woman. Don't you think she has a good heart?"

Exasperated, Nona Fortuna tries to explain the ways of the world. "Your Aunt Sophie is generous only when someone is shorter than she is and kisses her feet. You think that's kindness? That's arrogance, that's someone who's full of herself, that's your Aunt Sophie."

"Where do you see this, where?" Grandpapa Jacquo asks with a mixture of awe, respect, and distaste.

Most foreign of all to him is coldness of heart, the sharp, unsheathed thought that tears an abyss between men. Grandpapa Jacquo tries to bind people together; he craves brotherhood and yearns for an all-embracing harmony that will flow among those who love him and those whom he loves and those who are neither—that will buoy them up in delight, all plump and pleased, bobbing on their backs, their mouths open to receive grapes and marzipan sweets tossed from above and to utter words of adulation and honey-tongued praise.

High, high above all this he places Nona Fortuna, so high the top of her skull all but pierces the ceiling, her white, muscular legs dangling beneath her dress, her arms sparring with the stars. "Take care, Ota, don't catch cold up there," Grandpapa Jacquo warns, but she never listens to him. She runs to her father, instead.

Her father sits for hours in the company of his manservant, a tall, silent Sudanese who proffers polite, almost imperceptible bows, indicating yes or no with his magnificent dark head. "Is that you, Fortuna?" her father asks, sensing her presence though she herself is lost in the wonder of his room, sucked in through the doorway and consumed by its plush purplish browns and the scent of jasmine bubbling in water, the long, white-clad figure of the servant a filament of light. She sits at her father's feet, caressing the joints of his long, soft fingers as they move across pages punctured with Braille. Grandpapa Jacquo does not visit there often. They fill him with dread, the learned blind father-in-law who translates Shakespeare into Arabic and his Sudanese servant. Nona Fortuna scolds him. "Papa has a great secret in his heart, a sorrow he will take to the grave."

"Don't say such things," Grandpapa Jacquo pleads. "Don't say things like 'grave,' God preserve us."

"I will say them. There are things you do not understand, Jacquo."

• • •

She made his life miserable, Nona Fortuna—go, come, fetch, say, don't say—until she relented. She was twenty-four when he first noticed her on the veranda and tried his charming patter on her: "What a thick book you are reading, Mademoiselle. You will need someone to carry it for you." She lifted her eyes from the book: luminous blue, penetrating, distant. European blood ran in her father's family, Italian or French. Both father and daughter had pale, fine skin taut as a glove, distinctively shaped but colorless lips, blue eyes damaged by retinal disease, and golden curls a full, deep, yolklike yellow that never fades.

"I don't know you," she replied. "I have never seen you before."

"Was it true you'd never seen him before, Nona?" I ask.

The blanket is pulled up to our armpits and stretched across our chests. Nona Fortuna runs the tips of her fingers ceaselessly over the little ridges of the blue coverlet. She loves to fondle cloth. "Touch it, touch it," she urges me, "see how nice it is." She takes my hands and guides them over the coverlet. "Isn't it nice?" she says with satisfaction, returning to the main story with a sigh. "No, it wasn't true. I'd seen him several times before."

"How many times?"

"Two or three, I can no longer remember, *sit al-banaat*. What does it matter?"

"Yesterday you said two."

"Did I? So I did. I saw him going in and out of his aunt's house across the way. He was beautiful, dark, a bit sullen."

"He had a gray hat."

"That's right, indeed he did."

"He used to watch you from the aunt's window; you noticed him watching from behind the curtain."

"The curtain in the aunt's window would move a little, I saw that. Back then I had my sight, and I saw that red curtain of theirs move and someone peering out from behind it."

"You pretended to be reading."

"The whole time. I didn't want him to find out."

"But in the end he did."

"In the end he did, *sit al-banaat;* he found out. Not everything, but some things he did find out."

"Why not everything, Nona?"

"Because I was very *renfermée,* very reserved."

"You were very proud, too."

"Proud?"

"*Fière,* you were *fière.*"

"Yes, I was."

"But in the end you got married."

"Not so fast, though. My father wanted to get to know him first."

"But your father was fond of Grandpapa; you said he liked that he was simple and good-hearted."

"Father was not fond of anyone. Jacquo—maybe he liked him a little."

"Why wasn't your father fond of anyone?"

"Because that was his way, *ya ruhi,* my dear. He withdrew from life at a very young age, Father. He withdrew from people—all except me and Suleiman."

"The Sudanese servant?"

"The Sudanese servant. Now there was a man! I would have sent them all to learn a thing or two from him, from that man."

"Why?"

"He was noble. Everything he did or said was noble. He'd been the servant of the British attaché in the Sudan, that Suleiman," she says heavily, haltingly, her voice seeping slowly into the silence, the somnolence that descends on her in midsentence.

Grandpapa Jacquo died in Egypt five months after Uncle Sicourelle left for Africa. He died of diabetes, reckless neglect, and gluttony. During his last days in the hospital he would bribe the nurses, the orderlies—anyone who chanced by—to steal him trays of rich pastries swimming in butter and sugar glaze. The news of his death reached my uncle in Brazzaville, his first stop on the dark continent. He lay in a vile shack near the mines, burning up with malaria. The photograph Nona Fortuna sent with the news was swept into a swirl of feverish hallucinations, appearing suddenly in its entirety in vivid detail, then fading only to appear again disjointed, dismembered among the fever's nightmares and visions: a fez askew; an odd pole smeared with paint, leaning at an angle, pressing against his forehead; high windows widening; blurred faces drowning in space, their expressions enigmatic, like those on death masks. It took him forty-five days to recover; the Belgian priest who tended him called his recovery a miracle of medicine. The uncle detested the clammy feel of the priest's palms on his face, the sweaty smear of filth on the priest's collar. "There are no miracles," he said.

He had the photograph enlarged and framed. In the enlarged version the eyebrows—so similar—are many times darker and more dense, drooping, bleeding into the sockets of their eyes, which form black hollow circles like those of skeletons. Beneath the eyes break sly, grudging smiles.

I saw the photograph resting on the bureau in his room, beside other pictures and certificates of commendation from the governments of Cameroon and Gabon. Uncle Sicourelle caught me looking. "What are you looking at, *ya* Esther?" he asked, pressing tobacco into his pipe with his stained thumb.

"At this picture of you and Grandpapa."

"Ah," he said dismissively, turning and leaving the room.

• • •

"You did not know the grandfather, did you?" he suddenly asks at breakfast two days later, gulping his coffee standing up, poised to leave.

"He died in Egypt before I was born. I've only heard about him."

"What have you heard?"

"That he was a wonderful man and that he squandered the family's money gambling."

His face darkens. "That's nonsense, all of it. People love to talk."

That evening he comes to my room, entering without knocking. He looks out the window before sitting down. "What are you doing—writing letters?"

"Not exactly."

"So what are you writing?"

"A diary."

"A diary?" he marvels. "What have you got to write there?"

"Things that happen. What I think and imagine."

"You write about him?"

"About whom?"

"About your grandpapa."

"No, I write mostly about the present."

"Ah." He is silent a moment. "Write about him."

"What should I write?"

He paces the room, his hands clasped behind him, declaiming at the speed of dictation, commanding. "He was the best of men, the best of husbands, the best of fathers, the dearest of friends—*ektabi, ya* Esther, write."

"That sounds like the inscription on a gravestone, *mon oncle.*"

He goes to leave. At the door, he pauses. "That is the gravestone."

Photograph: The Wedding: Monsieur and Madame Sicourelle at the Entrance to City Hall, Brazzaville, 1954

Monsieur and Madame Sicourelle are stuck between two wide pillars. She is wearing black with a touch of white in front; he is in white with a black bow tie, a penguin in reverse.

The pillars separate the entry hall from the stairs outside, slicing the photograph in two, into foreground and background, into two events that are contiguous but not distinct, like slices of watermelon. In the background, the hushed ceremony; in the foreground, the hint of a story. In the background, the crowd; in the foreground, emptiness. In the background, the eddy of guests, who cancel one another out; in the foreground, the enigma of an object: the furled carpet at the Sicourelles' feet, which two men standing by a pillar point at in amazement or dismay.

The pointing men, troubled by something, are what draw us into the photograph. Clearly they belong there, dressed in suits and wielding an easy authority evident in their stance and their accusing fingers. They are preoccupied; they ignore the camera, the subdued splendor of the ceremony, and the couple positioned at the top of the stairs in the camera's honor. Their preoccupation disturbs the formality of the photograph, yet the sole purpose of the disturbance is to ensure proper orderly procedure. These men are masters of ceremony, perhaps self-appointed. Unwittingly they are the clowns who insist on tying the acrobat's laces mid-cartwheel. In spite of themselves, they provide comic relief. The onlookers' puzzlement at their presence turns to laughter. The guests cannot see the men's high-wire tricks, their odd, prissy fussing; they don't quite get what's so funny, but they laugh anyway. Thus the photograph's enigma is amusing; it lacks the sting of something truly dark and sinister. The two men stand in an empty spot, away from the crowd in the entry hall, pointing at the stone stairs where the carpet lies furled, at the blank stretch of sidewalk below. They are one step ahead of the guests in the entry, who chatter gaily and clink glasses; they worry about the future, about what will happen, about the threshold the couple must yet cross at the bottom of the stairs. Still, our hearts are not with them but with the convivial celebrants, who smile at their worries, making their fuss over the empty spot seem ridiculous— and rightly so.

But Madame does not think so. Worry clouds her face, which is cast down toward the furled carpet, toward the pointing fingers of the men to her left. Her mind is not on the camera; she is distracted: she must find the defect, worry about it. Her arm is entwined in the uncle's, disappearing behind it. Only with effort can we discern her white gloved hand on his white jacket sleeve, white disappearing into white. She is ready to descend the stairs, her leg extended in midstride but frozen because of the men who point, because of the camera. Madame Sicourelle is at the heart of things, attentive. The uncle is not. The uncle smiles, as he should. What is he smiling about? Another enigma: is he smiling at the camera? At the pointing men? At the ceremony interrupted by something unexpected? At the distracted woman whose arm is entwined in his? At all of it?

Nona Fortuna was happy he was smiling but she was suspicious. "Is he really glad, does he really look happy?" she asked.

"Really," I promised. "He looks very happy, Nona."

She paid me five agorot a photograph; that was our agreement. Every few days she would sit me down with her photographs and I would describe them to her. I was willing to describe anything for five agorot. On good days, when she did not argue with me over what was in them, I could earn as much as thirty or forty agorot. Afternoons after she had doused her arms, armpits, and face with soapy water and put on a thin cotton slip she would call me from the porch: "Esther! *Ya* Esther!" Absorbed in what I was doing, I would silently curse her. Sometimes I wouldn't answer. I didn't care about the money—let her yell. I would hide in a tin barrel, startled by her shouts ringing against the metal. Our neighbor the carpenter believed children should come when called. He'd yank me out of the barrel by my ears and drag me into the sandy yard, goose-stepping me around and around the electric pole, my earlobe in his hand. "You'll answer next time your grandmother calls you, eh? Eh?" We'd cross the road, climbing the small hill with one "Eh" after another until he had delivered me into her hands. She would wrap ice cubes in a towel and place them against my ear. "What did he do to you, *le monstre!* Tell me."

Humiliated, I would whimper, "Please, no pictures today."

"No pictures, no pictures," she'd promise.

"You won't ask me who's this and who's that and what are they wearing?"

"I won't, *ya ruhi,* I swear."

She would feed me apple compote with a spoon, humming something, the spoon clinking against the sides of the pan, hunting for slices of apple, spilling sweet juice. Nona Fortuna would put on eyeglasses with clear lenses just for the hell of it, for the look of it, so people would notice her eyes. Mother would quarrel with her. "You'll confuse people that way. They'll think you can see."

"Let them think."

"You're so stubborn. Just wait—one day you'll fall and no one will help you."

"No one helps me anyway. If someone wants to help they don't need a reason."

I helped her; I was her eyes. "You are my eyes," Nona would say. "Look good and hard for both of us, *ya ruhi.* We are one soul, you and I." We'd wander through town hand in hand, looking for bargains. One of her arms, much fatter than the other, was swathed in an enlarged sleeve that she ordered specially. I would hold on to her fat arm, loving the soft wobble of the flesh in my hand as we walked. "What are you laughing at?" asked Nona Fortuna.

"Your arm—it jiggles!"

"It's not nice to laugh at that, *sit al-banaat,*" she would say, laughing herself.

I'd measure her fat arm with a tape measure. "Don't move now, Nona." She would stand still, staring ahead blankly, giving herself up to my pricking and poking. "Does it hurt there if I prick you with a pin?"

"Of course it hurts—what am I, made of rubber?"

"And here on top?"

"There too."

"That's a sign you still have nerves. Did you know you have nerves there? That's a good sign."

She looked for signs, Nona Fortuna; she jumped from one sign to the next as if they were stepping stones in a stream. "When you were in your mother's belly there was a sign."

"What sign?"

"A sign; you shouldn't talk about such things. Just a sign that the baby would bring luck."

Mother had seven abortions before I was born; she used to get rid of babies like they were kittens. "Just like kittens," she said. "I'd get right up and go back to work."

Father would be away on one of his trips, would have vanished to some European capital and then to Africa, sending back newspaper clippings and little mementos. She had wanted to get rid of me, too. Nona wouldn't let her. "Don't get rid of it—give it to me. It will bring good luck." She had pleaded with Mother a whole night, fingering the long belt of Mother's robe.

So Mother had given me to her and gone to work in the homes of the rich, minding their dogs while they were abroad. Once she nearly choked one. For hours she had watched it sleep in its straw basket, its breath rising and falling under its little blanket and bow. Finally she had grabbed it by the neck and squeezed until it gasped. "Cookie. They called it Cookie," she said.

Photograph: Mother in the Yard

Mother is standing beside a strange bush that looks like a heap of sticks and leaves ready for a bonfire. Near the ground it is broad and thick with branches; on top it is pointy, a cone whose tip—one broad leaf—tilts toward her breast to the left, as if to touch it.

She is holding something in her left hand, a rope or a stick of uncertain length that is attached to the bush; she is either pushing it in or pulling it out. She is surrounded by sandy ground dappled by light and shadow, a pattern of dark and light grays that reaches back to a line of trees behind her. A smooth, slender stump sticks up from the ground to her left, like a pole.

She turns her profile to the camera with a bashful half smile, her left leg extended, echoing her profile in a clumsy effort to lend her sturdiness a model's nonchalance.

How slim, almost fragile, is the ankle in the open-backed sandal compared to the thick body in the pale sleeveless summer shift whose straps slip off her shoulders. Below her neck there's a near-symmetrical spot of tanned skin, evidence of some other piece of clothing with a triangular cutout.

Her black hair—either short or tied back—blends into the darkness of the trees behind her, a black gully sucked into the trees.

Almost parallel, in the lower half of the photograph, is the triangular shadow of the photographer, who failed to remove his presence. He invades the photograph, his shadow going before him. The sharp angle of the shadow suggests the photographer might have been bending his arm in a salute instead of reaching to press the shutter.

The photographer's shadow ruins the photograph, barging in like an author suddenly speaking in the first person, shattering the illusion of the photograph's omniscience, destroying the story it tells, which seems to unfold by itself, without an author.

Me, me, me, says the shadow.

You, you, you, retorts the photograph.

"*Vous,*" says Mother, using the formal pronoun. "You can see your shadow there, Robert, did you notice?"

"It's the sun," he says, embarrassed. "I wasn't paying attention to the sun."

They are sitting in the kitchen, crouched by the small electric heater, warming the palms of their hands, their faces burning. She glances at the brown suitcase at his feet, tied with string. "What have you got in that suitcase?" she asks, an expression of disgust contorting her face.

"Nothing, just some stuff—clothes and papers," he says, lighting a cigarette, leaning into the smoke.

He'd been seen on some bench in a park, sleeping.

"You were seen sleeping on a park bench," she says.

"So I was seen," he says. "What can I do? People see." The refrigerator makes a long buzzing hum, then falls silent. "What's the matter with the refrigerator?" he wonders.

She curls toward her thighs and hugs her knees. In a dry, dull voice she spits, "You've done a lot of harm, Robert. *Allah yisamhak* for what you've done. God forgive you."

"I don't care whether he forgives me or not. Do you forgive me?" he asks, brushing nervous fingers through his hair.

She rocks her body from side to side, hugging her knees as if soothing a baby.

"Just let me stay a few days, Inès," he says, then pauses. "Until I get settled."

She brings blankets and sheets from the bedroom, dropping them at his feet. "Here. Make up the couch in the living room."

He does, smoking until his eyes close, a yellowed butt still clasped in his yellow-brown fingers.

She wakes him at dawn as she turns the house upside down, spilling buckets of water, slapping the mop under his bed, dusting the shelf above his head. "*Yalla,*" she says, "up." He trails after her into the yard, bleary-eyed. She sticks a shovel in his hands. "Here," she says.

"What 'here'?" He looks at the other perfect holes dug in the ground. She demonstrates, tracing an exact circle. By eleven in the morning he has dug four holes. She follows him without saying a word, moving from one hole to another. She holds out a bottle of cold water, watching as he swallows. They do this every day for two weeks.

By the end he is exhausted. He spends the nights smoking, his mind working ceaselessly until *sabhat rabena,* until the light becomes visible through the square of window facing him, lending the young bushes, the round citrus trees, the taut laundry lines a hallucinatory, insubstantial, abstract air.

All the while he is drawing money out of their bank account and from Nona Fortuna's social security pension.

"Forget it, Inès," says Nona, warming herself in the weak sun on the porch, confused by the flurry of movement, turning her head to the right, to the left, and to the right again, talking to the place in the yard from which banging and panting emanate.

Mother is in the yard, quietly absorbed in the large bush with the broad, unyielding leaves, tying up its branches, making it look like a spiky cone, like a bonfire. She tosses on papers, sheet after sheet, photographs stuck to the black pages of an album, garbage gathered from the yard, withered leaves and twigs. Barefoot, she empties a bottle of kerosene onto the pile, then stands transfixed by the grand demonic conflagration. Mother stares at the tongues of flame lapping thirstily, licking the hem of her dress, singeing her ankles.

"Inès!" Father grabs her, forcefully dragging her heavy body back. "Inès."

Suddenly she regains her senses, looks at the fire, looks at the house, stunned at the connection between them. She grabs her head by the ears as if picking up a jar and, burning, breaks into a run toward the neighbors'. "The house, the house!" she screams, writhing with an involuntary shudder as they throw sand and water on her. "The house, the house!" She clutches the arms held out to her, several arms at once, digging in her fingernails: "The house, the house!"

Missing Photograph: Julien

He married her for her papers. Did you know that's why he married her, Julien?" the niece asks with her mouth full, dunking her *tartine* in a bowl of coffee.

"Everyone knows," Julien says. He is bent over the dishwasher, the upper half of his body naked. He has worked for the Sicourelles for six years, since he was seventeen. "Everyone envies me because of Julien," Madame Sicourelle complains. "Madame de Vilalville has tried to steal him from me more than once."

"Has she really?" the niece asks with interest.

"Yes," Julien says with a smile, baring his white teeth.

"That pleases you," she observes as she fishes pieces of bread out of the bowl and wipes her fingers on the silk bathrobe Madame Sicourelle just gave her.

"Surprise!" she had announced from the foyer, tossing her keys on the table. "Surprise!" The niece had been lying on the couch, watching a game show on television, occasionally extending her arm toward a bowl of lemon candies. "Surprise, Esther, did you hear me?" She placed a large shiny package on the niece's knees. "Open it."

"What is it?"

"Open it, open it, it's something you need."

The niece smoothed the silky purple fabric against her chest. "This is something I need?"

"Every woman needs a robe de chambre—at least one good one. Guests come, people stop by, you never know who's going to show up. This way you're prepared."

"Nobody stops by in the morning. Who stops by in the morning?"

"Don't split hairs, Esther. Besides, you know very well that Richard sometimes brings something to your uncle, or Erouan comes in. People stop by."

Esther tried on the robe, tying the long belt high under her breasts and turning around. "I've never had a robe like this."

"Come here," Madame ordered, pursing her lips in thought. She undid the belt and tied it again, this time around Esther's waist. "Here, like this. You don't want to look like someone who's just gotten out of an institution."

They heard the clatter of Erouan's keys landing on the table next to Madame's. He came in exuding cologne and engine grease, kissing their cheeks eight times, four kisses each. "Did you just get up now?" He surveyed Esther in amazement.

"I bought her a new robe," Madame explained. "What do you think of her in the new robe?"

He narrowed his eyes. "Fine, a bit long. Isn't it a little long?"

"It's a robe, Fufu, not a dress made to order. A robe needs to be a little long and a little wide so that it's comfortable," Madame Sicourelle insisted.

"She'll step on it, Maman. She'll be wiping the floor with it."

Esther took the robe off, tried to fold it carefully, and gave up, placing it in a heap in the wrapping. "It's all right. I doubt I'll wear it much anyway."

"Why not?" Madame Sicourelle lit a cigarette, waving the match in the air long after it had gone out. "Why wouldn't you wear it, Esther?"

"I don't know. It's for a lady—I'd feel ridiculous."

Madame Sicourelle stubbed out the cigarette in an ashtray. The reddish folds of her neck hung limply under her chin like a wattle, suddenly very obvious. "I'm going to rest for a while," she said.

Erouan poured himself something to drink and sat down beside Esther on the couch. They watched the game show. In an apron wrapped twice around his slim, bony waist, Augustin bustled about them incessantly, plumping up pillows, moving vases and china and brass objects from place to place. "I think I insulted her," the niece said.

"Maman is just tired. Don't pay any attention."

"She was angry at me, I'm sure of it."

"Don't be ridiculous."

"Didn't you notice her mood suddenly changed?"

"No."

He gulped down the rest of his drink and went to pour another. The niece looked at him contemptuously. His pants hung low on his hips, just barely clearing his flat backside. His wallet poked out from his back pocket. "How could you not notice that her mood changed?"

He came back and sat down on the sofa, two pillows away from her. He stared at the television screen. "He won a car, that guy." The large man in a diamond-patterned nylon shirt put his foot on the car's bumper, clapping his hands at the applauding audience. Erouan's eyelids dropped heavily, fluttered open for an instant, then dropped again. The niece turned the television off, got up, and straightened the pillows. "What are you doing?" Erouan asked, startled, rubbing his cheeks.

"Just tidying up a bit."

"Leave it. Augustin will do it later."

"Augustin is going home soon. It's almost five."

"So he'll do it tomorrow," he said with a shrug, stretching his arms and yawning. "I'm beat."

His face was pasty beneath the blue and red capillaries that formed a tangled network across his cheeks, the traces of too much drink and too much sleep. "Why are you beat, Erouan?" she asked.

"What did you say?"

"I asked why you're so beat. What have you been doing?"

"I was on the boat all day. The mechanic was supposed to come but he didn't show."

"Ah."

He paused. "I can take you out some time if you like."

"When?"

"One of these days, when it isn't too hot."

"It's always too hot."

"But some days are worse than others."

"Are they?" she asked, pulling the skin under her eyes toward her cheeks, revealing the red rims of her eyes.

"He's slippery. You feel like you're sliding down a wall whenever you talk to him," she tells Julien the next morning in the kitchen. Julien is slicing purplish onions, barely moving his rounded shoulders, shiny brown as if they had been rubbed with oil; only his wrists rise and fall in a steady rhythm.

"Mademoiselle does not like Monsieur Erouan," he says.

The onions make her eyes tear. "It's not that I don't like him, I just don't understand how his mind works."

He slides the thin onion rings into a pot. "She left him without taking a thing," Julien says, "just the shirt on her back. She went back to France."

"Who?"

"Dominique. His wife. Poor Monsieur Erouan."

Esther twirls some hair around her finger. "I didn't know he had a wife."

Julien turns back to the gas burners, flinching slightly at a spray of hot oil. "Mademoiselle does not know many things."

She is standing beside him, watching the onion rings turn golden in the pot. "Like what, for instance?" His arm, stirring vigorously, brushes against hers. Two thick droplets of sweat hang quivering from his left nipple, which is pink against the magnificent brown chest.

"Be careful of the oil, Mademoiselle," he says, lightly brushing her hand away from where it rests on the counter.

Her hand reaches for his long, damp neck. "Don't move, Julien."

He shuts his eyes. "*Ne bouge pas,*" the niece says. Her fingers fan out over the width of his nape, her pinky edging toward his bristly, shaven hairline. He drops his head back, mouth open, eyes closed, rubbing against her palm. The hand that holds the spoon is frozen in mid-air. Esther sees their reflection in the panes of the kitchen window: two heads, one upright silhouette, drowning in the broad outline of a tree visible from the other side, from the garden. A car door slams in the distance.

"Madame has come back," Julien says flatly without moving his head, without opening his eyes.

Julien has a nephew who is active in an underground movement agitating against the government of Cameroon. The nephew does not have a job. He sits for hours on a large rock by the gate near Augustin's hut, his head resting on his knees, dozing and waiting for Julien to finish work. Julien brings him food and sometimes alcohol in an empty oil bottle. The nephew's name is François.

"Why don't you get a job sometime, François?" Julien chides him.

The nephew teases him back. "Right away, boy. Right this minute, boy," he says, imitating Madame Sicourelle. Sometimes Julien shoos him away but he always shows up again, sharing secrets with the elderly Augustin, who scratches his chin in amazement.

"Why is François always making trouble? Cameroon is independent," the niece says now, trying to keep her voice casual.

"Begging your pardon, Mademoiselle, but you simply do not understand what is happening to our country," Julien says. "Everything here is corrupt. Everything."

"And François and his friends will suddenly make everything not corrupt?"

Julien has begun scrubbing a copper pot with lemon and steel wool, his breath rising and falling. "François says we shouldn't sleep with white women."

Esther straightens her glasses. "You're not sleeping with me."

"No, but it's like that."

"It isn't. You can tell your cousin not to worry."

"He's my nephew."

"Nephew, cousin, whatever. Maybe he's just projecting his own fantasies."

Julien's arm jerks away from the pot and he places the ball of steel wool in Esther's hand. He closes his fist over hers and squeezes hard. Beads of sweat fall from his forehead. Madame Sicourelle is out in the garden, giving instructions in a loud voice. After a minute Julien lets go and Esther's palm is scored with bloody scratches. She pats at her hand with a kitchen towel before Julien dips it into a bowl of tepid water, shaking her wrist lightly. Her slack fingers trace circles in the water. Cupping his own hand, Julien collects some water and pours it over his face, neck, and chest. He kneels at the niece's feet and the streams of water wet the thin cloth of her dress as it clings to her thighs. "You shouldn't have done that but I forgive you," the niece says, rubbing water over his feverish shoulders, neck, and lips.

Julien opens bloodshot eyes. "Who are you, Mademoiselle, to forgive me?"

Esther avoids the kitchen for two weeks. She watches Julien from the windows of her room, which face the wide kitchen window. His black shadow is blurred behind the linen screens. He moves silently, sometimes facing the window. "You've stopped sitting in the kitchen," Madame Sicourelle notes. The niece is reading; she moistens a fingertip with her tongue and turns the page. "I'm glad you've stopped sitting there."

"Why?"

"It simply isn't done. One doesn't talk to the help."

"Because they're black?"

"First of all because they're servants."

"But also because they're black."

"If you wish, yes, also because of that. Everyone is talking about Monsieur Sicourelle's niece who sits with the boy for hours."

"What else are they saying?"

"I don't know what they gossip about, but give them a chance and they'll spread all sorts of lies. Madame de Karini's boy said it. She overheard him."

The niece sits up and throws the book to the floor, her hands shaking. "What do you care what this one says or that one says? What do you care about all of this . . . this talk. It's racism, just plain racism." Eyes brimming, she runs to her room, dragging a small rug that gets caught in the buckle of her sandal. She shakes it free in a rage, then slams the door. Half an hour later, Madame Sicourelle knocks. "Esther," she calls softly. "Open the door, Esther." She waits a few minutes, then knocks again. "You needn't take it so personally. Please, I'm asking you."

In the evening the uncle returns, limping. He sprained his ankle going down the stairs, twisted something. Julien brings him a small footstool for the injured leg and sets the table for supper. "Where is she?" asks the uncle.

"She's been in her room all afternoon," Madame tells him. "She won't open the door for anyone, imagine that."

"What happened?"

"How should I know? She was hurt that I told her not to sit in the kitchen so much."

"Why did you say such a thing to her?" he says, kicking the stool aside. "Why do you pester her with your pettiness, tell me?" He limps to the door of her room, knocks forcefully. "Esther, do you hear me?" She comes out.

"I'm not very hungry, *mon oncle.*"

He pulls her by the arm into the kitchen. "You want to be in the kitchen? We'll be in the kitchen. Julien, set the table in here." Julien puts on his white waiter's jacket with the two deep pockets in front, padding silently on bare feet, moving among the three of them with a silver tray laden with baked potatoes and roast beef. Madame doesn't utter a peep.

An hour after the meal Julien is in the kitchen scrubbing tiles and the fronts of kitchen cupboards. Monsieur and Madame Sicourelle doze in front of the television in the living room. The niece returns to the kitchen to pour herself some cold water. "Are you still here?"

Julien wrings out the rag in the sink. "You know I am, Mademoiselle."

She watches his long fingers twist the rag. "Julien," she begins, then falls silent. He turns his face toward her from the sink. It has the terrible pallor of fatigue, a pallor that seems to collect in the lips. "A baby was born to me yesterday," he says. "A son."

"Congratulations, Julien."

"Thank you, Mademoiselle."

"Is it your first?"

"He is the first."

"Well." She leaves, only to come back seconds later. "I forgot my water."

"It's not so cold anymore. Shall I pour you some fresh water?"

"That's okay, I'll take this. Thank you, Julien."

She sinks into one of the easy chairs on the porch, smoking and listening to the noises from the road beyond the trees. A shrill screech pierces her eardrums. She walks toward the sound, looking up at the tangled treetops. "Strange bird," she says aloud. A wide ditch near Augustin's hut is dark and lumpy, smelling of good, fecund soil. Simon, the gardener, has stuck a hoe in the ditch and left it there. Esther sits, leaning against a tree trunk, her knees to her chest. She is careful to keep her body within the confines of the circular shadow cast by the tree. Soft feline steps move down the path: Julien is going home, the plastic bag with his work clothes rustling. The niece looks away from the path. Branches move and dry leaves crackle with a pleasing, spine-tingling sound.

"Are you there, Mademoiselle?"

From the corner of her eye she can see the hem of his pants and the soles of his feet in rubber flip-flops. "Yes. I'm all right, Julien."

"Are you crying, Mademoiselle?"

"I'm not crying, I'm just a little tired and upset, that's all."

"You're not used to this."

"What am I not used to?"

"The way people behave here. You're not used to it."

"Lucky me." She wipes her nose.

He stands on tiptoe and plucks a mango from a high branch. "It has a large pit but it's tasty," Julien says. "Shall I peel it for you?"

She shrugs her shoulders.

"Yes or no?" he asks.

"All right." He throws the skin into his plastic bag, presenting her with the peeled fruit.

"Tomorrow I'll buy a gift for your baby. I'll go choose something nice."

"Monsieur Sicourelle has already given me five hundred francs."

"Money is money and a gift is a gift. They're not the same thing." She wipes the mango juice from her mouth with her arm. He laughs. He is standing facing her, legs apart. The smell of fried garlic and onion is strong.

She gets up and extends her hand. "Good night, Julien." He does not touch the hand. He moves aside, letting her pass.

Photograph: The Wedding: Monsieur and Madame Sicourelle at the Entrance to City Hall, Brazzaville, 1954

They were married in a simple ceremony at City Hall, with few people in attendance. The grand white entrance in the photograph, the loftiness of its three arches, offered some compensation, lending the occasion more festiveness than it had. He had arranged the wedding in haste lest she suddenly change her mind, have second and third thoughts, those termites that gnaw at decisions.

Lacking French citizenship, he was about to be expelled from an African country for the fourth time. He wanted to put an end to it. And there was Marie-Ange, a young widow in her early thirties, who fell in love with him—to her misfortune, as she never tired of saying.

"*Malheureusement,* I fell in love with Monsieur Sicourelle. *Malheureusement,*" she says again with feeling, like a little girl who gets more satisfaction from pronouncing a word than from its meaning.

They are lying side by side, trying to get some sun. On the far right Justine de Karini lies in a metallic gold bikini that seems to have been poured onto her still, smooth body; next to her Hélène, a wet towel over her face, keeps pulling her bathing suit down to hide her pubic hair; beside her Madame Sicourelle sits up and lies down by turns, smearing herself with suntan oil and fingering the blue veins on her legs with dread and loathing.

"Why *'malheureusement,'* Marie?" Hélène snickers from under the towel.

"I don't know, maybe my life would have been simpler without this marriage."

"Really," Madame de Karini says, expelling air impatiently, barely moving her lips. "Alone with a child—in Africa!"

"I would have gone back to Brittany, to my parents, that's what I would have done."

"With your father telling you to do this and do that? You wouldn't have been able to stand it, Marie, I'm telling you. At least here you're free."

Madame Sicourelle digs a hole, gathering sand in her fist and letting it fall slowly, slowly onto her stomach. "Perhaps you're right." The sky changes, its shades of blue turning a steely gray.

"Now it is a pearly gray," writes the niece, thinking for a moment, sticking the pencil in her mouth, then erasing and writing: "Now it is nearly gray." She is sitting on a mat nearby, surrounded by sundry bottles of lotions against mosquitoes, sunburn, and allergic rashes, at the opening of a makeshift tent Erouan has made of flowered sheets.

"Don't you want to put on a bathing suit, Esther?" Madame de Karini asks.

"No, I'm comfortable like this. I can't stand the heat."

"But it's awfully hot in Israel, too, I've heard," la belle Hélène puts in.

"True. I suffer there, too."

"It's strange anyway," Madame Sicourelle muses aloud. "You, with your Mediterranean genes. Your uncle doesn't even feel the heat."

"He also doesn't feel the cold," la belle Hélène says, laughing.

Gabriel, her husband, approaches, holding a hot dog on a skewer. "Who wants one?"

Madame de Karini wants only a piece, just a taste. "Where is everyone?" she asks Gabriel.

"Fufu is on his boat, as usual, fixing something, and Claude is helping him."

"He's something, that boy," says Madame Sicourelle. "Doesn't rest for a minute."

Jean-Luc flops down beside Esther, rubbing his wet hair with a towel. "The water's fabulous! Aren't you the least bit tempted to go in?"

Esther gathers her knees up beneath her dress, turning away from the spraying drops. "Not at all," she says, narrowing her eyes and gazing at the endless, placid gray-green surface of the ocean. "Well, maybe a little," she concedes with a laugh.

"So put on a bathing suit and come on, let's go for a swim."

"I haven't got one."

"You went out on the boat without a bathing suit? You really are a strange girl."

"If you're in a boat you're on the water, not in the water. What's so strange about that?"

He is quiet a moment, looking at the sea. "Do you want to know what I think, honestly?"

"Go ahead, if you like."

"I think you're ashamed. I've been watching you for a while, and I see how you hide your femininity."

She smoothes her hands over the mat, brushing away the sand. "Where'd you get that from, a magazine?"

"Come." He grabs her arm and pulls her to her feet. "Let's take a little walk."

"Where to?"

"I want to show you the beach. It's amazing."

"Where are you going, Esther?" Madame Sicourelle asks, still supine, eyes shut.

"I'm going to show her the area a little. She should see something besides Douala."

The sand is brown and hard to walk on; its coarse dark grains seep into Esther's sandals. "It's so different from the Mediterranean," she says. "Have you ever been there?"

"I've been to Tunisia, Italy, and Spain. I've never been to Israel. I would actually like to go there someday."

At some distance from the beach is a thick, deep stretch of green: green upon green, ever more dense, muggy, and dark. The gray green of the ocean looks clear and motionless next to the muddy brown strip of shore that lies taut as a zipper between the dense growth and the ocean. "Is this jungle?" she asks as they duck under low branches better suited for the passage of small animals.

He laughs. "Of course not! This doesn't even come close."

"I'd like to go to the jungle. It's hard to imagine it."

"Ask your uncle to take you. I don't think he likes it very much, but maybe for you he'll go."

"Why do you think he doesn't like it?"

"I'm not sure. It's not uncommon among the whites here, a sort of denial of nature. Perhaps it's fear, too. Don't forget that the people who came here to make money have taken advantage of the place. It's a terrible tragedy."

"What is?"

"Africa. On one hand, there's all this." He waves his arm. "This extraordinary beauty. On the other hand, there's the suffering of the people. You've never seen such suffering. But then again"—he pauses—"you know, sometimes it feels like they're part of the same thing, the beauty and the suffering."

She stops to stare at a huge bloom of stiff orange petals speckled with yellow pollen; it could be artificial, made of plastic. "Look at this flower," she says, sliding a finger the length of one pointed oval petal, repelled.

They come to a clearing where children have gathered. Smoke rises from a fire.

"What's going on?"

He grabs her arm. "Shhh . . . you'll see in a minute."

They watch from a distance. Half-naked black children hang off a circular barbed wire fence, shouting with excitement and terror at the sound of an inhuman screech.

"This is a kind of zoo," Jean-Luc explains. They move closer. A graying female gorilla sits in a ditch inside the barbed wire, hiding her face in a red cloth. The children back away, making a path for them.

"This is a zoo?"

"Incredible, isn't it?"

Esther nods, studying the gorilla as it chews something and spits a greenish arc at her.

A swarm of flies lands on the gorilla's brown pate. The gorilla does not stir, chewing and spitting greenish arcs, staring straight ahead.

"She's lovely. I never could understand why people get insulted when they're compared to apes. Apes are so much more sophisticated than stupid lions. I'd be happy if someone told me I looked like this gorilla."

"You look like that gorilla," Jean-Luc says.

"Who asked you to volunteer?" Esther asked scornfully.

"Come on, my gorilla, we should head back before it gets dark. Let's go and tease your favorite lions, Sicourelle and de Karini."

"Wait, just a little longer." She is mesmerized by the gorilla's blank expression, by the eyes that slant up toward the fly-studded forehead, by the slack pinkish lips, moist and quivering. Beyond the barbed wire is a barren patch ringed by vegetation that obscures the ocean; the space is dotted with fires on which ears of corn are grilling. "Do they come to see the gorilla?" Esther asks.

"I think so. There are always people here, no matter what time of day." Jean-Luc strikes at stubborn branches with a stick, clearing a path for her.

The beach is nearly empty. The yachts and sailboats at anchor have filled with passengers and their gear, passed from hand to hand through the water and then hoisted on deck.

"You're back," says Madame Sicourelle.

"We thought you'd kidnapped the niece, Jean-Luc," Justine de Karini jokes, massaging the strip of white skin that cuts across her burning shoulders.

Jean-Luc pulls a shirt over his head, then looks at her coldly. "You were in the sun a long time today, Madame."

The boat sets sail quietly at first, borne slowly away from the shore, bobbing aimlessly like a large tub; then all at once the fury of the engine propels it out toward the open sea, churning foam, tearing the water's still green surface and stirring up a wind. The sky has an orange flush punctuated by spots of steely blue that hint at the sky's earlier color like bits of memory.

Ahead, two banks of lush foliage lean toward each other, forming an arc above the water. When the boat reaches the green
archway Erouan cuts the engine and lies back to wait; he lights
a cigarette. Falcons call from the undergrowth, a new sound filling the stillness. The passengers crane to hear the cry of the falcons while they wait for Monsieur de Vilalville's boat; they have
arranged to drink a toast under the green archway. The boat
bobs from side to side, from bank to bank, as if buffeted by the
strange sounds all around that scratch like fingernails at a blank
board of silence.

La belle Hélène snuggles into her husband's arms, her face
hidden by a sheet of red hair—a different shade from that of her
long fingernails, which rest like drops of blood on his thigh.

"Fufu," Madame Sicourelle calls suddenly, "please throw me
that towel next to you." For the first time since they embarked
Erouan turns from the helm and strides the length of the deck.
He wears sports clothes, green as the water.

"I'll take over if you want a break," Jean-Luc offers.

"Fufu would rather die than give up his helm," Claude de
Karini says.

Erouan takes off his baseball cap, showing his forehead, split
by the sun: the bottom half is dark, seared by sunburn; the top
pale. He squashes the cap in his palm. His spindly arms hang
limply at his sides; his gaze is fixed on the niece, who is leaning
over the railing, immobile, her eyes dull as painted glass. "You
could fall that way, Esther," he says sadly, as if in disappoint-
ment and reproach.

"Hey ho! Hey ho!" Monsieur de Vilalville calls from his
boat, trumpeting his arrival. He is standing on the upper fore-
deck looking through binoculars. His hairy belly spills over his
pants. Beaming, he holds up a bottle of champagne. Crystal

glasses appear along with two more bottles of champagne that have been chilling all day in a cooler. The two boats float alongside each other, their bows touching. Madame de Vilalville, in a cloth wrap draped Hawaiian-style, wants to come aboard "to chat with the girls." With one hand she holds her wrap closed while with the other she clasps a glass of champagne; she jumps, nearly falling into the space between the boats. Jean-Luc catches her, giggling, in his arms. "Careful, Jean-Luc," Monsieur de Vilalville calls from his deck. "Don't let your fingers do too much walking."

"He's done his bit for the day, haven't you, Jean-Luc?" says la belle Hélène.

"We have to marry him off, that's what we have to do," continues Monsieur de Vilalville, gulping straight from the bottle. "Why shouldn't he suffer a little, too, the bastard? Why only us?"

Madame Sicourelle is not pleased; she tips her champagne into the ocean and urges Erouan to head back. "*Allez*, Fufu, it's time for us to go. Some people's manners . . ." she mutters, sitting down next to the niece.

"He's just joking," says the niece.

"I don't like such jokes. They're not my style."

The darkness comes slowly, softening the sharp lines of Madame Sicourelle's profile, hiding the wrinkled skin under the eyes, the faint birthmark beside the mouth. Drained by the sun, she closes her eyes.

The boat sails toward the lights of the city, the passengers spent from champagne and the relentless sun. The niece watches them, humming. "What are you singing?" Jean-Luc whispers so as not to wake Madame.

"Nothing. Just an old song about a boat and some sailors."

"Sing it."

"It's in Hebrew—you won't understand it. I really loved it when I was a child."

"Tell me the words. I'd like to know."

She takes a breath. "Okay, it goes like this: 'A little boat, with two sails, floating / The sailors sleep, they watch no more / But if the sailors don't awaken / How will the little boat reach the shore?' "

"It's very nice. A little sad but very nice. It's full of the melancholy of sailors' songs, the fear of death."

"You have something to say about everything, don't you?" Esther says tersely, her hand shaking, spilling cigarette ash on his thigh.

"What's wrong with what I said?"

"Nothing. It's just a little too slick, that's all."

"I thought you liked poetry."

"Poetry, not poets."

"You're so arrogant. Why are you like that, Esther?"

"It's not arrogance; it's just the opposite."

"I don't understand."

"It's not important."

The boat bangs against the pier, shudders, and lurches. The dock is deserted; the heavy iron doors of the warehouses are closed; the floodlights shine cruelly. Uncle Sicourelle emerges from the darkness and comes toward them. He waits, smoking. "I was getting worried," he says. One by one the passengers extend their hands and jump onto the dock, greeting him with embarrassment and deference.

He examines Madame's flushed face with alarm. "What have you done to yourself, Marie? Now you'll be in pain all night."

"I guess I was in the sun a little too long," she says, hobbling after him toward the car.

He is tense; he had a terrible day. "Two fishing boats came in late, the buyers were on my back, Richard disappeared, and now this—this is all I need."

Madame cracks her knuckles, tugging at her large diamond ring. "What, Chouchou?" she asks anxiously. "What do you mean?"

"You don't take care of yourself, Marie. You do foolish things, just like a girl. You won't be able to move tomorrow— look at you!"

"It's only a bit of sun, Chouchou, don't exaggerate," she says weakly.

He is silent the whole way home, his lips pursed and his thick, close-knit eyebrows revealing something of the zeal with which he fans his anger, cooking it slowly like the herring he loves, grilling first one side and then the other, then each side once again.

Madame Sicourelle knows his anger well. She looks out the window, turning away from him lest some of it fly at her. She is waiting.

The uncle trades everything for anger—affection for anger, concern for anger, tenderness for anger, anything that is not anger for anger. But he is also miserly with it; he does not waste his anger. He husbands it, cultivating and tending it like a farmer compulsively checking his land at dawn's first light, making sure everything is still there.

"He was always like that, your uncle," says Madame Sicourelle. He even proposed to her in a rage, as if she had done something wrong, as if he were cursing her in his heart, as if she had forced him to propose. She was insulted—she didn't yet know his ways. "You don't *have* to marry me, Monsieur Sicourelle," she had responded in a huff. He hated feminine coquetry, those tiny Ping-Pong balls of insult and pride that fly about for no good purpose. "Stop it, Marie," he had interrupted rudely. He had arranged to meet her at eight-thirty in the morning at the entrance to City Hall—"the way people make an appointment for the doctor," she says. At the last minute she'd invited a few friends, who, out of politeness, kept their opinions to themselves. He had not invited anyone. "I don't have any friends," he had said. She had pressed him: "Not even one, someone from work perhaps?"

He had softened somewhat; his face had cleared. "Maybe Pierre; he works with me," he'd assented. Then he changed his mind: he couldn't leave the factory unsupervised. "I'll tell him about it later," he said.

At eight-thirty she appeared with Erouan and a friend who would mind him. The uncle was already waiting impatiently—a striking figure in his white jacket, especially compared with the cleaners who were still sweeping the streets. He looked as if he had just ended a night full of gambling, drinking, and beautiful women. Madame was satisfied that the building was respectable. She examined the large arches and stately pillars, quietly glad. "Did you at least tell your family in Israel?" she asked as they climbed the stairs to the justice of the peace. He'd forgotten; he'd do it tomorrow, today or tomorrow.

For two years the wedding photographs lay in a drawer until he deigned to send one. "It's all your fault," he said to Madame.

"My fault? Who's been pleading with you to write to them and send a picture?"

"I would have sent a picture already if you hadn't nagged me to write as well. They would have known it was a wedding. After all, what does it look like—a hen?"

In the end he wrote: "To my mother, sisters, and brothers, a picture of the wedding, leaving City Hall."

The edges of the photograph are slowly yellowing; it is speckled with tiny brown spots like pinpricks. Above the three arches the picture is fading. The fading patch of photograph—the imprint of time—blends with the building's gray wall. It is no longer possible to separate what the photographer saw from what time has done to the photograph. The future has wormed its way back into the past, tugging at the instant of the photograph's becoming.

Missing Photograph: Nadine

It's hard for me to believe that I'm really here. Sometimes it seems like I'll be stuck here every day for the rest of my life, morning, noon, and night, with the card games, the shopping expeditions, Madame Sicourelle's nagging. She just doesn't leave me alone. Yesterday I told Madame I was going to read for a while at the American Cultural Center. Of course I lied. I really went into town. I knew it would impress her if I said I was going to spend my time reading. The other day Jean-Luc said Madame has the brain of a game-show addict. We had a good laugh, but then despondency set in: Jean-Luc is supposedly closer to me than Madame is, but I'm putting on as much of an act with him as I am with her. The most important thing in the world to me is not to put on an act, and here I am doing it, living a life that's not mine.

I thought Madame wouldn't notice that I was going out. I snuck out the back door at around eleven, when she's usually in the study pestering Richard about the accounts. He agrees to everything she says and then does exactly what he wants. The respectful face he puts on always makes me laugh; I can't believe she doesn't see right through him. It's not that she's totally blind—after all, she suspects his every move—but it's as if she understands his craftiness in only the most stereotypical way. She thinks all blacks are liars and thieves, and therefore he must be one too, but in fact she completely misses his particular sort of cunning. He's very shrewd. All these years he's managed to work his way around the two of them—and Fufu, too, of course. Yesterday Jean-Luc told me where the nickname Fufu comes from. It's Claude de Karini's invention. Fufu is a character in the Tin-Tin comic strip; he's Tin-Tin's friend, a lazy dolt who lies around and doesn't do a thing. I told Jean-Luc I thought it was pretty cruel to call Erouan that, and he agreed. "So why do you do it?" I asked. He said I always ask difficult questions. Whenever he wants to avoid something, he gets this look on his face, as if he's suffering.

Yesterday he tried to kiss me. I couldn't help staring at his nose as he moved closer: it looked broad and squat like Mount Tabor. I tried to keep my eyes closed, but I kept peeking at him the whole time. It was pretty strange. His lips were too moist, too soft; they kind of sank into my lips, as if I had no lips at all, only a hole for a mouth. It didn't last long, thank God. I think he probably felt the same way. Afterward he looked rather sad. "We're not much, are we, Esther?" he said. "No," I agreed. "Not much."

Sometimes, though, we do seem to speak what Madame Sicourelle calls "the same language." "He's very standoffish, that Jean-Luc, but you and he certainly seem to speak the same language." "Really?" I say to her. Sometimes she drives me crazy.

Yesterday I'd gotten only as far as the front lawn when I heard her voice behind me, "Esther! Are you going out?" I didn't answer, letting her think that I had left. I caught a cab pretty quickly, within two minutes. The cabs zigzag down our street like bumper cars in an amusement park. They look like they're about to crash into each other just for fun, for the hell of it. "Aqua Palace," I said to the driver. That's about the only place I know in town—it's a hotel for wealthy whites who come to do business in Douala. I sank into the backseat, which was practically on the floor, and prayed this ride wouldn't be my last. From that uncomfortable angle, I couldn't see what the driver was doing, but my guts churned with every crazy turn he took. The distance from the house to the center of town is no more than two kilometers and I could easily have walked it, but the uncle doesn't allow me to. "This is no place for whites to go walking," he says. Once he found out that I had gone on foot and he made a huge scene. I don't have the energy for another one, so now I go by taxi. I wonder who told him. This town is full of tattletales, black and white, bastards all of them. Oh, well, what can you do? I've noticed that when I write the way I talk, everything flows better, drips from my fingers. I don't know whether that's a good thing or a bad thing. Anyway, it's easier to put my energy into writing—it gives me a sense of doing something.

I got out at the Aqua Palace and started walking. I intended to go to the market where they sell vegetables and trinkets for tourists. A few days ago, when I went shopping with Madame, I

saw a string of beads there I really liked. I asked passersby where
the market was, but every one pointed in a different direction.
After an hour I gave up. I went into an air-conditioned shoe
store to cool down a bit. Women kept coming in and out, all of
them black, all of them smoking, tottering on five-inch heels,
walking like ducks. After a while the salesgirl came over to me
and I found myself trying on pair after pair of high-heeled shoes
in pink, yellow, green. I started to enjoy it—the shoes piling up,
the salesgirl's attention, the way the other women kept offering
their opinions.

We started to talk. The salesgirl—her name was Beatrice—
told me about her troubles with her boyfriend, Johnny, who hits
her and drinks all the time. I just listened, trying to look sympathetic. I told her I was from Israel and she said, "Of course,
Mademoiselle Sicourelle." "How do you know?" I asked.
Oddly enough, the question created a barrier between us and
she clammed up. Her sudden withdrawal unnerved me more
than her knowing who I was. We parted friends, though, anyway. I invited her to come to Uncle Sicourelle's pool one day, and
she said, "Of course, of course," counting the two thousand
francs' worth of bills—nearly all the money I had—that I'd
given her in exchange for shoes I'll never wear. One good thing
came of it: she told me how to get back to the Aqua Palace. I
decided to forget about the market for that day: Madame gets
upset when people show up late for lunch.

While I was in the shoe store the street had become even
more crowded and sweaty; there were hundreds of people, some
carrying bundles, others pushing carts, and I could barely
squeeze my way through. I noticed that people were watching
me. They have this way of watching you without you noticing
them, as if they can make themselves disappear. It's unsettling.

Three children, beggars, followed me to the corner, shoving burnt ears of corn and bananas at me from every direction. I couldn't tell whose skinny black hand was holding which burnt ear of corn. In the end I bought all the corn and bananas, then threw them in the garbage.

As I got to the café of the Aqua Palace, I had the uneasy feeling that I was being followed. I checked. The beggar children had vanished, but a spindly teenager in a blue-and-white striped shirt was leaning against the wall of the building opposite, sipping a bottle of beer. Clusters of people blocked him from sight, but after they passed he was still there in the same spot, watching me. I sat on the café terrace facing him and ordered peach nectar—it's a sickly sweet drink, thick as mush, and it makes you thirsty, but I love it anyway. I stared at the boy over the cars, the street stalls, and the chaos; I wanted to see what he would do. Nothing. The terrace was empty; everyone else was in the air-conditioned bar. The waiter tried to persuade me to move. "It's nicer there, Mademoiselle," he said. I refused his offer politely; I wanted to keep my eyes on the boy. The waiter punished me by not bringing me my juice for twenty minutes. I wondered what was going through his head. It's hard to tell. You get the sense that behind the most ordinary exchange there's another, hidden conversation, and still another behind that. It's something like hypocrisy, but not exactly. I can't quite explain.

Anyway, I talked about this with Jean-Luc. He said that most of the blacks who adopt the white man's behavior and live in his world leave something of themselves behind. It's as if they maintain a secret, hidden life with their families and their tribal beliefs, which we can't understand. In a way, they're torn in two. According to Jean-Luc, the blacks developed complicated codes of communication during the colonial years, and ambiguity and

their layered language help them protect their secret life from
the whites' intrusiveness. It sounded very complicated but I
thought I understood what he was getting at. But Jean-Luc said
I'd have to live here a few years before I could really understand—if I didn't get ruined in the process, like everyone else.

Jean-Luc reads all the time, and I'm jealous of his education.
I wish I were that educated, but there's no chance. I'm too impatient, I tire of everything too quickly: of reading, of writing, even
of thinking about myself—but especially of writing. After I'd
sworn I would write every day, a week went by without my writing a thing. On the days I don't write I leave blank pages with a
date so that I'll have to confront my laziness.

I don't know why, but I told Jean-Luc what went on between
Julien and me. I exaggerated a little, saying that Julien had
touched my breasts. I watched Jean-Luc to see how he would
react, whether his face would change. It was strange: I almost
felt as if I wanted to hurt Jean-Luc, the way you do someone you
care about. He started to ask all kinds of questions and suddenly
I lost interest. "It's none of your business," I said. He seemed
disappointed. "Okay," he said, "if you say so." He took his car
keys and left the house and I haven't talked to him since. I've
sworn that if I do talk to him again, I won't expose myself in
such an embarrassing way. Sometimes I think that talking is far
more clumsy than actually doing, worse even than if I was to go
ahead and sleep with Jean-Luc.

Anyway, I had just finished my peach nectar when I spotted
Monsieur Sendrice, the Cypriot merchant whose house we had
dinner at several nights ago. He's insufferable. He sat down at
my table and wouldn't shut up—spitting, coughing, lighting
half-smoked cigars, laughing like an old lech, telling bad jokes,
all the time poking me a little with his elbow. Still, I was happy

to see him; for some reason, I like him. He makes great stuffed vegetables. He stuffs everything—tomatoes, onions, potatoes, carrots—all by himself, without a cook. He began interrogating me. "So, what do you think of Erouan?" He was obviously dying to know whether a wedding would come out of this. I played innocent. "I love my cousin very much," I said. The word "cousin" confused him a little. "Yes," he admitted, "he really is your cousin." Then suddenly he had a brainstorm: "But he's not a blood cousin!" "That's not important," I said. "We're just like brother and sister, Erouan and I." We said nothing for a few minutes, then he offered me a ride home.

The uncle had come home for lunch and invited Sendrice to eat with us. Madame was ready to kill him. Not that she has anything against Sendrice, she explained to me later, she just wants to be warned ahead of time. The uncle likes Sendrice and his jokes. When he was young, Sendrice spent a few years in Alexandria and they love to sit together and reminisce. They polished off a bottle of pastis, imitating the way Greeks in Alexandria speak Arabic and laughing themselves silly. Erouan laughed with them but you could see by his face that he didn't really understand, poor thing. They sat together for several hours, drinking one glass after another, and all of Madame's hints—that they had to rest, that the uncle had an important meeting—were to no avail. Later, when Sendrice had finally gone, we went out to the garden, Uncle Sicourelle and I, to wash Titus. The dog was so scared of the water he was trembling all over. I held Titus so he wouldn't bolt, and the uncle hosed him down, spraying water on the terrace, on himself, on me. My hair got completely wet and the uncle yelled to Julien to bring me a towel. I was drying myself off and shaking my head when sud- denly the uncle looked at me and said in a choked voice, "You are so very much like your Aunt Nadine. You have no idea how like her you are." I asked if he meant Father's sister and he nodded and said nothing more, as if he had forgotten I was there. I told him I'd never seen Nadine. "Not even a photograph?" he asked. "Not even a photograph," I said. Father never spoke about her, only Mother. Once she said that Nadine was so hard and resentful she even resented the shirt on her back. I didn't understand it then and I don't understand it now. What does it mean to say that someone resents the shirt on her back? I repeated this to the uncle, but he didn't respond. Afterward the uncle brought out Madame's hair dryer and we tried to dry Titus. The dog was so startled by the noise that he ran off. We laughed and the uncle said that in Egypt they always had a dog even though Grandpapa Jacquo was afraid of them. Once they had a fantastic black German shepherd called Shimshidian, who was caught stealing a piece of meat off the kitchen table.

Uncle Moise took out his rifle to shoot the dog. He said a dog that stole couldn't be trusted; dogs were supposed to be man's best friend and if a dog broke that trust he had to be put to sleep. So Moise killed Shimshidian. He cried, but he killed him. He'd been very attached to that dog. I asked if they ever had another dog after that. "No," said Uncle Sicourelle. Six months later Uncle Moise went off to Palestine, to his kibbutz.

Missing Photograph: La Terrasse. *Madame Sicourelle and the Niece, Douala, 1978*

Facing the terrace is a smoky-brown hill that looks as if it has been drawn by a child. It is two-dimensional, with orderly wisps of green grass scattered evenly across it. This is the hill.

In her dream the niece sees a dizzying vista. But the watchful eye cannot be hers; it is omniscient, too calmly surveying the entire landscape; the eye slides over the terrain as the edges of a shawl drape over an object without changing its form. It is only the memory of the touch, the sight, that leaves a mark.

A beam of light signals a gathering: five people sit at the crest of the hill in a circle of light. The niece climbs with ease and joins them: Uncle Moise, Uncle Sicourelle, Mother, Uncle Edouard, and Marcelle—the siblings.

The siblings are crying wordlessly, crying tears that are whipped against their cheeks by the wind; they sit erect and cross-legged at the top of the smoky-brown hill. Like statues of Buddha, they do not move, they do not touch one another, they abandon simple human gestures. Yet effortlessly they find perfect reconciliation on this arid hilltop, as if reconciliation were the universal condition.

The niece leaves them and descends the steep hillside. Hidden at the foot of the hill are dense Andalusian gardens with shaded paths, stone benches, bouquets of pale blue and pink hydrangeas, and low, rounded citrus trees. In the distance, at the garden's edge, is something blinding, stunning, white as a ship just christened: *la terrasse.*

The terrace is like an island unto itself, snobbishly turning its back on the house behind it, the thing that gives it meaning: long, white, a waist-high railing embracing the three open sides, empty porch chairs in three colors, a green card table with rickety legs, a pitcher of water sweating droplets of chilled liquid, a huge Sèvres china bowl filled with fleshy fruit swarming with black flies. The terrace has a human face, but without eyes, lips, or nose; all the human details are erased yet its expression is still clear beneath a thick impasto.

She wakes from the dream with a dry throat. Fat frogs are croaking in the pool just beyond her windows. She often sees them gather around the pool by the spherical lamps whose purplish light is meant to repel mosquitoes. The pool looks ghostly, distorted in the purple glow, its buoyant plastic swans beset by drifting yellow leaves and fat, insistent frogs.

There is something enigmatic about the frogs. In the mornings they disappear into the lush greenness, silent as the red ants or the grass itself. Esther asks Uncle Sicourelle where the frogs go in the morning. Surprised at the question, the uncle straightens in his chair, blinking. He thinks she is hinting at something else. He is swift as a gunslinger when it comes to a hint or a suggestion. The careful, sparing way he speaks leaves gaps that must be filled by the imagination, by gestures, by hidden, oblique shades of meaning, by ceaseless interpretation of his silence, of the spaces opened up by his missing words.

He does not answer, calculating as he carefully folds the pages of the morning paper. "Madame!" he roars suddenly without turning his head. "*Ya,* Madame!"

Madame Sicourelle hurries out to the terrace, her heels tip-tapping. "Has something happened?" she asks, shading her eyes. "What has happened, Chouchou?"

"Change the girl's room! Change it today. Those animals won't let her sleep."

The niece protests weakly. "They don't bother me, *mon oncle,* I was just asking."

He leaves. They see him at the gate, beside the car, emptying brimming ashtrays onto the ground and driving off in a cloud of dust, ash, and cigarette butts.

Madame and the niece remain seated on the terrace, their pale ankles resting on the white railing. The niece scratches her head, then examines her fingernails, using one to clean the brown scum under the other. "Simon has not come today," Madame says. "Typical." She puts on sunglasses and stares, transfixed, at the sprinkler twirling on the lawn.

"What's typical?" asks the niece.

"At least two or three times a week he doesn't come, that *cochon.*"

The niece spreads jam on a croissant that has cooled. She licks the knife. "I think he's kind of nice, Simon. He always has some story I can't understand because of his accent."

Madame Sicourelle slaps the back of the niece's hand. "You watch that diet of yours. You're like your uncle when it comes to sweets."

The niece tears her croissant. "Want some?"

Madame Sicourelle purses her painted lips. "I'll have a yogurt. Yogurt and an orange, that's what I'll eat today. Why don't you have a yogurt, Esther? It's very healthy."

"I hate healthy food. It makes me miserable to eat lettuce and peppers," she says with her mouth full.

"Lettuce is not so healthy," Madame Sicourelle says. "It's not fattening, but it doesn't have the nutritional value people think it has."

Simon arrives pushing a wheelbarrow full of rakes, hoes, brooms. He is wearing a white crewel hat that Madame Sicourelle once gave him. He passes under the railing, bowing slightly. *"Bonjour, mesdames!"*

Like water repelling oil, forcing it to float to the surface, Simon's innocent, indulgent smile deflects Madame's cold, spiteful look.

She tightens the belt of her robe, closes her eyes behind her dark glasses, and turns her face to the sun. The air is humid, damp, and gray. The heat advances from behind the low clouds. At eight in the morning the terrace is littered with the previous night's debris: tiny winged corpses belly-up in a line along tiles dusted with insect repellent, easy chairs tossed to the floor by the scornful wind, a thin layer of sand everywhere, especially beneath bare, sweaty feet.

"I'm going to wash my feet," says the niece, studying Madame Sicourelle's face and sneaking a cigarette into the pocket of her pajamas.

"I wish you wouldn't smoke, Esther," Madame says, distracted, now preoccupied by the filth at her feet, drawing up her legs and shrinking from it as if from bitter frost. "Just look at *la terrasse* this morning—just look," she mutters sadly, her voice faltering, then slipping into another register. "He's a monster, that's what he is—a monster," she says, dissolving into tears, dabbing her face with the lapel of her orange robe.

"Who?" asks the niece. "Who's a monster?"

"Your uncle. Didn't you hear how he spoke to me before? As if I were a servant, some black woman working for him."

The niece fixes her eyes on Madame, riveted by the sobs that add years to her aunt's face, consuming time with stunning speed. "Have a tissue," she says, pushing a packet toward her. The niece is waiting for quiet, for the hunched back to cease its shaking under the robe. "You should leave him. Do something worthwhile with your life. Why don't you leave?"

Madame Sicourelle hiccups. "That's easy to say, *ma fille,* very easy to say." She pulls at the lid of her right eye, trying to fish out an eyelash. "How could I? I have nothing but him and Erouan. Nothing."

Simon approaches with the long rake, staring. "The roses, Madame. Shall I prune the roses today?"

• • •

Simon, the gardener, is Augustin's cousin, Julien's nephew, and brother-in-law to Marie-Ange, who's just been hired to do the laundry and ironing.

Madame Sicourelle dislikes sharing a name with a washer-woman. "How can we both be called the same thing?" she had said the night before from the far end of the long dinner table.

"That's her name, Marie," said the uncle as he dipped his bread into spicy tomato sauce and pushed strips of calamari to the edge of his plate. "That's the name they gave her, what can you do?" Madame Sicourelle was not appeased.

In the afternoon she pulls the young woman aside for a chat.

"Come, come, *ma jolie,*" she says, sitting in a garden chair above which hangs a mosquito lamp lit day and night. The thin black girl is like a scorched stalk of grain with a protruding belly, a loop on a rope. She scratches her ankle with the toes of her bare foot.

"Do you like working for us, child?" asks Madame Sicourelle.

"*Oui,* Madame."

"You iron the master's shirts very nicely. The master is very pleased and so am I."

"*Oui,* Madame."

"Tell me, child, who gave you your name?"

"I don't know, Madame, who gave it to me."

"Let me put it another way. From now on, in this house, we will call you Madeleine. When you go home you will be Marie-Ange, but here you will be Madeleine. Madeleine is a very pretty name."

"*Oui,* Madame."

Madame Sicourelle taps her fingers on the arm of the chair, watching the girl step lightly across the garden to the laundry room. She waits a few minutes. "Madeleine!" she calls. "Madeleine!" There is no response. She groans, throwing her head back in despair.

The whole time the niece has been watching the scene while thumbing through the pages of *Paris-Match*. She uses the opportunity to take the cigarette out of her pocket, lighting it at the filtered end, then waving it about in alarm. "You'll burn the house down, Esther," Madame Sicourelle scolds her.

"You can't ask the girl to change her name," Esther says, stubbing out the cigarette. "You can't expect a person to do a thing like that."

"I changed my name," says Madame Sicourelle. "Until I was thirteen I was Marie-Annick, then I changed it to Marie-Ange. It's not such a big deal."

"Yes it is. Besides, that girl only works for you. You don't own her."

The heavy gate shuts noisily. Monsieur Sicourelle has come home early unexpectedly. He stands at the edge of the terrace in a light linen suit, cheeks flushed, all red and white, white and red. "*Voila mes fillettes,*" he says. "Just where I left you this morning." Uncle Sicourelle is very pleased; he has come from a successful meeting. They will drink to the good deal Uncle Sicourelle has just closed. Madame goes to her room, returning bedecked and perfumed and wearing a dress covered with yellow sunflowers. She tightens a loose earring, tipping her cheek toward her shoulder coyly. "Your niece," she says, "has a great many ideas in her head. Did you know that, Chouchou?"

He did not know. He bends over the niece, rests his lips on the crooked part in her hair. "What ideas does she have?" he asks, adding in the same breath, "Tonight we will eat at the Aqua Palace, Marie. What do you say to that? We'll eat at the Aqua Palace!"

"Tonight?" asks Madame, surprised, cautious, anxious.

"Tonight," he promises.

In the meantime, the green table on the terrace is set for a quick snack. Monsieur Sicourelle only wants something light: melon, olives, spicy roasted peppers, slices of mortadella sausage, halvah, and bread. He breaks some bread and wraps it around herring, gulping beer. Madame is beaming. The sunflowers flutter with her every movement. "Chouchou! How can you eat herring and halvah together? I don't understand?" He can.

"What ideas do you have, Esther? Tell me about your ideas," he says.

"Esther thinks we take advantage of our blacks," says Madame Sicourelle. "That's what she thinks of us."

"Really?" The uncle is amazed. "Why do you think that, my child?"

"I didn't say that, *mon oncle*. I didn't say you were mistreating them in particular. It's just not right that all of the blacks are servants and all of the whites are masters."

"Who told you that—Jean-Luc?"

"I don't need anyone to tell me. I can see for myself."

"Because if he's filling your head with that garbage, you should ask him exactly what he's doing on that project of his, which is costing billions of dollars. Ask him. We'll see who's taking advantage."

"What has his project got to do with it?"

"How old are you, Esther? Sixteen?"

"Nearly seventeen."

"What makes you think that after visiting here a few weeks, even a few months, you'll understand everything?"

"I don't understand everything. No one understands everything, not even you."

"True, not even me. I've been here thirty years and I still change my opinion of the situation at least three times a day. Do you think I like the way things are here? I've seen no less than ten revolutions in Africa, I've seen the French come and go in three countries, I've seen the blacks fight the French and one another. Whole villages tear up railway tracks, power lines, water pipes, damaging everything good purely out of hatred. There are no easy answers."

"But everyone deserves their freedom."

"Even the freedom to slaughter one another?"

"Even that."

Madame Sicourelle taps her fork on her plate. "Enough quarreling, *mes enfants,* we have finished quarreling for today. You need to rest, Chouchou. Go lie down for a while."

Monsieur Sicourelle does not want to rest. "If I rest now I won't fall asleep tonight," he says.

"You never fall asleep in any case," notes Madame. "Last night you were up until three. I heard you."

"Four," he corrects.

"Four?" She is aghast. "What were you doing until four?"

"I was reading something," he says rising, stretching, and striding the length of the terrace, brushing away dry leaves with his foot.

The air is slowly changing. The light, which is now a deep violet, seems to weigh like a heavy, limp blanket on the treetops, which stir with the cool, irregular breezes. Uncle Sicourelle peers over the niece's shoulder. "I see you're still writing."

"Constantly," interrupts Madame Sicourelle. "She never stops. Why don't you read us something you've written in your notebook?"

The niece closes the notebook, her face, too, closing shut in insult, hard and haughty. "It's in Hebrew," she says.

"How many notebooks have you filled?" the uncle asks with interest.

"One. I just started the second."

"That's a lot," he says, impressed.

They sit there until it gets dark, until Julien's shadow passes on the grass below the terrace.

"We must get dressed," says Madame. "What will you wear?"

"The same thing," says the niece.

Half an hour later they are back in the easy chairs, waiting for the uncle. He is still splashing in the bathtub, singing at the top of his lungs. "How he sings, that man," Madame says from behind a curtain of hair, bending over a blister on her heel.

Later he comes out to them, folding his jacket over his arm. He is pleased. "How pretty you look, just like mother and daughter."

In the photograph the niece is turning aside, warding off the light of the flash with her arm; a dark blotch of hair blends with her dark dress, forming one large smudge. Madame Sicourelle is staring straight ahead, touching the string of pearls at her throat with a finger, as if pointing at something, and opening her wide, painted eyes in vanity or alarm. Uncle Sicourelle is taking the photograph.

Photograph: The Look

The face still has the semblance of looking, the habit of look-ing, of muscles poised to look though the woman can no longer see, though her gaze cannot return another's.

She stares with frozen pupils. "What are you doing there, *sit al-banaat*? What are you looking for?" "Nothing," I say, search-ing through her wallet, stealing money. She is silent a moment. "Leave some for the cab ride to Dr. Pinchas," she says.

The doctor shines a bright beam of light into her wide eyes. "If only I had my eyes," she sighs. "But you do, you do," he says, indulging her. "Blindness, madam, is not a handicap; it's a trait."

"He loves trains, that Dr. Pinchas," Nona observes as we descend in the dim cell of the elevator. "He's always talking about trains."

"Traits," I tell her. "Traits, not trains." The whole way she turns this over and over in her mind, wearing her thoughts on her face. "Is what he said something good or bad, *sit al-banaat?*"

"It's good, he said something good. I promise."

"How do you know it's good?" she asks, suspicious.

"I know. I saw his face when he said it. He said it good-naturedly."

"Ah," she says, reassured. "You saw."

She sleeps on it that night. "You saw the whole time?" she asks the next day.

"Saw what the whole time?"

"His face when he said that. Did you see it the whole time?"

"Most of the time."

"What did you see when you weren't looking at his face?"

"Nothing much—his office, a table, two chairs, what he has on the walls. You think I remember what I saw?"

She ponders this. "It's not very big, his office. Just a table and two chairs. It's not very big at all."

"There's a couch on one side," I add, tormenting her.

She is confused, stricken. "There's a couch too?" she repeats. "A couch on one side? You didn't say anything about a couch. A couch, a table, and two chairs then," she says slowly, drawing the space and arranging things, faces, colors in it. "You forget colors last of all," she says. "Faces are the first to go. At the very, very end you forget colors."

She dreams people are colors. "You were yellow, *sit al-banaat,* like the sun," she says.

"And you? What were you?" I ask.

"Blue," she says, "like my eyes."

"Your eyes are light blue, not deep blue."

"Light blue then," she consents impatiently, continuing, "Your mother was brown, Edouard was white, Moise was red,

Marcelle was orange, and your Uncle Jacquo was green. They said I could touch their faces."

"*Merci*," she told them, "*merci pour votre générosité.*" She graciously declined their offer, forcing her hands down into her lap and fixing her eyes on a distant point, withstanding the greatest temptation, the one she can never yield to, the one without substitute: to see.

Photograph: Nona Fortuna, Uncle Edouard, and Grandpapa Jacquo, Cairo, 1947

Over time many of the photographs were destroyed, lost, or stolen. In the siblings' neglect, in their prodigal disregard for the few photographs left, there was something brazen, as if they were rejecting the burden of proof, denying the need to record who they were and where they came from; as if the very idea were an affront; as if photographs, mere objects, were an insult to their memories and to the boundlessness of the imagination.

The siblings went their separate ways. Different times and places, different needs and experiences divided them; the few surviving photographs left great gaps in the story—empty spaces that the family filled with words, gestures, childhood yearnings that had become tainted by later hues, a desire to link past and future and a longing for other days, for the people they had been in other days, and for a place that had never been a homeland but that they had called home.

In the last photograph taken of him, it is clear that Grandpapa Jacquo knew that the end—of their Cairo, of everything familiar—was near: there is a kind of defeat or humiliation in his eyes, a fatigue or despair. He did not want to believe there was no future for them. "What's so terrible here? What's so bad?" he would ask as he hobbled through the house after Uncle Moise, clutching the Zionist pamphlets in Arabic and French that so upset him they made him wheeze—or so Grandpapa claimed. All that paper.

Uncle Moise was both secretive and determined in his comings and goings, disappearing for nights on end. Once a whole detail of soldiers came to the house in the middle of the night, searching the closets and under the mattresses. Grandpapa Jacquo had no idea what they were looking for. The next morning over coffee, bleary-eyed, he said simply, "We're moving to another apartment. This business will bring us bad luck."

Nona Fortuna protested vigorously, but in vain. Grandpapa Jacquo was never as insistent as when it came to his fears. She called for his mother—also Umm Jacquo—a large woman who had terrorized and embittered the lives of the eighty construction workers in her employ, to prevail upon her son.

She came huffing and puffing up the stairs, her gold bracelets jangling, and looked him over as if he were terminally ill. Her conclusion: there was nothing to be done. She advised Nona Fortuna to give in gracefully.

That afternoon the two women found another apartment. The agent, owner of a stand that sold rice milk, brought the landlord; within minutes the deal was closed. Toward evening, the Sicourelles arrived at their new house with their clothes, the servant girls, and Nona Fortuna's expensive china. Grandpapa Jacquo looked out a back window, saw the cemetery across the street, and shuddered. "We will not spend the night here beside those dead people," he announced. And so they spent the night at his aunt's house, moving the next day into another new home in Cairo, their last, a noisy four-room apartment facing the street on Shari'a Sakakini, Street of the Knives.

The family's money quickly ran out. Grandpapa Jacquo sold their last articles of value to pay off his gambling debts and his creditors; he was ruined. His face took on the pallor of a worn old suit. Every day, beginning in the afternoon and continuing until the early hours of the morning, he would squander his time at the gambling table, seeing every loss as a sign that something good was bound to come, as the last hurdle, the last hell heralding true victory. One of the siblings—usually Uncle Moise, sometimes Edouard or Marcelle, even Uncle Sicourelle, who did his best to evade the unpleasant task—would pry him away. It was hard to uproot Grandpapa Jacquo. He believed a plot was being laid against him by Zionism, his rich family, and his creditors; he particularly loathed Zionism, placing it above all other enemies. Human beings he could never spurn—every face evoked compassion. Ideas, abstractions, and ideologies were another matter. And yet he knew nothing of ideas; he thought he supported Mussolini. Out of patriotism and nostalgia for his birthplace, Livorno, he flew the Italian flag on his roof during the first year of World War II. Uncle Moise climbed onto the roof and took down the flag. "Have you gone completely mad?" he asked. They argued. Uncle Moise explained about Fascism and the Italian alliance with Nazi Germany. Grandpapa Jacquo took it very hard, insulted on behalf of Mussolini and the Italian nation. "You won't have a family!" he cried in a frenzy. "You'll forget where you came from!"

Years later, Uncle Moise told this story with bemused affection, now sympathetic to the ties that grow from shared memories, shared landscapes, loyalty toward someone from the same neighborhood.

He became a farmer, first on a kibbutz in the Galilee and then in a village at the foot of Mount Tabor. Uncle Sicourelle ridiculed him, both to his face and behind his back, trying to entice him with business ventures in Africa every few years. Coffee plantations, mines, tanneries, corn importing—what didn't he try? Moise would read his letters with an abashed smile, holding the paper with the tips of his fingers so as not to stain it with grease or wet black fertilizer. "What does he write?" his wife would ask. "Tell me what he says." Moise's large, childlike face would open slowly, like a curtain that draws back in jerks because something has stuck in the track. "Nothing special. My brother wishes I were near him."

Uncle Sicourelle really did want him near. Lacking any religious feelings or aspirations to a higher morality, he had come to see Uncle Moise as a paragon of purity, a symbol of uncompromising virtue and integrity, a heroic figure whose mere existence elevated life itself. He was not completely blind to the pioneering Zionist vision: traces of it touched him, too, even in his colonial outpost. Warily, he allowed himself to be just a little impressed. His long years in Africa, during colonial rule and the first years of independence, had sown in him bitterness and suspicion toward the dogma of any national liberation movement, as well as toward liberals white or black—and intellectuals of any kind, Jewish, non-Jewish, African, French, or American. When their ideologies resulted in violence, he said, they simply "washed their hands of things, hiding behind their Third World slogans."

"All this claptrap ends in killing and corruption," he had said to Uncle Moise. He wanted to tell Moise something important: to watch out for himself, to not get sidetracked or disgrace himself. They were standing on the summit of Mount Tabor, waiting for Madame Sicourelle to end her tour of the Franciscan Church of the Transformation. It was the late 1950s, and the uncle and his wife had come to Israel for a brief visit. They had hired a car and driver and allotted five hours to Uncle Moise and three hours to everything else.

Uncle Moise had been stunned. For the first time he experienced the depth of his brother's cynicism, both personal and political, a great bottomless pit of distrust that swallowed every aspect of his life.

"Whose side are you on, anyway?" Moise had asked, a little confused. "Our side or the Arabs'?"

"Yours," answered Uncle Sicourelle. "What do I care about anyone else?"

They said nothing the whole way down to Moise's house, where they ate okra in tomato sauce and lemon that he had prepared. Madame Sicourelle took the recipe. When the time came to leave, Uncle Moise had disappeared. His wife apologized for him. "It's his shift at the cowshed."

"He's ruined, your brother," Moise complained to Mother when he visited several days later. "I don't know what's happened to his head over there."

"Maybe it's the heat," Mother suggested, half serious.

"It's hot here, too, Inès. So what?" Moise answered her in disgust, stern and humorless, like the saint Uncle Sicourelle imagined him to be.

Eleven months separated Uncle Sicourelle and him; Moise was the eldest. By age five he already had the wisdom of a clan elder, a reflective quality, keen judgment, and a rare gift for restraint. When he was angry he would crush plates and cups with his bare hands. He studied without cease. By age ten he was boss of the kitchen, giving the cook advice. He stubbornly insisted on washing his own clothes; he knew every stone, store, and stall on the street, every salesman by name, every cart owner. By age twelve he had taught himself to read and write in Arabic while Uncle Sicourelle, Mother, and Marcelle were busy terrorizing the strange Arabic teacher Grandpapa Jacquo had brought home. He learned to place bandages soaked in lavender water on Nona Fortuna's forehead during her long illnesses, both real and imagined; he raised Edouard, youngest of the siblings, "to be a real man."

Grandpapa Jacquo tiptoed around him, hiding the unpaid bills in a large vase in the living room. "He doesn't act like a child, that boy. What's he so worried about all the time?" he said to Nona Fortuna.

"He's *my* child," she informed him with pride. "That's what you don't understand."

But he did understand. When Uncle Moise stopped trying to educate him and found other interests, Grandpapa Jacquo breathed a sigh of relief. He was even generous enough to predict a brilliant future for his eldest son: "He'll be a great statesman like your father, Ota."

"My father was not a statesman," Nona Fortuna corrected him dryly. "My father hated politicians. He spent his whole life avoiding those people."

"It doesn't matter what he'll be exactly," Grandpapa said, defending himself. "You know what I mean."

But she did not want to know. Nona Fortuna avoided the intimacy of knowing; her face wore a mask of pain and pride, as if she felt herself unappreciated, misunderstood, as if she felt she never got what she deserved. She was aloof. She faced the camera even though she had turned her back.

This is their last photograph in Egypt, taken with Edouard, the child of their old age; a few months later Nona Fortuna and the children followed Uncle Moise to Israel. Her asymmetrical eyebrows, the left one lower and thinner than the right, make her face look lopsided. Her wonderful strong neck is erect, as if she were standing, but she is sitting down. She is no taller than Grandpapa Jacquo, who sits by her side, though she seems to be. Glasslike and motionless, her large, serious doll eyes seem not quite real. Having her photograph taken is a serious matter to her, a moment of control and restraint. She puts her heart and soul into it, showing the viewer what she thinks is her best self: the ears half concealed by carefully arranged hair smoothed like a scarf, the clean neckline of her dress with its two neat lapels, the absence of jewelry. Darkness closes in on the three of them from behind. The solemnity of the formal pose is a premonition of grief. Two months after this photograph was taken, Grandpapa Jacquo died. A tempered, gentle knowing shines from his eyes. He looks trim and proper. His flaplike ears are the only evidence of his characteristic playfulness, the right one lower than the left. The tall child standing behind, just where their shoulders meet, separates rather than binds them. He appears there as if he were pasted in later, part of a montage.

He *was* pasted in later: Nona Fortuna gave birth to her youngest at age forty-five. When he was six, he was sent to live with Uncle Renato, Grandpapa Jacquo's childless brother, who loved the boy as if he were his own.

That was the end of Edouard. He hated the rigid order of the household, the puritanical fussiness of Uncle Renato and his wife, the quiet, dark rooms, the servants who feared their own shadows, and, above all, the lessons in religion, history, and law that were forced on him hour after hour with the interminable patience and dull zeal reserved for the pursuit of minutiae.

He ran away more than once, coming home to Nona Fortuna filthy, battered, and numb from hanging off trolley cars and endlessly wandering through the city streets. Nona did not want to hear about his troubles. Lips pursed, she would wash him, dress him in clean clothes, feed him, and march him back to Uncle Renato's. Grandpapa Jacquo thought she had no heart.

"You have no heart, Ota," he told her.

"I wish I didn't," she retorted. "Maybe then it wouldn't hurt so much."

Their home had fallen apart little by little, without even the magnificence of decay that clings to a house past its prime. Grandpapa Jacquo had sunk into debt and ever more foolish attempts to get out of it; Nona Fortuna devoted herself to the cult of infirmity and its paraphernalia of milk baths, compresses, and endless confessions to her former teachers, the nuns of St. Anne's.

She brushed aside Grandpapa's sentimentality. Above all she prized a good education and the proper orderly life that made it possible. Uncle Renato was a respectable jurist who led just such a life, though she wasn't so sure about his other qualities. He blew his nose loudly, haggled with his servants over every half penny, never saw what was not shown him and never heard what was not intended for his ears; he bored those around him by sanctimoniously quoting legal citations, as if to prove his inalienable rectitude. Really, he was no more than an "*abu nafha*," an old windbag. Grandpapa Jacquo was confused. "So why do you send the child to him?"

"That's all there is," she'd explain. "It's better than nothing."

For six years Edouard lived with Uncle Renato, complaining bitterly but growing wiser in his way, learning to wear the protective camouflage of the weak, an air of obsequious courtesy that deceived the uncle into believing that his careful grooming had paid off well indeed.

Uncle Moise visited regularly, taking the boy out for fresh air. Overwhelmed with joy and a sense of release, Edouard would tear at everything in his path: leaves, papers, ice-cream cones devoured one after another, Uncle Moise's book bag, the tablecloth at Café Groppi, the scented onionskin paper that Moise's friend Jacqueline would give him to get him to sit quietly and draw. Every two weeks Moise would take the boy to Jacqueline's large, well-lit room, full of enormous colorful pillows and young men and women smoking and talking with incredible speed and earnestness. Jacqueline always wore the same dark dress, black or blue, with the same white lace collar. The same wan smile adorned her face, and this disturbed the child: he never knew whether her smile expressed happiness or displeasure at their arrival. The young women pressed cakes and sweets on him, and one of them, Nadia, taught him to play chess, praising his skill until she tired of him and crossed the room to join in a lively conversation. Uncle Moise and Jacqueline would shout at each other and flail their arms. One time Moise abruptly grabbed Edouard and stormed out, slamming the door.

"Why do you visit Jacqueline if you fight all the time?" the child had dared to ask.

"We are not fighting," Moise had explained. "We're arguing. Sometimes people disagree."

"You always disagree," the child had insisted. Uncle Moise had laughed. "Maybe, but that doesn't mean I don't love her. I can love her *and* argue with her."

They were eating yellow lupine beans from paper cones, spitting out the tough translucent skins. "Does she love you?" Edouard had asked.

Uncle Moise had thought for a moment. "I don't think so. I don't think Jacqueline loves anyone."

Edouard ran into her twenty years later in the heart of the newly captured Sinai desert, several months after the Six Day War. The jeep in which she and other curious Israelis had been traveling had broken down. They had been withering in the sun for hours, waiting for a passing car to help. When Jacqueline saw Edouard in his army vehicle she stared long and hard from behind her dark sunglasses before running toward him, crying his name. The two soldiers with him restrained her, splashing water on her face. They thought she was suffering from sunstroke. When she removed her sunglasses he recognized the familiar wan, intriguing smile. "So what are you doing here?" she asked excitedly. He stammered something evasive. He was the head of Israel's secret service interrogation team in Gaza.

Photograph: Jacqueline Kahanoff, Uncle Moise, and Mother, the Banks of the Nile, Cairo, 1940

Jacqueline hated having her picture taken, but she liked this picture because of its "literary" blurriness, as she called it. "Literary! Everyone in it looks seasick," Mother said. How strange and brutal the placement of the dark diagonal line to the left, which slices through the photograph arbitrarily, barely missing the three figures but dividing the foggy, dreary, inconsequential landscape. The diagonal line is itself a figure in the photograph. It is insistent, more definite than the pallid people in the photograph or the photographer's uncertain intentions. The three figures are poised between visibility and invisibility, flickering before our eyes like a mirage.

Years after the photograph was taken, Uncle Moise sent it to Jacqueline. He had found it tucked between the pages of an

Arabic edition of *The Thousand and One Nights*. She wrote back in English: "This is the story of our lives, Moise." He didn't know what she meant by "this," but he liked the bittersweet nostalgia of the sentence. When, in the early 1960s, he heard that she had published an article on their "Levantine generation" in an important literary journal, he was filled with a childlike happiness. "I always knew Jacqueline would make something of herself," he told Mother.

Jacqueline had vanished from his life, but he heard that she had moved to Paris and back to Israel, moved to America and back to Israel, that she had published essays and stories and gotten married and divorced, that she presided over a "salon" for local intellectuals in her Tel Aviv apartment, that she was highly respected. Then he heard that she had a fatal disease.

He went to visit her at the nursing home where she had been brought during the final weeks of her life. He spent hours in the visitors' lounge; she refused to see anyone.

"You're wasting your time, Moise, you might as well go," he was advised by Jacqueline's sister Josette, who had come from Paris to care for her.

"I've been her friend for ages," he explained.

"She is nobody's friend right now, least of all her own," Josette answered.

He paused. "She may not be my friend, but I am hers," he said slowly and strode toward her room, Josette at his heels.

She did not recognize him. Josette explained, "It's Moise, Jacqueline. Don't you remember?"

She closed her eyes for a long while. "Stubborn ass," she mumbled when she opened them, waving weakly at the chair beside her bed, inviting him to sit.

They talked for more than an hour. "I'm tiring you," he said at last.

She could no longer speak; he gave her a pen and some paper. "Fatigue has no meaning for me," she wrote in a wobbly, pale script.

"Be strong," he said.

She glared at him, pressing the pen into the paper as hard as she could. "Don't be a fool. I'm more than half dead already."

He rose, hands by his sides, and stared at the floor. Finally he said, "I brought you some oranges and apples, our best this year. Next week I'll bring you strawberries. You used to love them."

Tears welled in her eyes. She tried to brush at them with the back of her hand. She wrote, "I don't love oranges or strawberries. I love you."

When he came the next week she was somewhat stronger and had been propped up on large pillows. Her face was clear and her features as sharp as they had once been. When she saw him standing in the doorway she said, "Here comes the Zionist farmer with his oranges!" They laughed and reminisced. As he was leaving, he said, "When I sent you that photograph of us, you wrote, 'This is the story of our lives.' What did you mean?"

"What difference does it make?" she asked.

"It's important," he insisted. She slid her arms under the blanket and pressed her head back against the pillows. "I wrote something about that photograph once," she said.

"I've read everything you've ever written; I don't remember that."

She laughed. "Why should you remember? It was never published. It was in the first draft of 'A Childhood in Egypt.' "

"Why did you take it out?" he asked.

"I didn't. The editors took it out. I was so grateful they were publishing my work that I didn't object. You know how we good girls were raised in Egypt, Moise. We'd say 'Excuse me' if someone stepped on our toes."

He nodded. "I'd like to see the piece anyway," he said. "Does Josette have a copy?"

She shrugged, her sharp shoulder blades poking from the wide neck of her nightgown. "Forget it, Moise," she said. "It's just *kalaam fadi,* empty words."

She died a few days later. After the funeral, as they lingered by the cemetery gate, Josette handed Moise an envelope. "Jacqueline wanted you to have this," she said.

He read it on his way home, as the bus lurched toward the Galilee, making the words jump before his eyes. The title typed on the first page said, "A Childhood in Egypt"; under it some-one had scrawled, "First Draft." That evening, after he had showered and eaten, he read a passage aloud to his wife. "Some time ago a friend from Cairo sent me a photograph. Three blurry figures—my friend, his younger sister, and myself—against a blurry cityscape. Although it was taken on the banks of the Nile, the picture could have been taken anywhere, in Warsaw, Berlin, or Tokyo. It is nearly impossible to make out the details of the place. This photograph occupied me for several days, not because of what was in it but because of what was not: a real sense of place or time. Its ambiguity was somehow famil-iar. The photograph resonated within me: after all, the blurring of figures and landscape, of general and specific, is exactly what typified our Levantine experience. The light that floods the pho-tograph, obliterating distinctions, is my light, the light of my Levantine generation. Questions—What is our language? Our nationality? Our place?—rise from the painfully beautiful haze of this photograph." When Moise finished reading, he looked up at his wife. She had fallen asleep, curled in an armchair.

Missing Photograph: Left to right: *Esther, Inès, and Uncle Edouard, Tel Aviv Beach, 1965*

Edouard is kneeling in the sand, one leg folded beneath him, the other bent at the knee. His left arm is resting on his belly and his right, shiny with suntan lotion, is extended, fist clenched and muscles flexed, to show off his strength. His bony profile with the hawk nose tilts downward toward the display of muscles, his mouth twisted in pride and exertion as he spits, "Take the picture already, take the picture."

"You're such a baby," Mother says, running a hand through his tight curls. "Such a baby!" she repeats, suddenly frowning: her large ring is caught in his hair, tangled in curls that tug at her fingers as she tries to break free. That's how the photograph catches her: one hand buried in Edouard's thick curls, leaning toward him, her mouth slightly open in alarm.

She is wearing a corsetlike bathing suit that sculpts her body into a large rectangular box. Her short, soft hair is windblown, revealing her forehead and a thin, barely discernible scar.

I am lying to their left trapped beneath a thick layer of sand, my wet head glinting like a skull. Uncle Edouard has buried me like that, carefully pouring bucket after bucket of wet sand over me and patting it down, forbidding me to move. "Stay like that until we come back," he instructed me before taking Mother for a short walk up to the kiosk.

Uncle Edouard has an impressive set of false teeth. Whenever I misbehave he pulls out the upper row and waves it at me. "Do you see this? Do you want to see the other half?" he teases me.

I hide behind Mother, peeking around her. "Stop that, Edouard," Mother says with a laugh, half scolding. "You're frightening the child."

"Eddie," he corrects. "Eddie, Inès, not Edouard."

"Your friends can call you Eddie. To me you're Edouard. Eddie—what kind of a name is that anyway?" says Mother.

"It's a perfectly good name," Edouard says, briskly drying his curls with a towel and then shaking them out, batting his eyelashes, pretending to ignore the girls who pass by, ogling him.

As they walk away he studies their small behinds, encased in even smaller bikinis, the cheeks rising and falling. "Ah, Tel Aviv," he sighs longingly.

Edouard has a passion for the good life, fantasizing about the bounties that surely await him if only he works hard enough. In the meantime, in indulgent compromise, he snatches everything that comes his way: women, good times, food, investment opportunities. "He's like a girl who just lost her virginity and wants to make up for lost time," Uncle Sicourelle says.

At twenty-two he arrived at the uncle's doorstep in Gabon looking for work, for a "chance." Uncle Sicourelle scrutinized the pointy black-and-white shoes, the hip-hugging pants, and the gaping nylon shirt with yellow rectangles exposing the hairy chest. "First put some decent clothes on, then we'll talk," Uncle Sicourelle had said in disgust, passing his hand in a razor-like movement over Edouard's long sideburns.

The things he had cultivated with such childish determination made no impression in Africa: his gruff Israeli manner, his army swagger, his smugness over his success with women. Frustration and arrogance, an alternating sense of inferiority and superiority—the legacy of his youth as an outsider on the kibbutz—suffused his every encounter with the world.

He was thirteen when Uncle Moise had brought him to the kibbutz, after Nona Fortuna and the children arrived in Israel. Edouard had mastered Israeli ways and the Hebrew language with astonishing speed. His years in Cairo under Uncle Renato's thumb had taught him something about pleasing authority and feigning indoctrination: he never met things head on, ducking confrontations, draping himself in the colors of his surroundings with engaging charm and flexibility, lying incessantly.

Nona Fortuna had let go of him. He was the youngest of her children and the most complicated. His flirtations with girls and with various ideologies, his running around, his perfect Israeli accent, his broken French, in which he expounded on the virtues of the kibbutz and collective living—all this simply amused her. "The child doesn't know what he's talking about," she'd say.

When he came out of the army, he had changed his tune. He began denouncing the kibbutz, dressing in fancy clothes, and pestering Nona Fortuna with endless questions about his brother in Africa who had "made it."

"What has he 'made,' *ya ahbal,* you fool?" Nona Fortuna said. "What is it you think he's done, tell me?"

"He has everything he wants," Uncle Edouard mumbled in reply, spread-eagled on her bed, stroking his bare belly, his eyes closed.

"So what? He lives like a dog over there with those *sauvages.* He doesn't enjoy any of it."

"You don't understand, Maman," he protested. "You don't understand a thing."

Day after day he nagged her to write to the uncle, "so he'll send for me." At last, she gave in reluctantly.

"What should I write?" she asked, irritated, impatient, smoothing the paper.

"Tell him about me. Tell him I'm hard-working, honest, and willing to do any job he'll give me. I'll even work in garbage— tell him that."

She laid down the pen. "I can't write that."

"Why not?" he pleaded.

"You're not hard-working, you're not honest, and you're not willing to do any job, Edouard," she said.

In the end she wrote something vague and grudgingly complimentary. Uncle Sicourelle understood perfectly. "Let him come for a trial period," he replied.

He watched Edouard from a distance, noting with amazement how different he was from the rest of them: there was no trace of the austerity, the abstinence, the great pride they all took in restraint and circumspection—he, Uncle Moise, Inès. "That brother of mine really likes the good life," he said to Madame Sicourelle.

She prayed Edouard would leave. "He's taking up with the servant girls, Chouchou," she said, attempting to sound nonchalant.

Uncle Sicourelle made Edouard a foreman at the leather factory he owned in Gabon, putting him in charge of six men. "Only six?" Edouard complained, disappointed.

"Be glad I'm making you a foreman. I should have kept you as a worker, but I can't because of the blacks."

Edouard did not understand. "What about the blacks? Why do you care what they think?"

"I can't have a brother of mine working side by side with blacks. It's not good for them, and not good for me."

Edouard tried to learn. He adopted his brother's authoritative, distant tone of voice, wore a tie, kept notes on a small pad purchased for that purpose, and harassed the workers. But the harder he tried—enacting a cheap imitation of control and competence—the more the real thing evaded him: the subtle, intimate understanding of his surroundings and the gentle wielding of authority that Uncle Sicourelle had labored to acquire and that he now, after much experience, wore like a second skin, never forgetting that his laborers were his allies, that power and those who held it were mutable and fleeting, and that only by grace— not by right—only by the ephemeral smile on fate's countenance did he sit where he sat.

Once Uncle Sicourelle found Edouard shaking one of the laborers by the neck. "*Mais qu'est-ce que tu fais?*" Uncle Sicourelle asked, horrified. "Have you gone mad?"

"He came late, the bastard," Edouard explained. "It's the second time."

"Follow me," Uncle Sicourelle commanded, striding toward the office. He closed the door and faced Edouard. "Tell me, who do you think you are?"

Edouard was confused and when confused he turned insolent. "Either give me a free hand or don't, but I can't work with you breathing down my neck and humiliating me in front of those blacks."

"A free hand?" Uncle Sicourelle sneered. "And what will you do with your free hand when I give it to you? Will you use it on them, *ya* Co-lo-nel?"

Edouard left the office with a slam of the door, flushed from head to foot. "I'm leaving!" he announced to Madame Sicourelle, piling his clothes in a heap and dumping them into his suitcase. But he didn't leave. He stayed for another two months, painting the town red, rising late, splashing in the pool with Erouan.

The child adored him. Erouan would wait for hours for Edouard to get up, sitting outside his room like a beggar, listening for sounds of movement. The gurgle of water in the bathroom was the signal. Erouan would race to the kitchen and bring Edouard a large tray laden with a coffeepot, *pain au chocolat*, freshly squeezed juice, and a dish of thick cream studded with slices of mango and banana. "*Bonjour, mon petit jeune homme*," Uncle Edouard would call gaily, combing his hair, a towel around his waist. "What shall we do to amuse ourselves today?"

They would dive into the pool, throw stones at the trees to scare away the birds, set water traps for Richard, frighten Arlette, the governess, or dress up in Madame Sicourelle's old clothes. The child beamed as never before. Edouard's intense vitality, his charming flippancy, his inflated stories of heroism in the army, which he turned into a kind of endless Western, imbued Erouan with a new confidence. Edouard sensed this and seized the power it gave him. He set the child against his surroundings. "Tell them what you don't want! Be a man!" he would exhort.

He had a way with children and women. He never tired of seduction, his truest role, in which his pure self broke free of the adult constraint and pretense he had learned at Uncle Renato's; he became all body and desire and will.

As if by accident he would rub against Arlette's bare dark shoulder, enjoying her embarrassment. "Excuse me, Mademoiselle Arlette, I didn't see you there," he would lie. The governess would flush with excitement; no one had ever called her Mademoiselle Arlette. He vaguely remembered Levantine gestures of courtship from his childhood in Egypt; in Gabon he took them out and aired them, as he did his French. He showered the tall, awkward girl with flowers, cheap perfume, and wooden beads—not because he could not have won her any other way but simply because he enjoyed doing so.

Erouan stood watch when the couple were alone in the toolshed until Madame Sicourelle discovered them one day and nearly fainted. Leaning on the flimsy door, Erouan had not wanted to let her pass.

"Let me in or I will call for Monsieur Sicourelle," she hissed at him. When he still refused to budge, she slapped him and shoved open the door. As she stood in the entrance, straining to see, Erouan sank his teeth into her arm and would not let go. Squealing with pain, Madame Sicourelle saw the girl lying on the carpenter's workbench, her legs spread and her skirt rolled up to her waist. Madame Sicourelle fired her on the spot and ran to tell the uncle.

"What are you getting so excited about?" he said. "These things happen." What concerned him most was the child's biting her. He pondered this for some time until he came up with the appropriate punishment: he locked Erouan in the toolshed overnight so the boy could give serious thought to his deed. That night, his cries shook the house. Madame did not shut her eyes for a second, begging Uncle Sicourelle to drop the whole affair.

"Forget it, Chouchou, I've already forgotten it myself. You see, it's all over," she said, covering the purple welt on her arm.

Edouard had shut himself up in his room, where he sat sweating over his packed suitcases. In the end he raced to the yard, broke the lock on the toolshed door with a long wooden pole, and grabbed the child, who was soaked with urine.

"Why don't you pick on *me*—that's something I'd like to see! It's easy to pick on a child!" he hurled at Uncle Sicourelle, who stood in the garden watching, blinking back his anger.

On the morning of Edouard's departure, the uncle gave him two thousand francs. "Take it, do something with it," he said, throwing the envelope at Edouard and walking away. Edouard left the envelope on the dining table, face up. "For Mademoiselle Arlette," he had written.

"You can tell he's never worked for money, that brother of yours, wasting it on a black girl like that," Madame Sicourelle said bitterly.

The uncle was pleased, though. "Maybe he'll straighten out in the end," he said.

For years afterward the uncle heard nothing from Edouard and did not try to contact him. Whatever was beyond his immediate world became increasingly vague and obscure, almost nonexistent, relegated to a netherworld where it could not thrive.

But Uncle Moise kept him informed; he would not let him escape. Every month he sent a detailed letter, uninflected and devoid of extraneous adjectives, calm as the sea in August. Detail followed detail with monotonous clarity, like a bedtime story told to a child for the thousandth time.

"Edouard has become a policeman," Uncle Moise wrote two years after the uncle left Gabon, where he'd lost his property in a military uprising. Moise went on to relay with great thoroughness his daughter's trimester grades, the state of the crops, Robert's loss in recent local elections, and a new recipe for mayonnaise.

Madame Sicourelle usually read these letters aloud to the uncle, interjecting her own comments until it was no longer possible to distinguish between them.

"Is that what you say or what he says?" the uncle would ask, annoyed.

Moise's letters always provoked an uneasy mix of affection and irritation, calm and disquiet, longing and estrangement. More than anything they made the uncle conscious of the distance, which he would rather forget; the effort to imagine the other and so remember his separateness left him exhausted and despondent. He almost never answered Moise's letters unless he wanted to propose some entrepreneurial venture. "Write something," he would tell Madame Sicourelle. His silence in no way deterred Uncle Moise—quite the contrary. He felt the uncle's evasiveness increased his own responsibility for the family's unity, for the integrity of its members, for their collective memory and shared past, for their offspring and their future, for the ingathering of their scattered fragments.

Moise was good at this. With interminable patience he wove his apologia, turning, as he did, everything bad into something good, never averting his gaze, not for a moment, as if his persistence, his will, could change all things intransigent; as if his very gaze had the power to soften and ripen the obstacle, melting it in the heat of his constancy.

Once, he had fixed his devotion on one of the cats in his yard. It was a speckled cat, skittish and suspicious, which Moise came to call Margot. He was in love with cats; he plied them with chunks of white cheese and bread crumbs—but only in the yard, since his wife objected to their presence in the house. He had had his eye on Margot "from the beginning," he said. She was the most agile, the most cunning and aloof; she was the first to steal the food and run off. Her independence and pluck commanded his respect. He wanted to befriend her. At first he had left the bowl of food for Margot at the edge of the yard. She had come up to the bowl, grabbed the food, and fled as usual. Several days later Moise moved the bowl a few inches closer to the porch, and then a few more, little by little. Within a month he was placing the bowl right on the doorstep to the house. Another month went by and he was extending a hand and petting her arched back. He and Margot made an agreement: one stroke only, no more.

He called her "my cat," not out of a proprietary sense but out of affection and respect for the stringent terms of their relationship, which never altered, thanks mainly to Margot, who continued to keep her distance—until one day she was crushed under the wheels of Moise's tractor.

He hadn't heard a thing, he said. He had stopped the tractor and there had been one faint cry, then silence. He found the bloody pelt caught in the front wheel. He lifted it with a dustpan and threw it in the garbage.

"You could have at least dug her a nice grave if you loved her so much," Mother had said.

He had shrugged his shoulders. "What difference would it have made, Inès?"

Like Grandpapa Jacquo, he loathed graves, headstones, memorial services—anything in life that was evidence of death. Unlike Grandpapa, he was not haunted by mystical fear; rather, it was the sanctity of the secular that made him loathe all such religious trappings.

"You and your principles," Mother hurled at him after Nona Fortuna's death, many years later, when he forbade them to observe shivah, the seven-day mourning period. Nevertheless, she didn't dare defy him. Moise exuded a firm sense of knowing the right thing, however radical his views.

Sorrow had hardened his features, lending them an air of brutality. "These things aren't for us, Inès. We're not believers. Why on earth should we start lying now?" he said.

"It's got nothing to do with believing," Mother said. "We can't just go home like this, as if nothing happened."

"We can," Uncle Moise said.

Edouard made a scene and then sat shivah at his own house in Dimona. "I won't have that Communist goy tell me how to live!" he fumed later.

"Stop, stop with the dramatics. I haven't got the strength," Mother said, climbing a flimsy aluminum ladder that barely bore her weight and crawling into the tiny space between the ceiling and roof of Nona Fortuna's house, her behind protruding, ballooned out like a pillow, as she pulled out large dusty bundles and threw them down with a heavy thud.

"Be careful, Inès," Edouard called, skipping aside in alarm as a box landed at his feet.

"You be careful," she retorted, plunging a broom handle into the space and pushing out great thick clouds of dust that turned their hair white.

Edouard's explosions of rage annoyed her. "He's become just like an Arab, that one," she would say to Uncle Moise. He would nod his large head pensively. "Yes," he agreed. "Yes."

Edouard had become a big boss. "King of Gaza," they called him. He kept a little apartment there, with a cook and a mistress, returning to the house in Dimona only once every other week, for the Sabbath. Night after night he lay in his living room on a mountain of plump embroidered featherbeds, watching

Egyptian sitcoms and picking at the large trays of snacks hurried in to him.

Having made a name for himself on the police force as the toughest and cruelest of interrogators, he had been appointed head of the security service's interrogation team in Gaza. "Those poor Moslems tremble when he walks down the street," Mother says with amazement and infinite sadness, looking at the photograph of Edouard on the beach. "Look what a child he was!" she says, bringing the photograph closer, right up to her eyes, straining to see more, to plunge into it.

They rarely meet, an obscure screen of suspicion and bitterness having risen between them. "He's the one who's changed," Mother says.

The years have chipped away his desire for play, his restless pursuit of different identities, and his promiscuous sailing among people and things. What has been exposed is a core of extremism and tyranny: he is now hard, solid. The change happened slowly, far from the family. He speaks Arabic almost exclusively and with a strange, demonstrative aggression, taking every opportunity to deride both the "Ashkenazi assimilation" of Uncle Moise and Mother and their naive conciliatory feelings toward the Arabs. He fans some small flame of the past with elaborate Oriental gestures of respect and honor that embarrass Uncle Moise on the few occasions when he visits. It is not that Uncle Moise feels ashamed but that he knows that the past Uncle Edouard would make his own was never, ever his.

"He never saw such things in our home—all this hoo-ha," Uncle Moise marvels. "Were there such things in our home, Inès?" he puzzles, doubting himself, his memory.

"Perhaps there were and we didn't know it," says Mother. "Perhaps there were but we didn't see."

Photograph: *Uncle Sicourelle, the Port of Douala, Cameroon*

R̲egarde, Inès, he's got a face like an animal. Look at Jacquo's expression," said Marcelle.

Mother stared at the photograph, narrowing her eyes in pain or in strained concentration. "He really does, doesn't he?"

"Who does?" I asked, trying on the green jade beads and silk scarves Aunt Marcelle had brought from Thailand.

"*Il est abooha.* Just like Father, *tu sais?*" said Mother, mixing French and Arabic and swatting away the cat that purred around her knees. "Scat! You're like glue."

"Inès!" Marcelle was horrified. She hurried to the spurned cat, its back arched, its eyes fixed stupidly on the floor, and took it in her arms.

"Raphael, *mon pauvre mouton.*"

Lips curling, Mother watched Marcelle bury her face in the gray fur. "You with your cats, you're disgusting."

Aunt Marcelle held the cat with one hand while with the other she thawed a hunk of frozen liver under hot running water. "*Tu ne peux pas t'imaginer,* Inès, how Raphael suffered on the flight. They nearly killed him. When he got out of the cage he could barely make a sound—meow, meow, meow . . ." Marcelle whimpered weakly. "That's what he sounded like, Inès."

"*Ya farhati!* Joy of my old age!" Mother muttered, rolling her eyes. She turned to watch blood dripping on the floor as Marcelle swung the liver gently, slowly, back and forth under the cat's nose. "Give him some fried onion, too, why don't you?"

They had crossed half the world, Marcelle and that cat: Arizona, New York, Singapore, Thailand, Cameroon, Paris, Amsterdam, Israel.

At three in the morning she had pounded on the door with a shoe whose heel had broken off. For hours she had been wandering the darkened alleys of the neighborhood, searching for the tall cypress at the front of the house—her sign.

"I cut it down," Mother explained. "A few months ago. Its roots had grown into the septic system and were causing blockages."

"How could you have done that?" Marcelle was aghast. "That tree was practically a monument, Inès. How could you have cut it down?"

"With an ax," said Mother. "I gave a couple of kids a few shekels to help me. It wrecked all my flowers when it fell, that tree."

"It's a good thing it didn't fall on you, *ya choucha mankoucha.*"

They laughed, their eyes damp. Marcelle was born with a thicket of hair black as a goat's. Grandpapa Jacquo had taken one look at her and said, *choucha mankoucha,* wild forelock. For years her pale triangular face had peered out from behind the great mass of hair with its large, dark, heavy curls.

She suffered much anguish because of that hair. Countless times she had cut it, set it, smeared it with oils, and straightened it, and once she had even burned it trying to flatten the curls with an iron. All in vain: the black intransigent strands had sprung back over her forehead and out from behind her ears, overrunning hairpins and barrettes, elastic bands and velvet ribbons, ruining the *comme il faut* look she had so wanted to adopt.

Mother suddenly turned serious, catching Marcelle's narrow wrist, squeezing, and then letting go. "*Anestina, ya uhti,*" she said softly. "You have delighted us, my sister."

She came once a year, always in the middle of the night, surprising and surprised and thoroughly pleased with her excellent tricks. There she would stand on the doorstep, her slanted eyes with their glorious curling lashes shining in the darkness, lively with a story she was bursting to tell, a ruse, a scrape that had turned out all right in the end.

"*Tu sais,* Inès," she began, gulping cold coffee and wolfing down slices of pickled turnip straight from the jar. "I didn't believe I'd get out of it alive." She had been on a boat, she said, in Australia. A storm had whipped up the sea, rocking the boat violently from side to side. The wind had whistled terribly. "Whoo, whoo . . ." Marcelle blew, puffing out her cheeks.

All the passengers had been screaming and vomiting. Marcelle had vomited and then lost consciousness. When she came to she found herself on an island. "The ship was torn apart at sea. Inès, it was an island of savages," Marcelle swore, placing her hand over her heart.

Mother was spellbound but skeptical. "But you weren't in Australia. How come you were on this boat?"

"This was earlier. Don't you remember I was at Renato's in Adelaide? It happened after I left his place. You should have seen those savages, Inès, every one of them a gorilla, a mountain of a man three times your size."

Mother nodded, slicing bread and picking the crumbs up one by one from the cutting board. Exaggeration was habitual with Marcelle; it came as naturally as eating, sleeping, or breathing. Without a second thought she lied about everything, giving reality infinite leeway, the possibility of ceaseless metamorphosis. She lied for the passion of the story: lying served her no other purpose. On the contrary, she often lied against her own best interests, or just for the hell of it. Even when asked the time she would fib, just to be on the safe side, as if telling the truth were an act of apostasy that would invite incalculable danger.

When she was six Uncle Sicourelle burned her tongue. "You'll stop your lying or I'll show you," he said, bringing a cigarette lighter close to her mouth. She pursed her lips, extending her hand to him instead. "No, your tongue," he demanded. "Open your mouth." She did not open it but fled to the home of the "big lady," Grandpapa Jacquo's mother, who hated little girls. Out of fear, she stayed there for three days, placidly accepting the old woman's idiosyncrasies. She polished dozens of copper pots, waded through sacks of rice and lentils picking out pebbles, slept on a straw mat in the kitchen with the servant girls, and every afternoon suffered humiliation at a fierce ceremony of the big lady's devising. The old woman would gather her grandchildren around a small coal grill in the garden, seating the boys and girls separately. Then she would begin roasting. On one side of the grill she would sear fresh pieces of meat, on the other hard-boiled eggs. The children would sit with their hands behind their backs as she passed her fork from one child to the next, from mouth to mouth: meat for the boys, eggs for the girls. After the children had taken their bites from the fork they would continue to sit in perfect silence, arms and legs crossed, as the big lady indulged in her water pipe. Rose petals floated in the bubbling water in the glass body of the pipe. It was Marcelle's job to pluck the petals for her and throw them in. If a petal was torn or had not been pulled from the very base of the flower, the big lady would force Marcelle to begin the whole procedure from the beginning— spilling out the liquid with the torn petals, cleaning the glass bowl, filling it with fresh water, lighting the pipe, and throwing in new petals. When at last the big lady would suck on the mouthpiece, her eyes closed, Marcelle would breathe a sigh of relief, then stare, transfixed by the swirling water and the dance of the red and pink rose petals bubbling inside.

On the fourth day she returned home and opened her mouth. "Burn it!" she said to Uncle Sicourelle. And he did. Years later she would stick out her tongue at every opportunity, pointing to the small dark spot on its tip.

She showed it to Mother, sticking out her long, purplish tongue, arching it down toward her chin. "Look what that Jacquo did to me. Do you remember?" she asked in a quavering voice, still insulted.

Mother did not remember. Marcelle's adventures, her many crises and afflictions, aroused terror in Mother. "Stop it already, stop it," she scolded, swiping the coffee cup and placing it in the sink.

Marcelle followed her, poking among the dirty cups, searching for hers, and complaining. "Why did you take it away from me? I hadn't finished."

"So make yourself another," Mother said impatiently, jerking the kitchen curtains aside and letting the dawn light creep into the room. They stood at the window, shoulder to shoulder, their elbows on the ledge. Fat pigeons clustered on the grass below, pecking at the green weeds and puffing out their wings. There was a large pit to one side.

"Is that the hole from the tree?" Marcelle asked.

"I covered that one," Mother explained. "This is a new one, for a lemon tree."

"You used to have a lemon tree," Marcelle recalled. "The lemons were as dry and shriveled as a witch's tit."

"Lemons don't work for me," Mother said sadly. "It's because of the earth here: just sand and more sand."

She was constantly pulling up and planting, moving things from place to place. Her plans were hatched in the early hours of the morning, over her first cup of coffee. Wearing the pale nightgown that revealed her thick, strong thighs, she would survey the garden with the careful attention of a general looking for signs of disobedience. Dismay would spread across her face, the slow poison of displeasure: here the weeds had gone wild, there a large stone from her beautiful rock garden had rolled to one side, a bush had withered. "One thing leads to another," she would explain two hours later when the work had been finished—the rock garden dragged in a wheelbarrow back behind the house, the rose bed torn up, the mango tree divested of its branches, left scrawny and bare. She attacked them all with a dull vengefulness, steady as a monk. Large thorns would stick in her palms or her legs as she tied a cactus plant with rope, tugging and tugging until both she and it had nearly expired; her arms would be black to the elbows, the front and back of the white nightgown—its hem pulled to one side and tied in a knot—stained as if on her wedding night, the tough skin of her feet scraped and bleeding. Afterward she would wash her feet with a hose, assessing the damage. "I really did some work today," she would say.

"It's a good thing I can't see her," Nona Fortuna would sigh. "God had mercy on me that I shouldn't see her like that, with the hands of a man."

But Mother had no pity—she spared Nona nothing, placing the sprinkler smack in the middle of the path that connected the two houses. Nona Fortuna would stand a few meters away, listening to the spray of the water, waiting. "Inès!" she would call, "Inès! Is that the sprinkler there?" Mother would watch her from the porch, silent. Nona Fortuna would venture three steps forward and get wet, a stream of water running down her glasses. "Inès!" she would try again, coming a few steps closer, arms spread, bending toward the water. She would grab the two spinning, spraying nozzles of the sprinkler as one grasps a writhing puppy. Mother would go to her then, holding her arms forcefully. "Why didn't you say you were here?" Mother would lead her back to our porch and sit her down to shell fava beans and peas for us.

There she would stay until afternoon, singing softly, the towel on her lap covered with empty hulls. Marcelle helped her whenever she came. "I'll do some, Maman," she volunteered gaily, blowing on her freshly painted nails, scattering the hulls.

"Leave it, leave it," Nona Fortuna pleaded after several frenzied minutes. "I'll do it myself."

On the back of her pack of cigarettes Marcelle scribbled the recipe. "So, first you shell them," she ventured knowingly.

"Of course you shell them. What are we, cows? You shell them and sauté them a little with the usual mixture—garlic, coriander leaves, and scallions."

"No water?"

"God forbid. Just a little water later, but not so it becomes a soup. Let it cook in its own juices."

"A little tomato paste," Mother added from the kitchen.

"I crush a fresh tomato," Nona Fortuna whispered, sharing a secret. "It tastes better that way."

"What did you say, Maman?" Mother's voice rose, threatening.

"I said instead of tomato paste you can use a tomato. We used to use a tomato."

"When was the last time you went into a kitchen? You always had cooks to make it for you."

"I always cooked, Inès," she protested. "They would put the kettle on the fire and I would add the taste."

Mother brought out a tray of wafer cookies and a pitcher of lemonade. "Ah, you would add the taste," she repeated, drawing out the syllables in feigned awe. Her leg swung back and forth nervously as she glanced at her watch. "It's already noon. Where has the day gone?"

"The day hasn't gone yet, Inès," Marcelle said, yawning. "For me, it's just beginning. When I was in Africa at Jacquo's I never got up before one in the afternoon. That is, if his concubine didn't wake me before that."

"Stop with that filthy talk," Nona Fortuna scolded. "She's your older brother's wife."

"So what?" Marcelle chewed her wafer, reaching to take another. "The truth must be told. I never understood what he saw in her."

"And what does Henri see in you, tell me that? He never says a word, *le malheureux*."

"He's not such a poor thing. He's lucky he found me."

"Some luck! You don't sit still for a minute—not for a minute, like a yo-yo."

"I amuse him, Maman. No one can make him laugh like me, isn't that right, Raphaelos?" She brushed the cat's tail against her cheek, petting him.

Mother's face darkened. "In the end he'll leave you, Marcelle, with all your nonsense."

"He will not," said Marcelle, plucking at her mustache with a pair of tweezers. "He'll never leave me. I know how to hold on to a man, Inès. Give him a lot of rope—you pull a little, give a little. Like that."

Henri did leave once. That was before they moved to France. A Parisian of Polish origin whose family was killed in Europe, he had come to Israel during the War of Independence, joining the foreign volunteers. He had met Marcelle on one of his leaves and fallen in love instantly. But Marcelle drove him crazy. They lived with their baby, André, in a squalid one-room apartment in Magdiel, a dusty little town in the center of the country, tearing each other to shreds, then making up. In the middle of one of their fights he had suddenly been overcome by despair. He had left the house and begun walking. Walking all night, his head pounding, he had reached Kalkilya, just over the Jordanian border. The Jordanian soldiers who stopped him thought he was a spy, beat him soundly, and threw him in jail. He spent three months in a special interrogation wing until Marcelle managed to get the French consul in Amman to intervene on his behalf. The protracted torture had changed Henri. He had lost much weight and become grim. Once back in Israel, he experienced the alienation he had first felt during the War of Independence. He was fed up with everything and within weeks he had sorted out his affairs and taken Marcelle and the baby to Paris—forever, he swore. Years later, after the Six Day War, he returned to Israel and visited Kalkilya, now part of the occupied West Bank, out of nostalgia. He stood in the main square, his face reddening from the sun, and wept. "Did you free Kalkilya?" he was asked by men carting melons and watermelons under their arms. "Not exactly," he mumbled, ducking into a side alley.

After his release, Henri became accident-prone; his arms and legs were frequently in casts and he easily lost his balance. Quick-tongued, quick-tempered, tormented by persistent insomnia, he was constantly slipping on the wooden stairs in their house in the Paris suburbs. Aunt Marcelle loved to polish them with oil, stair by stair. A great thud and cry would be heard from upstairs, followed by a second shout as Henri toppled the shelves full of Simenon books. "Is that you, Henri?" Marcelle would call from downstairs, slowly placing her cigarette in an ashtray, shouting to make herself heard above the sound of one radio, a humming dishwasher, a whirring coffee grinder, a whooshing, gurgling espresso machine, and a television that stayed on night and day. She had a passion for electronic gadgets. She purchased one after another, finding novel uses for them that allowed her to reinvent herself again and again.

Perusing the classified advertisements every morning, she would excitedly circle finds. In pursuit of a used bicycle in excellent condition, or a lawn mower, or the electric deep fryer that a bankrupt restaurateur billed as capable of producing twenty kilos of French fries at a time, she and Henri would travel about for hours, to far-flung suburbs, coal-blackened slums, and remote villages where cows chewed their cud in vast green pastures. Henri would drive, seething, chomping on hunks of carrot and cucumber in his effort to cease smoking, pressing the car to ever faster speeds, and braking suddenly for no evident reason as Aunt Marcelle studied large maps and kept an eye on the road. "Now, Henri, you can pass now!" she would exclaim excitedly, hunching toward the windshield and urging him on whenever they got stuck behind a truck. He would obey, his tongue clenched beneath his upper lip, until suddenly, in the middle of passing, he would remember to explode. "Would you please not tell me how to drive?" he would cry, swerving to the side of the road.

They went from one scene to another, dragging André behind them: entrances and exits, minor scandals, the slapstick of domestic accidents, sales and purchases, airline schedules, brimming ashtrays, and meals *à la minute*. Uncle Henri searched for relatives all over the world. Seconds after they had set down their luggage in hotel rooms in Shanghai, New York, Addis Ababa, or Guadeloupe, he would be attacking the local phone book, looking for a Lehman, a nephew thrice-removed, or just any Jew—even one would prove something.

"Prove what?" Marcelle would say. "What on earth do you have to prove?"

"That they didn't win."

"Who didn't win?"

"The Nazis! Haven't you ever heard of the Nazis? *Mon Dieu!*"

The Jewish diaspora excited him, as if the worldwide dispersal of Jews promised opportunities to find lost Lehmans, extensions of his own existence, emissaries of his self who had been planted, by chance, somewhere else in the world. He imagined them all engaged in a global conversation that went on over his head. He kept in touch with scattered Lehmans by telephone and letter, sending greeting cards even at the Christian New Year and at Easter.

On one visit to Israel he sat with me over a map of the world, excitedly drawing lines connecting countries: "You have family in Colombia (a line), Brazil (a line), Philadelphia (a line), Cameroon (a line), Australia (a line), Paris (a line), Italy (a line), and Israel of course (a line). What do you say to that, Estherkeh?" He beamed with pleasure.

"That's not family there in Australia, Henri," Marcelle interjected. "*Ces sont des cochons.* They're pigs."

"They're still family. You don't have to love them."

"We haven't heard from them in years, those misers. Don't you remember how they treated me?"

"I'm sorry, but that was your fault. Who goes to stay with strangers and brings three girlfriends and a cat?"

"They're not strangers, Henri, they're family."

Marcelle had never got over that trip. She immediately took steps: she tore up all the photographs of Uncle Renato, his wife, and his brother Mario, stuffing the shreds into a brown envelope taped to the back of one of her albums.

She had four of them, with leather bindings: red, green, blue, and gray. They held more than two hundred photographs. Marcelle sucked up photographs like a black hole; every picture that ever belonged to anyone found its way to her. No one knew how she did it. "Last time she was here I watched her like a hawk, but when she left nearly all our photographs had vanished," Uncle Moise once reported in astonishment to Mother. "Tell her she should learn not to steal." Moise wavered, hesitant, a dreamy smile appearing on his lips. "*Il ne faut pas embarrasser les gens.* You shouldn't embarrass people, Inès."

Mother was disappointed. "Moise. He's so trusting." Whenever Marcelle came, he would spread his dwindling collection of photographs before her, shutting his eyes. He turned

Marcelle's weakness into something charming, making it part of family lore, protecting her the way one protects a backward child from taunting neighbors.

And she treated her photographs the way a thief treats stolen property: she moved them from one drawer to another, disguised them, blocked out incriminating information on their backs with blots of ink.

"Show the photographs already," Mother would insist. "Everybody knows you have them."

"I have nothing, Inès," she would swear. "Nothing. Everything's gone."

"The photograph of Papa and Jacquo in Egypt," Mother might plead. "I don't have a single picture of Papa."

Marcelle would break down, slowly opening her heavy drawer. "Just a look, Inès," she would warn. "I'm missing a lot of pictures."

"You're missing a screw in your head, that's what you're missing," Mother would snap, waiting for Marcelle to turn away so she could sneak a few photographs into her own pocket.

They'd been stealing from each other for years. Full of self-righteousness caught in an endless game of gentle retaliation, each was merely reclaiming what was properly hers. In their puzzlement and fury, neither admitted the reason behind it all: that the photographs, tangible remnants of their past, were the emblems of their love.

The last time she came—between her son's two suicide attempts—everything went awry. Sick, quieter than usual, and with a new, soft roundness in her movements and her voice, she seemed to have shed something of herself. She sat on the porch for hours, her hand burrowing in the cat's fur; suddenly cold, she'd turn her face to the December sun, which could not warm her. A thick checkered blanket was draped around her shoulders.

Mother bustled about her, offering things, crazed with worry and a desperate anger. "*Yalla,* get up already, do something," she would say at least once an hour. They went to the cemetery to visit Nona Fortuna. "We haven't visited her for a long time, *tu sais,* Inès?" Marcelle said one morning, lighting a cigarette before her coffee. That night she had had a dream, she said; she had dreamed of Nona. It was the day she died, the day they had buried her.

"You weren't here," Mother corrected. "You were in Tunis."

"It was a dream, Inès," Marcelle protested, defending herself, "not reality. We were all walking in procession, wearing white hoods like the monks in Tibet. It was so beautiful, Inès, *tu ne peux pas t'imaginer.*"

"So?" Mother asked, hostile. "What happened?"

"Each of us was playing an instrument. There was no one else there, just us with our little band and the trees all around. I don't remember what we played. We were carrying Maman with our hands, way up high—you know, like those dolls they used to hold up at the demonstrations against Farouk. We were happy. We were so happy we cried. It was very strange, that dream. I wonder what Moise will say."

"What can he possibly have to say? Was it his dream?"

Marcelle stirred her Turkish coffee, waiting for the grainy brown silt to sink.

She left the next day. All afternoon the scent of her Gitanes and patchouli clung to the rooms, until, toward evening, it was overpowered by the acrid smell of insect repellent that Mother sprayed everywhere as she went about opening all the windows.

It was dark. Mother curled up beside the cupboard in the bedroom where she keeps her photographs, taking them out and putting them back into the brown envelopes, counting them over and over. Her cheeks glistened with a sheen of lotion and the tears that streamed over it, softening nothing in the harsh profile, falling and falling, clinging to the edge of her chin like stubble. "She didn't take anything this time," she mumbled, hunched, shrinking into her flesh.

Missing Photograph: Uncle Sicourelle, the Port of Douala, Cameroon, 1972

That's Uncle Sicourelle standing there like a man. "Stand up straight, Jacquo," Marcelle commands from behind the camera. "Not like a great big sack, *mon Dieu,* like a man."

The plaza is clear, bright, and empty. It is early morning and the sharp light shines down mercilessly, with no reticence or restraint. Blinded, the uncle is squinting, his face scrunched up. He looks like a ferret, with the mean, skeptical, narrowing of his eyes, his thick eyebrows, and the frown that sends little wrinkles down to his chin.

He has gone outside with Marcelle, leaving the rancid office against his will. "There isn't enough light in there. How am I supposed to take your picture without any light?" says Marcelle. "Your office is like a tomb."

He is always happy when she comes to Douala and even happier when she leaves. She makes his head spin, he complains. Now, obedient, he mechanically folds his arms behind his back: he always holds himself that way, like the master of the house, or an overfed sloth, or just an old man worrying amber beads, enjoying them out of eye's reach. One flap of his thin white shirt is lifted by the sea wind, revealing low-slung pants with a partly unzipped fly and a waistband folded down to accommodate the bulging belly.

"Suck your stomach in, Jacquo," Marcelle pleads.

He cannot hear her because of the wind. "What?"

"Your stomach. Hold it in."

He ignores her. "Hurry up or I'm going."

Marcelle shuts one eye, pressing the other, wide open, against the lens. *"Quel type!"*

She takes a step back—she wants to capture the sign hanging over the air vent above the great steel door—then stops. "Your name," she says. "Why isn't your name up on the sign?"

"What am I, a clothing store?" he says, exasperated. "Next you'll want me to put a tag on every fish I catch."

A burst of laughter from Marcelle. "I'll tell that one to Henri—he'll die."

The uncle's face softens a little; he likes her appreciation. His self-love is too wary and discriminating to show itself easily, to be bought cheap. But despite his gruffness and humility, seemingly against his will, he is more than happy to bathe in admiration; he likes being talked about.

"Maybe we'll put your name up there, Marcelle," he goes on, encouraged by her laughter. "We'll write in big letters MARCELLE, CAMEROON FISHERIES."

• • •

She visits twice a year, bringing *nouvelles de la famille,* cheese, dried fruit, anise candies, escargots, choice sausages, her own homemade quince jam, and chocolates. Like an excited child, he stands over her as she opens her bundles. "What did you bring, what's in there?" he demands impatiently, squatting down beside her on the floor amid the torn wrapping paper and empty boxes, searching through the pile. She prolongs the pleasure the way one holds a candy on the tip of one's tongue; each item is proferred with an endless story full of twists and subplots, jokes and digressions, references to things someone told her or she read in the newspaper. Every one of Marcelle's stories has a sting in its tail, a punch line, always promised with the same assurance, "You'll thank me for this, Jacquo, you'll see. You'll thank me yet."

Marcelle whirls about the household like an excitable child—amusing, exhausting, tireless, but grouchy in the morning. She interferes in Julien's orderly kitchen and scandalizes Madame Sicourelle with the latest reports on the sex lives of middle-aged couples, but mostly she just tries to put things right. It takes only a glance for her to see how the object of her scrutiny could be immeasurably improved. This time she wants to improve Erouan.

"What's the matter with the boy? Why does he skulk about like that?" she wonders, watching him.

"What do you mean 'like that'?" Madame Sicourelle says, carefully pulling back the foil cover from a yogurt container and wiping her finger across the white circle imprinted on its underside. She is clearly offended. "He works very hard, Marcelle. He runs himself into the ground."

"Sure, sure," Marcelle says, ignoring Madame. "But why is he so . . . joyless? There's not a shred of joy in him."

Madame can scarcely contain her annoyance. "What do you mean, 'joyless,' Marcelle? He's not out having fun all the time, but he does have his moments of happiness."

"What happiness? He always looks like he swallowed a mouthful of bleach."

Madame is struck dumb. She restrains herself until the evening, when she hurls at Monsieur Sicourelle, "*Ta soeur!*"

He has no patience for her complaints. "Don't start with "*ta soeur*" this and "*ton frère*" that. Don't say a word, you hear?"

But Uncle Sicourelle's anger conceals his true feelings. In fact, he is worried about the boy. Since childhood Erouan has been clinging to Uncle Sicourelle's side like a vine that needs something to hold on to—an iron grating or a wooden pole—lest it grow slack and crumple to the ground. Watching him, Uncle Sicourelle chokes with rage and desperate pity. "Fight for her, for God's sake! Why don't you fight for her?" he raved when Dominique, Erouan's young bride of eight months, left him, fleeing to the South of France.

"How?" asked Erouan. "How am I supposed to fight for her? She doesn't want me."

"So make her want you! Get hold of her and force her! She doesn't know what she wants anyway. You have to decide for her."

"I can't," Erouan said in a small voice. "I just can't, Papa."

"It's not that you can't, it's that you won't. You don't want to."

"Okay, then. I don't want to."

"You see?" the uncle spat. "I told you so. You don't want to."

Dominique was six months pregnant when she fled, taking only the clothes on her back.

"Dear Erouan." Madame Sicourelle is reading the letter Dominique left. "Do you hear that? 'Dear Erouan.' The nerve!"

Marcelle urges her on, impatient. "Read."

"Dear Erouan. I am sorry to leave you like this, but I simply cannot go on any longer. If I stay in Douala one more day I will suffocate and die. This life is not for me. I do not want to die. I have tried to grow accustomed to it but have not succeeded. It is hard for me to live with you—you are always absent. Even when present, you are absent. I will be with my brother in Arles. I hope to find work there. You may join me if you wish. Perhaps there we can truly begin again."

"You see?" Madame Sicourelle sputters in scorn. " 'Even when present, you are absent.' So now she's a poet, poor little Cinderella."

Marcelle lights a cigarette and closes her eyes, her long lashes fluttering. For a moment she says nothing. "It's terribly sad, Marie. Really, it breaks your heart. What did Erouan say about the letter?"

"Say? What could he possibly say, the poor boy? He showed me the letter and went off to work on his boat. We didn't see him for two days."

For years Uncle Sicourelle has devoted himself to salvaging Erouan's honor. He has sent a swarm of lawyers after Dominique, blighting her life whichever way she turns; he has paid thugs in shiny suits to visit the tiny boutique she has opened; he has refused to recognize her child as his grandson. Erouan bowed out at some point along the way, leaving the stage clear for the uncle, feeling a mix of acceptance, apprehension, and the euphoria of the weak sucking at the veins of the strong. He would spend days on the deck of his boat, moving from port to starboard, repairing, painting, polishing, dismantling the engine, then starting all over again. He practically never took the boat out; for months on end it would sit in the boatyard, resting on two thick beams. After Dominique left, Erouan gave up his apartment and returned almost furtively to his parents' house.

When some time had passed and the apartment remained empty, Richard was sent "to settle accounts" with the owner.

Once a year, when the de Karinis return from their annual visit to France, they bring news: they saw Dominique, they saw the child, both are fine. Not a muscle moves in Erouan's ruddy face, swollen as a lump of dough. He drinks relentlessly, lying on the leopard-skin couch in the de Karinis' living room. He drinks away entire evenings, speechless and glassy-eyed. In the wee hours of the morning he is thrown into the backseat of a car and driven home. Several honks bring Augustin out to lend a shoulder.

Uncle Sicourelle tries to get him to snap out of it. He and Richard hatch plots. "Shall we send him to the factory in Abidjan? What do you think, Richard?" the uncle asks.

"That's an idea," Richard agrees. "We'll have to tell Pierre to keep an eye on him."

"Pierre won't like that," the uncle recalls.

"No, he will not, Monsieur."

"So what should we do? Should we send him to Dakkar as our agent? What do you say?"

"This deserves investigation."

He is sent to Dakkar, where he spends two months in heartening silence, until something happens. The buyers are displeased; there is an urgent telegram from the local agent, followed by snippets of a rumor about entanglements with native girls of questionable repute, charges of blackmail, a demand for compensation.

Erouan is sent back. At first he says little, spending most of his time sleeping or sitting on the edge of the pool, splashing his legs in the water. Eventually he falls into his old routine, the boat.

He has three full-time workers as lazy and shiftless as he is. Uncle Sicourelle calls them the Three Musketeers. The four men are bound in a covenant of silence, drunkenness, and long breaks spent lying on the deck side by side in the withering sun. Erouan's status among them is vague; he is entirely lacking in the natural authority of a boss. The men despise him for this—despise him and like him by turns. He skulks in his corner, unnerved by their displays of both scorn and affection, each of which obliges him in its own way, making him responsible to them, to himself.

. . .

"That Fufu is the quintessential product of colonial life," Jean-Luc declares, sipping his Campari and soda and rubbing his misshapen bare toes along the hard edge of the pool. The niece is walking around the pool wielding a long pole, one end in the water, spearing yellow mango leaves as they float by and piling them in a heap on the grass. The de Karinis' two young daughters, Priska and Eve, are splashing in the water, fighting over an inflatable life preserver with the head of a crocodile.

"So his wife left him. What has that got to do with colonial life?" the niece asks. "I don't see the connection."

"It's not just that his wife left him. It's the whole bored, empty, dissipated existence—that's what I mean."

These last words are swallowed by boisterous cries of jubilation and fear. The girls break into a run, chasing each other around the pool, spraying water.

"Can't you be careful!" Jean-Luc shouts at them, wiping his wet arm with a towel. "I'll call your mother right now if you don't stop."

The niece laughs. "Look at you! You should see your face."

He straightens his glasses sourly. "What's wrong with my face?"

"You look like you've been bitten. You don't have patience for kids, do you?"

He puts on his shirt. "That's not it. I just don't like aggressive, spoiled children, that's all."

Eve is hanging off the niece's neck. "Tell her to give it to me, Esther."

"Give you what?"

"My crocodile. She's always taking it from me."

"Give her the crocodile, Priska."

Priska is hiding around the side of the house, panting. "It's not hers!" she calls.

The girls have been left with Esther since the morning. "You don't mind keeping an eye on them for an hour or two, do you Esther?" Madame de Karini asked. "Their nanny is ill and I don't know what else to do with them."

"Esther would be happy to look after them," Madame Sicourelle interceded. "She hasn't got anything to do this morning anyway."

"I wanted to go to the American Cultural Center," said the niece.

"On a Sunday?" Madame asked. "But everything is closed, child. Besides, Jean-Luc said he would come over to take a swim."

Now Jean-Luc is stuffing his feet into his rubber thongs. "I'm off. Good luck."

The niece sullenly watches his slim back as he walks toward the house.

"Want to make chocolate balls?" she asks Eve, brightening.

The girls dry off and follow Esther into the kitchen, leaving wet footprints behind them. "Julien, are there any old cookies around?" the niece asks.

Perched on a ladder, Julien is wiping the pane of a large window. He finishes a wide circular sweep, then folds the rag carefully and descends the ladder. Without a word he produces a large bowl, *petits-beurre,* chopped nuts, butter, chocolate, and liqueur. "Anything else, Mademoiselle?" he asks.

"That's all. Thank you, Julien."

He holds out a long strip of paper. "Monsieur Jean-Luc asked me to give you this."

Esther unfolds the paper and reads: "I'm sorry I left so quickly. I'll call you later. Jean-Luc."

"Throw it away, Julien. It's nothing."

Julien crumples the paper, watching Esther and the girls as they throw the ingredients into the bowl. "My advice would be to stay away from him, Mademoiselle."

"What?" she says, startled. "Stay away from whom?"

"From Monsieur Jean-Luc. Stay away from him."

Her face reddens. "What's it got to do with you, Julien? Who asked for your opinion?"

"Who asked you! Who asked you!" Eve and Priska mimic her, giggling.

"Do as you wish, Mademoiselle, but I must tell you what I think."

Eve sticks a finger into the brown mess, then puts it in her mouth. "Stop that!" the niece says angrily. "Don't lick your finger and then put it back in the bowl!"

"She's a pig," Priska says. "We've given up on her."

They form round balls of unequal size and shape and place them on a tray. "Now we need coconut," says the niece. "Is there any coconut, Julien?"

He is hanging on to the kitchen window, scraping the frame with a knife. "No. You can use chocolate shavings and nuts, Mademoiselle; that is what we always use."

"Well, we'll use that then," the niece says, suddenly wishing she could escape. "Come, wash your hands, girls."

She makes a large tent of sheets and blankets for them in the living room. "Go play in there and don't dare come out," she orders them.

"Why can't we come out, Esther?" Eve asks.

"Why? Because this is the jungle. Whoever comes out gets devoured instantly. Cannibals will make her into soup!"

They play in the tent for half an hour, glancing out warily. The niece lies on the sofa, her feet on a pile of pillows. She stares at the television, smoking.

In the afternoon everyone arrives at once: Monsieur and Madame Sicourelle, Erouan, and Madame de Karini, with two large sweat stains in the armpits of her yellow dress.

"Did the girls behave, Esther?" she asks.

Monsieur Sicourelle is hungry as a bear. Stripped to his undershirt he stands in front of the open refrigerator examining its contents, then slams the heavy door angrily.

"There's nothing to eat," he complains.

"Nothing to eat, Chouchou? Julien prepared the veal you brought yesterday," says Madame.

"Veal and more veal. I'm sick of veal. It was like shoe leather a few days ago. Isn't there anything good to eat?"

"Like what, Chouchou? You always want what we don't have."

"So make sure we get it. That's what I say."

Madame de Karini hurries her daughters to get dressed, then pushes them out the door.

"Who gave her that idea?" the uncle asks, munching on a hot pepper, after the door has shut behind her and the girls.

"What idea, Chouchou?"

"That Esther should babysit for her children. Esther is not a servant."

"Don't exaggerate, Chouchou. All she did was spend a pleasant hour or two with them."

"Was it pleasant?" he asks the niece. "Tell me, Esther, did you enjoy yourself?"

"Not exactly. It was all right," the niece says flatly, avoiding Madame's gaze.

"You see?" He turns to Madame Sicourelle. "It was not pleasant. She did not enjoy herself. Next time tell your friends there are people whose job it is to do that sort of thing. Come," he says to Erouan, heading for the terrace.

Madame Sicourelle is silent a few moments.

"Are you satisfied?" she says at last.

"Satisfied with what, Marie?"

"With having made trouble between us. Do you see how angry your uncle is?"

"He asked, I answered. Do you want me to lie?"

"It never hurts to lie a little now and then, Esther. Telling the truth all the time won't get you very far."

"Depends who you are."

"Fine," Madame Sicourelle says, going off to her room to change.

"*Ma nièce,*" Uncle Sicourelle calls from the terrace. "*Où elle est, ma nièce?* Where are you?"

Esther steps through the large French doors. "Did you call me?"

"Come sit with me," he orders. Esther settles on the tiles, crossing her legs under her.

"Pull up a chair. Don't we have enough chairs?" he chides.

"I'm comfortable like this."

Dripping with sweat, the uncle fans the grill with a small, stiff piece of cardboard.

"Bring me some kerosene," he tells Erouan, who is standing nearby, transfixed by the filmy, hazy columns of smoke. "What?" Erouan asks, startled. "What do you want?" "Kerosene, kerosene. Are you deaf?"

Strain is visible in the uncle's back. Taut with tension and concentration, he leans toward the coals, the smoke, and the strips of herring frying on top. He shows Erouan how to turn them. "Careful, make sure they don't fall apart. Now you try," he says, handing him the spatula. "Go ahead, turn them over."

Erouan grasps the spatula and begins scraping the blackened metal grid of the grill. "What are you doing?" the uncle shouts. "You're getting ash all over them. Give it to me, give it to me," he says, taking the spatula from Erouan's hand.

Erouan smiles weakly at Esther, embarrassed. He starts to say something but then stops, as if lost in thought. "Perhaps you are thirsty, Esther?" he asks after a moment or two, his expression brightening.

"No, I'm not at all thirsty. I drank something earlier."

"Ah," he exhales, again falling silent. "It is hot today," he adds.

She is tracing the brown grooves between the tiles with a blade of grass. "Maybe later you could take me for a drive in your new car," she says.

The uncle perks up. "Take her to Adnan's and give him my regards, that bastard."

The tension in Erouan's face slackens; he pours himself a whiskey. "I hope the car is okay. The engine was rattling all day."

He trades in his car every few months, perpetually leafing through catalogs and waiting restlessly for phone calls from car salesmen.

"He gets a new car as soon as the ashtray is full," says Aunt Marcelle, who has stopped by for two days on her way to the Ivory Coast.

She wants to try out an idea for a business venture on Uncle Sicourelle: selling handicrafts from the Far East and Africa in Europe and Israel. The uncle is not interested. "It's a headache, Marcelle, a lot of bother, and all you'll see in the end is a few pennies."

They sit on the terrace until midnight, stretched out on recliners, dipping bread into a mixture of olive oil, cumin, coriander, and sesame and drinking chilled white wine. In the humid air, their voices fuse with the croaking of the frogs and the dim noise of cars and people on distant streets far from the quiet suburban villas shrouded in dark trees. Now these other sounds seem to overwhelm the conversation, then they are cowed by it, defeated by the words, their tone and music, by the hum of agreement and dissent that rises from the table, a light buzz, weightless, floating in the fragrant damp air beyond the terrace, out by the windows of the niece's room, past the fine linen curtains that form a gauzy barrier between inside and out.

At ten past twelve the chairs on the terrace are pushed back with a scrape and a thicker darkness falls: the large neon lights on the wall have been turned off, but not the round garden lamps with their milky, muted light.

Aunt Marcelle tiptoes into the niece's room; she has left her large suitcase there and forgotten it. Click-clack, the catches on the suitcase open and close and the pleasant smell of laundry detergent is released with the shake of a bathrobe. "Marcelle?" the niece whispers.

"Why aren't you asleep, Esther? I tried not to wake you."

The niece turns on the reading lamp by her bed, rubbing her eyes. "What time is it?"

"About twelve. I'm exhausted but I feel wide awake," says Marcelle, sinking into a chair. Her thick, heavy hair, threaded with strands of gray, rings her shoulders and neck like a fur piece. There is something childish about its unruliness, though age lines score the skin around her mouth and eyes. Marcelle gathers her hair up in a bun and lets it go, gathers it up and lets it go. "I must do something with this hair," she says.

"Can I have a cigarette?" the niece asks. They smoke, staring at the curlicues that rise and twist before them in the wan light.

"He's put my passport in Richard's safe; he won't let me go," says the niece.

Marcelle places two fingers on her temples and rubs, eyes closed. "I know."

"Tell him to let me go. I've been here long enough. Tell him to let me leave."

"He loves you very much, *tu sais*? I never would have thought he could love someone like that, like a daughter."

"What good does that do me?"

Marcelle is quiet. "I don't know," she says at last. "I don't know what good it does you, but he really wants you to stay. He and your father were such close friends—I can't describe it."

"He's a tyrant," the niece says bitterly. "He thinks everyone is one of his blacks."

"You don't really believe that. I know you don't."

"Oh yes I do. That's exactly what I think."

"Shh. You'll wake up the whole house. All we need is for Madame to walk in."

"Or Augustin." The niece laughs. "Imagine him standing in the door with his funny old monkey face."

"Stop it. Be quiet," says Marcelle, suddenly serious. "You know I have no influence on your uncle. You've seen what he's like when he's made up his mind. It's like talking to a block of wood."

"You're telling me I'm a prisoner."

Marcelle smiles, tired. Then a shadow flits across her dark, angular face. "For now."

Photograph: Left to right: *Uncle Henri and André, Aged Three; Aunt Marcelle; Father; Uncle Edouard; Uncle Edouard's girlfriend, Miriam; a Passerby with His Back to the Camera, the Port of Haifa, 1954*

Father is in the middle, next to Marcelle, leaning in toward her, shielding her with his stooped back. His long, bony arm extends across Marcelle's shoulders, pressing her to Henri. We can just make out two of Father's fingertips, clutching at Henri's left shoulder like the talons of a bird that is hanging on tenaciously, trying to peer over the people.

Father beams with smug satisfaction: he is the patron of this journey, this departure.

Mother is not in the photograph. She cannot bear partings and she can bear even less the quiet confidence, the sense of victory with which he has taken charge of this one, as if Marcelle's leaving were one more proof, one more validation of his loathing toward the country.

"Stop spreading your poison," Mother says.

"It's not me," he retorts. "It's this country."

"*Arrête*, Inès," pleads Marcelle. "Don't fight because of us."

Mother does not listen. From her corner she fixes her gaze on Father, like a big, patient spider watching its prey. "*Ça a rien à faire avec toi,* Marcelle. It's got nothing to do with you."

"You should have heard them fight," Marcelle remembers, glancing at the photograph, smiling to herself. "They used to raise the roof. Look how handsome your father was, Estherkeh. A regular Omar Khayyam."

"Sharif, Sharif," Esther corrects her, exasperated. "You mean Omar Sharif."

Marcelle and Henri left Israel in August 1954. Father gave Marcelle a good-luck charm, a small golden fish with a turquoise eye. "Be sure to take care of this, Marcelle," he instructed her gently, placing the charm in her hand and closing her fingers around it. On the voyage to Marseilles she had vomited without cease. For months afterward the mere mention of fish elicited horror.

Father stood a long while on the pier, waving good-bye with his skinny arm, the large sleeve billowing about it like a sail: one ship seeing off another. "Toward us his heart was always pure," Marcelle recalls.

He had come to Israel grudgingly, following Mother, who had followed Uncle Moise and Edouard and Aunt Marcelle and Nona Fortuna, who, in turn, had not been thrilled about coming but had accepted it. They stuck him on Uncle Moise's kibbutz, where he was supposed to work in the fields. Within a week, though, he went back to wearing his suits and raw silk handkerchiefs. He wanted to be the kibbutz secretary or something like it.

"You haven't even begun to understand how the place works," Uncle Moise said. "What's the big hurry?"

"I'm not interested in understanding," Father answered.

He moved to the city, leaving Mother behind. She didn't hear from him for a year. She darned the kibbutz members' socks until her eyes nearly fell out and downed meal after meal of beans and rice. "If you'd shot those things from a rifle, they'd have hit the wall and bounced right back," she said.

He reappeared one day out of the blue, bringing gleaming ripe mangoes, fine soap, marzipan, and a yellow fox stole with a pointy nose and erect triangular ears.

"Where am I supposed to wear this?" she asked. "To the dining hall?"

"We're leaving," Father said. He had found a place.

Uncle Moise was skeptical. "Just what kind of place?"

Father explained at great length, in flawless Hebrew. For three months he had devoted himself to learning the language. He had devoured the Bible and the newspapers and now spewed forth the Hebrew that would one day fill his political pamphlets, a mixture of low journalese, clichés couched in biblical syntax, and verses from the books of Isaiah and Jeremiah.

He took them to a *ma'abarah,* a tent camp for immigrants. Within two weeks, theirs was a "model tent." To Father's astonishment Mother hung bright curtains, arranged flowerpots, sewed her own lamp shades, and weeded, hoed, and planted, taming the surrounding plot of earth and threatening "the bastards who throw their garbage everywhere."

"It's only a tent, Inès," he said, trying to reason with her.

She did not want to hear. "It may be a tent, but for the moment it's our home."

He wandered the country, vanishing for a while, then returning, scraping together a living from this and that, making an impression on the people he met, quietly nursing the injured pride of a man whose true nature had been quashed, who had been denied the life he was born to, the life of a Levantine gentleman.

Mother made scenes: she wanted him to be like everyone else, a person who fit in.

"Who's 'everyone,' Inès?" he challenged her. "Who are these people?" He was never able to sustain a reasonable argument. Articulating his feelings, clarifying and sharpening them left him exhausted. He tired quickly—of debates, of people, of places, of ideas, of families, of need. For isolation and loneliness, though, he had greater tolerance. He did not exactly seek them out but he knew how to weather solitude, how to find joy in the anonymous and the covert; he liked to think he had something to hide.

Sometimes Father would be tempted by the real world and try to sustain interest in something concrete. For a while he joined a team of diggers. He was photographed with a hoe. His brush with manual labor hastened a decision that had been forming inside him; it settled the pendulum swinging between his personal desires and his ambitions: from now on, life would be political.

Bearing placards demanding "Bread! Work!" he staged a sit-in at the Ministry of Labor office in Petah Tikva. After he led a small demonstration protesting the privileged status of the Ashkenazis, the ruling Labor Party got scared; they gave him a job. Buying him off was easy: a kind word, a benevolent look, fine liqueurs, flattery, and cultured discourse, polite chat that managed never to get down to the ugly business of real life—all these made him melt. He was a true son of the Orient.

For two years he advised the interior minister, Israel Bar-Yehuda, on Arab affairs. He became a favorite of Yigal Allon, the labor minister, who was charmed by his talent for cultivating relationships, by the sparkle of his manner, the manner of a gambler who has happened upon the dull grayness of the political game.

Suddenly he disappeared, leaving everything behind, including his debts. Where he went, what he was doing, and why were the subjects of merciless rumors. Mother wrote to his stepbrother in Milan, a silk dealer, but he knew nothing. Then she wrote to Father's sister in New York, a librarian with a master's degree in French and English literature who had written a thesis on Emily Dickinson.

"*Ma chère* Nadine," she wrote. And again: "*Ma chère* Nadine." She did not know what to tell her. Nadine dwelled in a closed inner world Mother could not penetrate; any pity Mother might have felt for her withered in the face of Nadine's eerie, twisted air of suffering. In the end, Mother was blunt: "If you hear from him, let me know," she wrote.

Three months later a letter arrived in English. Mother was working as a maid in Savyon, a wealthy neighborhood, for a Rabbi Levin and his family. He translated it for her:

We passed through orange, brown, gold, and more gold, through leaves floating softly in air, falling upon us in the forest inferno, a cold, cold, red-sparked fire, until I could not breathe. It was as if my mouth were crammed with a density of trees, ocher and violet and so very tall. The more we lifted our eyes skyward, hoping for an end to the trees, for a soothing patch of sky, the more we gazed, the more we were lost in that gaze, which became a mirror reflecting only the brownish red-orange that suffused all like an impending illness, like the flash of color that precedes blindness, like distorted images unrelated to the

objects they represent. Reddish-brownish orange filled
our empty gaze that no longer saw pictures, no longer
saw an image of the world but only color. It was at this
moment that I understood: I must fight, I must not give
in; my fear of life grows out of an intense fear of beauty
and the death inherent in beauty, which—unlike evil or
suffering—dissolves the barriers between the body and
the world, between the spirit and the flesh. I was chilled
by my understanding, which I could not cast off for many
weeks after as I turned it over in my head. That landscape, the pictures of it in my memory became a synonym
for fear and for the thought of fear. So torn as I am, I must
nevertheless urge you, dear Inès, to go to Vermont: Go,
visit Vermont in October.

Rabbi Levin was flabbergasted. "What is this, Inès?" he
asked.

"She was a doormat," Mother explained, "just a doormat."
There was something comforting in this explanation, which,
having been handed down in the family from one generation to
the next like a recipe for cookies, had now stuck to Nadine as
surely as the shape of her face, the color of her eyes, or the shade
of her hair.

She was indeed a doormat. Tall, stooped, frantically voluble,
and sickly, she cringed if anyone attempted to touch her. Like
Father, she visited Nona Fortuna and Grandpapa Jacquo daily.
Grandpapa Jacquo swung between pity for her and a deep sense
of revulsion. "Where on earth did she grow up, that one?" he
would mumble to himself in the bedroom, pulling the quilt up
over his ears so as not to hear her tumbling stream of speech
below him in the kitchen, stemmed now and then by the hesitant
interruptions of Nona Fortuna.

Nona was oddly fond of her. Nadine's awkwardness, her feverish brain, her one, stained shirt, her lofty family connections—at least on her mother's side—but mainly her good education touched something in Nona Fortuna.

"It's one thing to wear a torn shirt but you can't go around in a dirty one. Jacquo noticed that your shirt is covered with stains. Better torn than dirty, *ma chérie*. At least rips have a kind of distinction," Nona explained to her.

Nadine understood none of these nuances; she was lost in herself. Nona Fortuna's philosophy of life, which held that one should always look neat and well put together and should keep one's suffering to oneself, went over Nadine's head. Certainly it failed to stop her from spilling out her life story in her strange, gushing style.

"And her life didn't amount to much," Mother told me, plucking a yellowed leaf off the overgrown philodendron and fanning her face with it. "From the time she was seven she took care of her mother, Nona Marguerite, who could hardly remember her own name."

Nona Marguerite's family, wealthy cloth merchants from Beirut, had been transplanted to Cairo. Marguerite had gone to the best schools, been taught by the best teachers, and had the best of everything else as well, from her white suits and colonial hats to the summer holidays in France and England. Insulated by the family's money and prestige, she was surrounded by an army of servants and governesses, who sheltered her from the world as much as they shielded it from her. Her self was never reflected back to her as others truly saw it; in fact, it barely shone forth at all, concealed as it was by the costumes and masks of social convention. The Levantine aristocracy was so scared of doing the wrong thing that it did nothing at all, frozen in a strange, worldly death of stultifying inner contradictions.

That is how Nona Marguerite grew up: without passion, without will, in a fog of indecision that obscured her feelings. It is not clear how or why she and Grandpapa Maurice married. It was his second marriage.

No one seemed to know him well, nor did anyone speak words of esteem or tell stories that did more than recount the bare biographical facts and vaguely convey distaste. No photograph remained. He married Nona Marguerite for her money and then stole her inheritance; he brought women into their bed and slowly drove her mad, which was not all that difficult apparently. In the end he left her and married a young heiress: he collected rich women like pigeon's eggs.

Nona Marguerite gave birth to Father and two years later to Nadine. She was overwhelmed by the diapers and the crying and the midnight feedings, by the disarray of the huge house, which accumulated layers of filth and garbage, its open spaces ever diminishing. Over the years the rooms were closed off one by one so Nona Marguerite would not have to bother with them; life was restricted to the large living room where she and Nadine ate, slept, and closeted themselves, reading aloud to each other until midnight, finishing the crushed cigarettes that Father left in the giant ashtray.

They drove him crazy. Stripped of their social standing, helpless, tormented by the ceaseless uproar of their souls, by their pressing daily needs on the one hand and their craving for words and beauty on the other, they clung to Father and would not let go, hungrily demanding that he bring them some scent of the outside world in which he roamed, begging him to shed on them, too, his beneficent rain, with its promise of hope, of change, of everything that wasn't the heavy burden of their selves.

Father fled. From the age of twelve he wandered, quick-witted and plucky, savvy about people and life, finding other homes. He was always changing occupations or working several at a time: he was a salesman, a journalist, a translator, and a consummate, perpetual student who picked things up here and there, making the most of his often meager knowledge and inflating it as needed. Although he coveted a life of wealth and ease, he was invariably drawn to one fringe group or another—to the Marxists and Trotskyites, the Copts, the Arab nationalists, Cairo's drug dealers and pimps, its actors and musicians. He ran with them all, drinking, carousing, switching allegiance, spurning his Jewishness in favor of Arab national identity and pan-Arabism. To the last, Nasser was his hero.

He spent much time at the home of Nona Fortuna and Grandpapa Jacquo. After a night on the town, he would fall asleep fully clothed on the couch in their living room, or in Uncle Sicourelle's bed with him, or on the carpet—anywhere. In the morning, sipping his first, second, and third cups of coffee, finishing everyone's cigarettes, he would cheer the family with his stories. Nona Fortuna loved a good story; it was enough to make her overlook this or that unsavory business.

He appreciated the Sicourelles' hospitality and valued their good opinion; he took care not to disappoint them. One day he ceased coming. The family waited for him for a week, two weeks, and asked after him in the coffeehouses and clubs. Finally, Uncle Sicourelle found him in the most unlikely place: locked in one of the filthy closed rooms of his house. The two of them shared a laconic mode: "I like Inès" was all that Father said.

Uncle Sicourelle did not approve. He tapped his cigar on the dusty tabletop three times, then hid his face in his hands. They were silent.

"What are you going to do?" asked Uncle Sicourelle finally.

"I don't know," said Father. "Perhaps I'll go away for a while."

Uncle Sicourelle had no illusions. His love for Father did not diminish his businessman's acumen. He studied Father with the same ruthlessness, the same exacting severity with which he judged a chancy venture—or himself.

"If you try anything I'll break your arms and legs," the uncle said.

"I know," Father said.

The uncle waited for him to get dressed and shave, then took him to a café. Uncle Sicourelle had missed Father, he had missed Father's dandyish outfits, and now he wondered with impatience and panic if Father's sudden neglect signaled some danger latent in himself as well. They never spoke of it again, but Uncle Sicourelle could not relax. And there was the other matter to clear up.

"Watch out for him," he told Mother.

She played innocent. "Why should I watch out? Isn't he your best friend?"

"What's good for me is not necessarily good for you."

Mother was the adored sister who was taken everywhere, a *basbousa*, a favorite confection. She had soft, smooth pinkish flesh like a baby's, her voice and her gaze were clear, she stood impressively straight.

"I know what's good for me," Mother said.

"You have no idea," the uncle replied angrily. "You don't know what bad is."

The uncle won a provisional victory. With the approval of Nona Fortuna and Grandpapa Jacquo, who ate out of his hand, he quickly married Inès off to someone else, a man with money who made her life miserable. She ran away from him when she was seven months pregnant. Father was waiting for her. Having no good name to preserve any longer, he took her as she was, with the baby, who died shortly after birth. Father mourned the boy for three years, keeping a fading photograph of a small, bluish face and spindly legs poking out of white lace.

I used to stare at it hard, searching for the details, but the effort blunted its immediacy instead of sharpening it. It's hard to convey what I saw. I remember a fuzzy rectangular structure behind the baby's nanny, three hazy trees leaning to one side, the woman's face inclined toward the tiny cloth-wrapped bundle, her white sock rolled down over a high white nurse's shoe, shades of gray indicating maybe a winter sky, maybe the poor quality of the photograph, maybe the damage caused by time.

Father lost the picture in one of the moves to another apartment. He was not a man who kept things: he left behind layer upon layer of himself, forgetting or willing himself to forget, burying old disappointments under a mound of new failures, under versions of himself that had lost their distinct identities, heaped as they were onto one dark pile of pain and oblivion. The loss of the photograph was the loss of one more memory.

Missing Photograph: Standing, left to right: *Father, Nadine, Uncle Sicourelle.*
Sitting: *Marcelle, Mother, Jacqueline Kahanoff, Uncle Moise, Cairo, 1945*

From "A Childhood in Egypt," in *The Sun Rises in the East,*
by Jacqueline Kahanoff

I did not know the words needed to express my thoughts. True, I was very young, but I also felt that none of the languages we spoke could express our thoughts, because none was our own. We were a people without a tongue and could speak only through signs and symbols. Our elders spoke of ordinary, every-day things or about religion. Their religion was to say *"Maktub,"* *"Inshallah,"* "Amen," "Our Father Who art in Heaven" and praying and fasting sometimes; but it offered no guidance about the things that were so difficult for us in life. Whether, for instance, it was right to want the British to go and wrong to hate them, right to learn so much from them and from their schools but wrong not to want to be like them or like the French, or our parents, or the Arabs. We were searching for something within ourselves that we had yet to find.

At school, we learned other things, but there, too, we learned nothing about ourselves or what we should do. We did not know how it had happened that we Jewish, Greek, Moslem, and Armenian children were sitting together to learn about the French Revolution. As for *la patrie, liberté, egalité, fraternité,* none of us had experienced any of these things. Not even our teachers really believed these words had anything to do with our lives. They seemed to think it was right for us to want to be like French children, but they must have known that we could not really become French, that the French did not want us to be their equals or their brothers, that we were in fact nobody at all. What were we supposed to be when we grew up if we could be neither Europeans nor natives, nor even pious Jews, Moslems, or Christians, as our grandparents had been?

It was impossible to question anyone about these things. We could not ask our parents, who kept saying that they spent so much money to give us an education and advantages they never had (and this was true). Nor could we ask our teachers, who would have laughed at us without trying even to understand. I could not share my feelings and thoughts with anyone, not even the other children, because I had no way of knowing if they were as happy as they seemed and as ready to believe that the world we grew up in was true and good or if they were only pretending, as I was, because they were frightened to speak out. It was only through fantasies that I could explain this inexplicable little world to myself and fit it into a larger world where I could find my place.

When I reached adolescence, these fantasies lost their grip on me, or rather they began to express themselves more deviously through rational thoughts and political sympathies. I was not entirely aware that I was pretending to believe in certain ideas because they were already clearly formulated, while I could not express my own, partly for fear of appearing absurd, and partly because a reflex of self-defense prompted me to keep secret what was my own. This measure of deceit and self-deception, which disguised self-doubt, was—and still is—characteristic of my Levantine generation. We thought of ourselves as Socialists, even Communists, and in the school yard we ardently discussed the Blum government, Soviet Russia, the civil war in Spain, revolution, materialism, and the rights of women, particularly free love. The only language we could think in was the language of Europe and our deeper selves were submerged under this crust of European dialectics, a word we loved to use. We talked and acted as we imagined young people in France talked and acted, little recognizing that they were still held within a traditional framework that we had lost. Blithely we dismissed everything that was not left-wing as reactionary, and because we were culturally displaced and dispossessed, without yet being able to define our predicament, we did not understand that our motives were not those of French youth and that we were neither as pure nor as generous as we imagined them to be. We wanted to break out of the narrow minority framework into which we were born, to strive toward something universal, and we were ashamed of the poverty of what we called "the Arab masses," ashamed, too, of the advantages a Western education had given us over them.

· · ·

Our parents were pro-British as a matter of business and security and we were pro-nationalist as a matter of principle, although we knew few Moslems our age. We hesitated between devoting ourselves to the masses and going to study in Europe, to settle there and become Europeans. In later years, many of us switched from one attitude to the other or attempted to achieve some compromise between them, the most usual being to help improve the lot of the Arab masses through social work or by preaching Communist doctrine. Some of us became cynics bent on enjoying our advantages while there was still time, but others of us were acutely aware of the difficult choices before us. We felt cut off from the country in which we lived and its people and knew that nothing would come of us unless we could build a bridge to a new society. Revolution and Marxism seemed the only way to attain a future that would include both our European mentors and the Arab masses.

There was in us a strong mixture of sincerity and pretense, a tremendous thirst for truth and knowledge, coupled with an obscure desire for vindication, for deliverance from both the arrogant domination of Europe and the Moslem majority which—we could not quite forget—despised its minorities.

Few of us Jews were Zionists, because we believed that for humanity to be free one had to give up one's narrow individuality. At most, we argued, the Jewish people had the same right to national existence as did all other peoples. A Jewish nation was but an inevitable preliminary to "international socialism." I said such things much as my friends did, but I wondered if they, too, only half believed what they said and were biding their time until the day came when they could speak out with their own voices. Our teachers expounded knowledge from on high, and most of us who sat, heads bowed, taking notes were Jews, Greeks, and Syrians, the Levantines, those whom the Moslems called with superstitious respect and suspicion, the "people of the book." The Greeks and we Jews were always there, had always been there, changing the world more than we changed ourselves, remaining the same behind our many guises. Other people passed us by, and we bowed our heads until their power spent itself. Our teachers, too, would depart, but we would continue to contribute to the ferment of knowledge, making history in our insidious, secretive way, without ever being totally subsumed by it. What would we Levantines do in that world which would be ours? The new world would have to wait for us—we who were still in the schoolroom—to give it a different color and shape.

Throughout our Mediterranean world and the vast continents it bordered, other young people were imbibing this knowledge from their teachers, never suspecting that the dormant seeds would suddenly sprout from under the silt of centuries. The Arabs and other colonized people were cultural hybrids by chance, while we, the Levantines, were inescapably so, as if by vocation and destiny. Our ways would therefore probably part, but together we belonged to the Levantine generation.

• • •

In later life our paths sometimes crossed, and we could speak in our own voices: Greeks, Moslems, Syrians, Copts, and Jews, Arab nationalists, Zionists, Stalinists and Trotskyites, Turkish princesses in exile, priests, and rebels. We talked of our youth, when our souls were so divided within ourselves that we feared we would never recover. Yes, we had mastered words, a language in which to frame thoughts that were nearly our own. Perhaps too late to make any difference, we discovered how close we had been to one another in our youth. Our choices had commanded other choices, and from those, in the adult world, there was no retreat.

Today, when we can no longer meet and talk, we know that history is our childish fantasies come true and that sometimes they turn into nightmares. In newspaper stories we see the names of those we knew, hear the echoes of things we said or thought long ago. We understand why we chose the particular roads we did. At last we recognize ourselves in events that happened *through* us, not only *to* us, though we grieve that the wicked sorcerer has cast his shadow between our dreams and our deeds and that none of us can turn back and start again.

Missing Photograph: Uncle Sicourelle and Richard, the Port of Douala, Cameroon

That's Richard to the right of the uncle, his brown arms crossed over his chest in satisfaction; he has left his work for a minute but will soon go back to it. He welcomes the well-earned respite afforded by the taking of the photograph: like the uncle, he even enjoys it, revels in it.

They stand shoulder to shoulder, sleeve to sleeve, their two bald heads shining in the sun. They pose not quite willingly, but as if they are doing the photographer a favor, leaning forward slightly, almost poised for flight, suppressing their pleasure with close-lipped smiles.

The workers watch from the plaza, pretending to be part of the stolen leisure of the photograph, to share the long-standing secret finally revealed: Monsieur Sicourelle's humanity has been unmasked.

Uncle Sicourelle and his secretary regard the workers with condescending benevolence and magnanimity. "Let the boys have some fun," they seem to be saying. Later Uncle Sicourelle claps his large hands and his voice takes on its familiar sternness, commanding, "Back to work, back to work."

The work has been there all along, seeping into the photograph, filling the space like Uncle Sicourelle himself, overflowing it. So much work everywhere you look, and the uncle there firmly in the middle.

He has dragged Richard over to the narrow pier where the large boats, berthed side by side, provide a backdrop. Then he has tried to make himself small against the boats, to become an inconsequential object to be ignored by the finger that points from outside the picture, directing the interested eye of the onlooker.

But the camera is indifferent to Monsieur Sicourelle's wishes. Though he wants to order the spectator to look elsewhere, the stubborn eye chooses him, settling on the one detail that exudes life. "What is this man?" it asks. "Who is he?"

. . .

"He has his morning routine," Madame Sicourelle notes tartly from her post at the far end of the long dining table. She is watching him cross the room, dragging his feet in ragged house slippers, heels flapping, his pajama top fastened by a single button over his belly. At the window he pulls the heavy linen curtain aside with one swift movement. "Chouchou," Madame Sicourelle pleads, shading her eyes with veined fingers weighted with jewels. "Chouchou, I've asked you a thousand times."

But he is long since gone. Where is he? In the kitchen, his head stuck in the two-door refrigerator, his fingers poking through plastic bags of pink shrimp that Nicola, a harbor worker, brought from the port last night; or by the stove, grilling a hot dog speared on a fork and humming some obscure private tune; or in the part of the garden that overlooks the road, shaking the broad branches of a tall tree and coaxing a cat down.

Madame Sicourelle shakes her curly head and sticks a wet finger in the sugar bowl. "*Voilà ton oncle,*" she concludes, half joking, half complaining.

A short, sharp ring of the doorbell. "That will be Richard," Madame Sicourelle says, hurrying to her room to make herself presentable.

He waits in the hallway as he does every morning, portly and perfumed, holding a large black folder under his arm.

"Good morning, Richard," the niece says, ushering him in as she has learned to do. "Come, sit down."

"Don't trouble yourself, Mademoiselle," he says, relishing the attention.

"It's no trouble," she assures him with feigned patience, twisting her hands in irritation. "Would you like coffee?" she asks.

He strides toward the table, placing the folder on it, leaning on the back of a chair, not yet sitting down. "Just a little, Mademoiselle. I already had some this morning."

The niece pours. "I hope it's hot enough." Richard sits at the far end of the table, settling his large behind on the edge of the chair. Eyes closed, he sips. The ceremony is complete.

"You've gotten new glasses, Richard," the niece notes.

He straightens them on the bridge of his nose. "Yesterday they made me the new frames, Mademoiselle. The old ones broke."

"Mine break by the month," the niece confesses. He opens his eyes wide and looks puzzled. "I sit on them," she explains. He chuckles. "I sit on mine sometimes, Mademoiselle, when I forget."

Richard has worked for Uncle Sicourelle for fifteen years, since the uncle started his business in Cameroon. "He's no genius," Uncle Sicourelle admits, "but he's loyal."

" 'No genius' is putting it mildly," Madame says. "He doesn't understand a word you say, Chouchou."

"He understands what he wants to," Uncle Sicourelle counters, rising to his assistant's defense.

"In that case, so much the worse," says Madame.

"So why do you ask him for help? Leave him be if he annoys you so much, Marie."

Madame tries to leave him be, forcing herself to manage the accounts without him. Like a heavy smoker who declares she's quitting, she announces every two weeks that she's going it alone. For two or three days there's no sign of Richard, but in the end she always calls him. She can never hold out. She sends word to his house to come the next day—there is something she'd like him to "go over." She is filled with scorn for herself and for him, the human mirror of her weakness.

They vanish into her tiny room at the end of the house to pore over Uncle Sicourelle's bills, half the time trying simply to decipher his handwriting on the crumpled, stained invoices.

Money matters cause Madame Sicourelle considerable anxiety. It's part of her basic insecurity, as she calls it. "Tomorrow they'll have another one of their coups and it will all go down the drain," she predicts. She persuades Uncle Sicourelle to invest outside the country, save something for a rainy day. Who knows? Within twenty-four hours they could find themselves under a bridge with nothing but the shirts on their backs.

"What bridge, what are you talking about, Marie?" Uncle Sicourelle asks. "There are no bridges around here, unless you mean the one Jean-Luc is building," he says, casting a glance at his niece. "Maybe we should ask him to hurry up and finish, so we can go sit under it."

He harbors a special dislike for European experts in general and for Jean-Luc in particular. He has held on in Africa for thirty years partly because he minds his own business and respects the social barriers; he is able to fade into the landscape or the human throng, to come and go without fanfare, without explanation. He has seen and heard much and been silent about even more. Like a sponge, he has absorbed first the self-righteous, self-serving blather of the colonialists, then the post-colonialists' talk of development, investment, and expertise; he has seen the young engineers, economists, and agronomists make their money and run. They don't know the first thing about anything as far as he is concerned. These foreigners are supposed to form his social circle, and occasionally he gives in to Madame Sicourelle's pleas, moving in their company, accepting their invitations and reciprocating. But the day always comes when, disgusted, he reverts to the habits that have earned him a reputation as a loner, an ill-tempered eccentric.

The distaste for Europe that he brought with him long ago from Egypt underlies his disdain for "those people." He doesn't like the way they attempted to show him his place. Nevertheless, he eventually found that place, choosing it willingly rather than by necessity. Alienated from the white elite, he was fearful of the black masses, scornful and suspicious, yet he felt an affinity for them, even a familial bond. Once a month he would spend a long evening playing bridge and drinking with Adnan Haled, a Lebanese chef and restaurateur, his British wife, Elizabeth, and Constantine Sendrice, a diamond merchant of Greek extraction who, like him, had spent many years in Africa. Like him, too, Sendrice had tried to leave several times but had always returned, drawn back by the fierce magnetism of the place, which seemed to exert a force very much like love.

They had all faced death at least once in their lives. They had fallen ill with dread diseases, buried a friend or two, nearly been murdered in this or that coup. They had witnessed epidemics and famines that had wiped out entire villages. Daily they had seen life teeter, then slide, without much protest, into the void. Yet they remained on the dark continent, mindful of the immediacy of death but reconciled to it, on intimate terms with it, having developed a stoic affability toward it. This they had learned from the blacks.

· · ·

Madame Sicourelle hated the bridge evenings. She had never managed to learn how to play and Monsieur Sendrice's crude jokes she found appalling—"Simply appalling, Chouchou," she announced.

The uncle, stoking his pipe, was unsympathetic. "Take a lesson or two, Marie, and learn. Or go for a walk. Why don't you go for a walk when they come over?"

Madame was furious. "Because it's just not done, that's why. When guests come over one does not go for a walk."

The uncle was exasperated. "*Mon Dieu,* why do you care so much about whether something is or is not done? When that friend of yours, that priest Didier, comes over, do I worry about the right thing to do? No, I go to sleep. That's what I do."

"And he gets very offended. You should know that the last time he was here you really insulted him."

"So let him be insulted. Do I care that he's insulted?"

Father Didier came to dinner every third Sunday. The uncle tried to keep track of the weeks so as to avoid the priest's next visit, but he always failed. To his great annoyance, he almost invariably ran into him.

Father Didier was a tall, gaunt man with a sallow face. He was forever rubbing his dry palms together. His voice was weak and whispery, ethereal, so that Madame had to lean toward him, practically laying herself on the table between them. "What?" she would say frantically. "What did you say?"

Uncle Sicourelle was convinced he did it on purpose, to torment his listeners.

"Do you always talk so that no one can hear?" the uncle once asked.

Hearing him, old Augustin had dropped the large tray of shrimp in garlic butter he had been bringing to the table. Augustin worshiped Father Didier. The hours the priest spent at the Sicourelle home were Augustin's most cherished. His wrinkled face would beam with joy so great that from time to time it could no longer be restrained. It would burst forth in the form of an enormous smile odd to those observing him, for whom it seemed to have no cause. He would listen intently, his entire being focused on what was being said, his body inclined like the stalk of a sunflower.

"Have you seen Jeanne lately, the de Karinis' little servant?" Father Didier whispers, holding his coffee cup with his pinky aloft.

"No, I haven't. I haven't been to their place in a while," Madame Sicourelle says apologetically. "I hear they are very proud of her."

"She came to mass today," the priest says, dabbing his mouth with a napkin.

"It's a good thing they have somewhere to go on Sundays. I ask myself, What would they do and where would they go without your church, *mon père?*"

"She is all belly."

"What?" Madame Sicourelle blinks with the strain of listening. "What?"

"She is all belly. The seventh or eight month, I believe. And all of fifteen."

"Oh," Madame sighs, sinking back in her chair and lighting a cigarette. "It really is too terrible. They get pregnant like rabbits. And then what? God knows."

"I wonder whether Madame de Karini will keep her on," the priest reflects.

Augustin has frozen at his post in the corner, stiff as a standing lamp. "Augustin!" Madame Sicourelle barks. Startled, he hurries to gather the dirty cups.

Father Didier turns to the niece. "So, my child, how do you like Douala?"

"It's interesting, but I haven't seen much of it. I spend most of my time here."

"Esther is a homebody, as they say," Madame Sicourelle explains. "You know, *mon père,* Jacquo has his opinions about such things, that girls should stay at home."

"And right he is," Father Didier says, nodding vigorously. "Absolutely right—especially in a place like this."

The niece suddenly shoves her chair back and gets up. "I'm going to go look for Titus. I haven't seen him for hours."

The garden is muggy, hot. Steam rises in puffs from the laundry room window at the far end of the garden; Marie-Ange, the maid, is ironing Monsieur Sicourelle's white shirts, spraying streams of starch from a bottle.

"Marie-Ange," the niece calls to her, "have you seen Titus anywhere?"

"He's here. Go on now, you Titus, go to Mademoiselle Esther," she says as she kicks him gently. "You Titus," Marie-Ange calls him.

The dog ambles toward Esther slowly, weak from the heat. "Come, Titus, let's take a little walk," she says. But Titus lies down at her feet, batting his tail feebly, refusing to move.

She goes to the pool, taking off a shoe and dipping her foot in the warm water. Stiff mango leaves cover the surface like a dense yellow skin. "I skimmed the leaves off just this morning and look how many there are now," she says to Julien, who is wiping down the white chairs, tables, and metal poles of the umbrellas with a damp rag.

"It's always that way," Julien says, watching her walk the length of the pool, dragging the long pole and net for fishing out the leaves. He dips his rag in a pail of soapy water, wrings it out, stifles a smile. "Mademoiselle is very diligent."

"Are you making fun of me?"

"Not at all, Mademoiselle. I merely said that you are most diligent—"

"I heard what you said," she interrupts sharply, suddenly dropping the pole and running to the gate.

Richard had stopped by for a moment; he'd come to pick up something he forgot earlier in the day.

She stands facing him, blocking his way. "I need to talk to you, Richard," she says.

His eyes are hidden behind dark glasses and a wide-brimmed hat casts a shadow across his dark face. He cracks his knuckles. "I cannot do what you want, Mademoiselle. I've thought about it. It's not possible."

"Of course it's possible. It's *my* passport, isn't it? You're just afraid of Monsieur Sicourelle, but I promise he won't lay a hand on you. He'll laugh when he finds out, you'll see."

Richard is silent a moment. "I am not so sure, Mademoiselle, that Monsieur will laugh. Madame will certainly not laugh."

"You're wrong. She's dying to get rid of me. Do you honestly think she's happy I'm here? She's terrified he's going to leave me something in his will. Don't you see? They'll only discover the passport is missing after I'm gone. Think about it for a minute."

"I can't do it, Mademoiselle. I regret this from the bottom of my heart, truly."

Esther pulls a wad of bills from her pocket. "Take it, take it," she urges.

He doesn't dare touch it. He glances around him. "Under no circumstances, no, absolutely not."

"Don't play the saint with me, Richard. I've saved it from what Monsieur Sicourelle gives me. I can get you more."

"That is not the issue, Mademoiselle. It is not what you think. I am sorry."

"What's not the issue? You yourself said that everyone greases one another's palms here. I know what goes on."

"You don't really know, Mademoiselle. I'm terribly sorry. I feel quite bad for you," he says, lowering his voice.

She watches him until the tall gate has slammed and she sees his hat bobbing along behind the brick wall.

Monsieur Sicourelle cannot bear that hat. He hides it from Richard or puts it on a chair so that Richard will accidentally sit on it. He stuffs it with shredded paper and chocolate candies, sticking things to its wide brim. Sometimes he himself puts it on, folding the brim up so it looks like a cowboy hat. Richard is not amused by this. He watches with a wan smile, occasionally extending a hesitant hand but then pulling it back, giving up like a dog that realizes a hunk of steak is just out of reach.

Monsieur Sicourelle does not want Richard to wear his hat in the photograph. "I can't stand here with my bald head if he's going to wear that hat, can I, Esther?" he says, pretending to ask her advice.

The niece, fiddling with the new camera, is not paying close attention. "What? Yes. No, it won't look very good."

They descend the stairs to the wet concrete plaza. Monsieur looks around and decides: "Take our picture in front of the ocean, over there."

Richard pads after him, the hat in his hands. "Let Esther hold your hat," Monsieur Sicourelle suggests pointedly.

"It's all right," Richard says, ignoring him and facing the camera. He holds his hands at waist level; the hat covers his belly.

Missing Photograph: Uncle Sicourelle, Madame Sicourelle, Erouan, and Esther on Esther's Seventeenth Birthday, Douala, Cameroon

Visited Julien's house on Tuesday evening. Jean-Luc drove me there and on the way he made fun of the giant panda I'd bought for Julien's baby. It was the biggest one I could find. "You could do all kinds of things with a bear that size," he said with a stupid, ugly smirk on his face. I wasn't in the mood for his jokes and I told him so. He puffed out his cheeks and got all red in the face and said as if he were terribly sorry, "Off with his head! Off with his head!" It made me laugh. He can be really sweet sometimes. We've been seeing each other a lot lately, almost every day, and practically everyone is unhappy about it—the uncle, Madame Sicourelle, Erouan, Monsieur Sendrice. Even Julien. After we said good-bye the other day it occurred to me that it's really just the disapproval that creates that spark between Jean-Luc and me. Maybe if we weren't both stuck here like this we wouldn't even notice each other. Jean-Luc said he thinks there's something rebellious about us both. Bullshit. Whenever he sees the uncle he sucks up to him right and left as though he were hoping for a job or something. It's just as well he doesn't know what the uncle really thinks of him. Then again, maybe he does.

On the way to Julien's I told him about Richard. He thought I shouldn't have offered him money, that I should have appealed to his feelings, his humanity. But I did, I said. I practically cried but he didn't budge an inch. Jean-Luc said he'd think of something, because it's pretty clear that Richard isn't going to help me—he's been with the uncle too long and they've gone through too much together for him to sacrifice it all for some girl. I think he was just kidding, but Jean-Luc said he'd marry me if that would help.

Meanwhile, I hadn't noticed that we'd come to one of those black shantytowns. We had to drive slowly because the alleys were so narrow and sandy. Everyone was staring at us, practically devouring us with their eyes. They were all sitting on the ground outside their tin shacks, men, women, and children, lighting fires and grilling fish and *manyuk*, that thing that's like leek. The smell of fish, smoke, and sweat was awful, and Jean-Luc closed the car windows and turned on the air conditioning. I was a little afraid. I didn't like the way the people stared at us and I tried not to stare back. I started changing stations on the radio. Jean-Luc asked if I was okay—he knew I was scared. I told him I was fine, I was sure there was nothing to be afraid of. He admitted he'd been scared the first time. Not of something specific, like a knife in his back—it was just a vague sense of anxiety, of distress, as if what he was seeing—the poverty and filth—would stick to him forever. I felt a little like that too. I was amazed he knew how to navigate the alleys and find Julien's shack without asking directions. I asked him how he knew the way, whether he'd ever visited Julien's place before. Once, he said.

Jean-Luc stopped the car several feet from Julien's house and walked me to the door. He said he'd wait in the car. The door to the house was ajar, but I knocked anyway. No one came. I knocked several more times and wondered whether or not to go in. In the end I did. The room was almost completely dark, although the floor was lit by some light that came in through the broken blinds. I saw a body lying on a mattress, someone sleeping. I thought of just leaving the bear there and going, but something made me stay. "Julien," I whispered. I was sure it was him lying there.

I heard the sound of heavy breathing. "It's me, Esther," I said. Julien sat up with a start and asked me what I was doing there. I told him that I'd come to bring something for the baby. He asked me which baby. "Your baby," I said, "the one that was born two weeks ago."

He opened the blinds, leaned out the window, and asked me how I got there. I told him that Jean-Luc had driven me and was waiting outside in the car. Julien stank of beer. He dragged a chair over and told me to sit. "So where's the baby and the baby's mother?" I asked.

He told me they were at the neighbors' and offered me something to drink. I refused politely. He sat opposite me, his legs crossed on the mattress. His skin shone like velvet in the darkness. He was half naked. We said nothing for several minutes. It was so stifling I could hardly breathe. "I will bring you something to drink, Mademoiselle," Julien said finally. He vanished into a dark hole—the kitchen, I guess. Suddenly there was a strange cry. "What's that? What's that?" he said. He'd stumbled onto the bear I'd left on the floor. I jumped up from the chair, picking up the bear and placing it in his hands so he could feel it. "It's a toy, see?" I said. He touched it with his fingertips, as if he were still a little scared, then laughed at himself. "What a fright I had! I thought it was a real animal," he said. We were standing close. His chest was soaked, maybe from sweat, maybe from water that he'd thrown on himself in the kitchen. I've seen him do that, stick his head under the faucet, then shake the water out of his hair. I felt very tense but I liked the feeling. I wanted it to go on, for Julien and me to stand there always. I knew that if I touched him, even with just a finger, the tension would disappear. I said something stupid—"You're completely wet" or something like that. I stared right into his face, something I had never dared do. His eyes were black and his pupils dilated; they looked full of hatred. I'll never forget those eyes and their dark, blank, hateful stare. No one has ever looked at me like that before. I couldn't understand what I'd done to deserve his contempt. For a second I thought that Julien was simply crazy. He was crazy, and I was crazy for going there. Then he said abruptly, "Monsieur Jean-Luc should not be kept waiting too long." I took a step back, toward the door. "You're kicking me out, aren't you?" I asked. He said nothing, just kept standing in the kitchen like a pole, his head grazing the ceiling. I ran out to the car, shaking.

Jean-Luc was concerned. He asked me if something had happened, but I didn't want to talk to him about Julien. I got in the car and we drove off. I leaned back and covered my eyes while Jean-Luc took a small bottle of cognac out of the glove compartment and offered it to me. I drank some and my head cleared a little. I still didn't understand why I was so shaken by Julien, but the familiar streets of the city calmed me. Jean-Luc suggested we stop and have a drink at the Meridian. He talked about all sorts of things and I was grateful that he didn't shower me with questions. We sat in the tropical garden at the Meridian drinking cocktails until it got late. When we stood up to leave, we were both a little drunk.

Jean-Luc asked if I was feeling better when we reached the house. I'd looked quite upset before, he said. I was light-headed and wanted to drive around some more, but Jean-Luc wouldn't. He said I was completely drunk and needed to go to bed. I tried to argue but I didn't really care one way or another. I felt totally numb and happy. Before I went into the house we sat in the car for a while and talked about what we'd like to be doing in a few years. Jean-Luc said he wanted to be doing exactly the same things as he was now but maybe in another place, Asia or America. Without thinking, I said I'd like to be a diplomat. That amused him no end. "A diplomat," he kept saying, practically choking with laughter. I was lying, of course, but was insulted anyway. "What's so funny about that?" I said. Jean-Luc wasn't listening—he was sputtering and coughing and writhing in his seat. The child wants to be a diplomat! You mean a diplomatic incident! I was suddenly sick of him. I got out of the car without saying good-bye and slammed the door. All the way up to the house I could hear his rude drunken laughter. Disgusting.

I took my shoes off at the entrance so I wouldn't wake anyone, but when I reached the door to my room, feeling the walls and the furniture to find my way, I heard the uncle calling me. "*Ta'ali hena, ya,* Esther," he called. "Come here." He had been sitting on the sofa the whole time, waiting, watching me grope the armchairs.

He asked where I had been. I told him the truth, that I'd gone to visit Julien, that he'd had a baby.

I stayed where I was, away from the uncle, facing the door with my back to him.

"Who took you there?" he wanted to know. I told him.

The uncle mumbled something and I could hear the sound of cellophane crumpling and then of a match being lit. "So, he's teaching you about Africa, is he? *El-mouhandes,* the engineer!"

I couldn't answer. I leaned my forehead against the door, hoping he would go away. After a few moments he told me to go to sleep. "We'll talk about this in the morning," he said. I heard him drag his slippered feet into his bedroom.

I was exhausted and drunk but couldn't fall asleep. Every time I closed my eyes I saw the tin-shack alleys, the fires, Julien's outline in his stinking, stifling room. What had I wanted from Julien, and what had he wanted from me? What had I done or said wrong? I felt a cold, wretched despair but no tears. I tried to cry, to force myself to think really sad thoughts about being trapped here, a prisoner, watching my life waste away before my eyes, not knowing when or how I would ever get home. I was alone in the world, no one would stand up for me—not Mother, not Father, not Marcelle, not even Nona Fortuna. Alone as a stone. I pictured myself dead, laid out on a bed of flowers in a white silk dress, my hair to my waist, in my hands a bunch of hyacinths, lovely and white as the walls. Everyone passing before me weeping: Mother and Marcelle holding hands, propping each other up; Father, even; Uncle Sicourelle, wild with grief and guilt. My high school teacher, Rachel, making a speech. "Like a rose among thorns, so was Esther among the maidens." That's what she actually wrote in my autograph book. She asked me not to show anyone: "Like a rose among thorns, so are you among the maidens." I wonder

what the other girls would have thought of being called thorns. I
would have called a few of them thistles, not thorns. In the end
I managed to whimper a little, but only when I remembered
how humiliated I had been when Katzowitz, the math teacher,
had ordered me to stand inside the wastebasket for an entire
class as punishment for throwing some paper out the window.

I dozed off around four in the morning: I saw the glowing
hands of the large clock before I fell asleep. As I was finally drifting off I remember wondering whether Jean-Luc was lying
awake, too, like me.

I opened my eyes at ten-thirty with a pounding headache. I
lay in bed for half an hour, watching the branches move behind
the curtains until I had the sensation that someone was looking
at me. The uncle was standing in the doorway, dressed and
shaved. He asked if I was awake and I said yes but that I didn't
feel too well and thought I'd just lie there a little longer.

He sat on the edge of the bed, covering my legs with the blanket. He reminded me that my birthday was in two days. I didn't
really have the strength to answer. He asked me how I wanted
them to celebrate and I told him we didn't have to celebrate. But
he insisted that we had to. And what kind of fabulous present
did I want?

I was overcome with rage; it seemed like part of the pain shattering my head. "Don't try to buy me, *mon oncle,* it won't help,"
I said, startled at myself. "I am not for sale!" I closed my eyes,
curled up under the blanket, and covered my face to my nose. I
didn't hear him move. "I want to go. Let me go home," I said.

"Why?" he asked. "What's waiting for you there that you
want to go so badly?"

"Everything is waiting for me there," I said. "My home is
there."

"You're at home here," he said. "This is your home too."

Augustin turned on the vacuum cleaner in the next room and I didn't hear the uncle leave over the noise. Fifteen minutes later Madame came in to see whether I had gotten up yet. She asked whether I wanted to go shopping with her. I told her no. What would I do all day? she wanted to know. Did I have plans?

I had no plans, I just wanted them to leave me alone. I stayed in the house for two days. I can't remember what I did exactly: clean out the leaves in the pool, eat meals, read newspapers, clean out more leaves. I would sit down with a book until I realized I was reading the same page over and over. Jean-Luc called. "You're on African time," he said when I told him what I was doing. I didn't want to see him, and I ignored Julien, looking right through him as if he were air, just like Madame does.

I wrote to Nona Fortuna and Mother. Get me out of here, I begged. Madame took the letter to the post office for me. I saw her read the address on the envelope. I've always suspected her of reading my letters, of maybe not even sending them, but I dismissed my fears. Madame has been acting strange lately. She's been very quiet, barely ever speaking to me, let alone pestering me. She has practically stopped eating too. At mealtimes, she moves a few leaves of lettuce and cabbage around on her plate and tells the uncle that the doctor has put her on some kind of low-sodium, low-cholesterol diet. The uncle usually goes crazy if someone isn't eating, but he swallows her doctor excuse.

Today, my birthday, I woke to a shriek coming from the garden. I ran out at once: Madame was standing there in her bathrobe, beating Simon, the gardener, with a rake, shouting that he'd stolen money from her. The uncle pulled them apart, sent Simon home, and took Madame to the bathroom to soak for a while. That usually calms her down. He left for work early but asked me to keep an eye on her and to call him if anything happened, God forbid. He sounded very anxious.

Madame stayed in her room all morning. From time to time I went in to see whether she was sleeping, but she just lay on her back staring at the ceiling.

In the afternoon she asked me to call Augustin. "Tell Augustin to come, *ma chérie,* I need him," she said so meekly and helplessly that I immediately forgave her everything.

When he came she asked for her crossword puzzle books. I could have brought them myself, I told her, but she changed the subject. She started asking questions about Mother, Father, and Nona Fortuna. I noticed that she was barely listening, surveying the room as if she were looking for something. Augustin returned with a huge pile of crossword puzzle books and a small stool for her to put her feet on, but it was as if she'd forgotten what she'd asked him for. "What are you doing with that garbage? It should have been thrown out weeks ago," she said. And what was the stool doing there? Why did he always move things and not put them back? The stool was a stand for the vase that was given to her by the consul's wife last Christmas. She had told him a thousand times, a thousand times. Was he trying to kill her? Was that what he wanted? Did he want to drive her out of her mind? She went on and on like this and then suddenly fell silent. "Augustin, bring the book," she ordered.

He brought over a leather-bound book and opened it to a marked place. She told me to leave and not say a word to Uncle Sicourelle. So I left. But I stood on a chair outside the room and peeked in through the pane of glass at the top of the door. "Read!" I heard her say. Augustin read something from the New Testament, repeating the same sentence several times. It sounded like Jesus addressing his followers, telling them to speak in light what had been told them in darkness. Augustin said this over and over, almost gleefully. "Speak ye in light, speak ye in light." Then there was something about death, that one had only to fear the death of the soul but not of the body, and what would happen to those who did and did not follow Jesus' commandments. Hideous things. I didn't understand most of what he read, but I heard the word "sparrows" a few times. The believers were sparrows, maybe, or as precious as many sparrows. At the end there were all kinds of threats: Jesus warned that he had come to bring not peace but something like death or the sword or war, to sunder people from their families. Woe unto them, said Jesus, if they loved their families more than him or, for that matter, if they weren't willing to lose their lives for him. Augustin repeated the words "loseth his life" about ten times. He was so carried away that even Madame's protests didn't stop him.

He read for a long time. It sounded like he garbled some of the hard words and skipped over others. When she didn't get angry or correct him, Madame would simply urge him in an angelic voice, "Go back, Augustin, please." And he would repeat the difficult words, spelling them out letter by letter until she could recognize them. The whole thing gave me the chills. I ran and called the uncle at his office, but I was told he had already left. By the time I returned to my post on the chair, Madame and Augustin had begun to argue. She wanted him to read the part where Jesus cures the young girl but Augustin stood his ground, saying, "*C'est trop,* Madame Sicourelle, it's too much. The priest does not allow it." Madame was furious. She pounded her fist into the blankets, insisting that he read it to her at once, that it was her will that counted, not Father Didier's. Finally they reached a compromise and Augustin returned to the passage he had read earlier.

"Esther," the uncle said, startling me, "what are you doing?"
I tried to explain. "How long has this been going on?" he asked.
"About an hour," I said. "Come with me," he said. We went in.
"What's going on?" he asked Augustin, taking the book from
his hands and hurling it to the floor. "What rubbish are you
reading her?"

Augustin bent down, picked up the book, and dusted it off.
He showed the uncle the page. The uncle looked at the page and
twisted his mouth in revulsion. "Abominable!" he said. Madame
lay on the bed with her eyes closed as if she were sleeping; she did
not look at the uncle even once, nor did she say a word. From
now on, the uncle told Augustin, he was to read her only *des
belles histoires,* only the nice parts, about how Jesus worked miracles and walked on water and all that. Not all this gruesome
nonsense.

Augustin glanced fearfully at Madame before he left the room.
"Come, get dressed," the uncle said to her. "We are going to celebrate Esther's birthday." She got up very slowly and then
remained seated on the bed for a while. "And as for that degener-
ate priest," he shouted, "I don't ever want to see him here again!"
"Yes, Chouchou," she said weakly. "If you don't feel well take a
pill, take two," he went on, "but don't read that garbage! Do you
understand, Marie?" She nodded. As the uncle and I went out she
whispered, "Judas."

Photograph: La Petite Florence

Father brought back about two thousand slides from his travels in Africa. "Beasts, beasts, and more beasts," Mother snorted when she saw gazelles, packs of wolves, zebras, deer, and silent antelope grazing in the silent green brush.

Years after his African adventure Father was still crossing the globe with his slides and stories like a one-man traveling circus act bringing out his dancing bear. One of the last times he showed them was when he was running on an independent ticket for head of the city council; he invited people to the house of his running mate, an electrician named Prosper Baruch.

Prosper had set up an open-air theater in a field of brambles behind his house: an elevated stage, long benches set in a semicircle, rows and rows of colored lights, and two projectors beamed toward a screen.

More than three hundred people crammed into the field on the eve of the election, hungry for entertainment. One by one Father's slides were projected onto the large screen: pygmies, copper mines, lions, straw huts, droopy-teated women with infants slung on their backs, tribal chiefs, wooden fires and cauldrons, the infinite green of the jungle, the rivers and the savanna, and Jacques Taieb, the leader of the treks, whose face or hat or arm or leg appeared at the edge of almost every picture.

Father explained the slides, speaking into a microphone that crackled with earsplitting shrieks. As his party lacked a platform, his commentary on the slides constituted his campaign speech. He was followed by a succession of ardent supporters, mostly neighborhood youths who admired him. Their spicy stories laced the night like strips of fat on steak, peppered as they were with phrases like "the corrupt labor regime," "oppression of the Sephardis," "the usual lies about national security," and "the ruling class's hatred of Orientals."

Mother lent a hand, decorating the large placards bearing the party symbol. Maybe he'd finally straighten up, get some kind of a job, she thought. Everywhere in the house there were coffee cups, brimming ashtrays, pamphlets, lists, aspirin bottles, loose slides and photographs, and neighbors and supporters who came and went at all hours. Mother thought she would lose her mind; she ran to Nona Fortuna to rest for a while and gripe. "*Al-subr wa al-zaman,* Inès," patience and time, Nona Fortuna reassured her over and over.

Financial backers were found: Prosper Baruch himself, who had managed to put something aside; seventeen-year-old Zion Amsalem, a welder's apprentice who was known as "wild Zion" for no obvious reason; Moshe and Rosa Antabi, the owners of a bicycle-repair shop. But it was all for naught: Father lost to the incumbent councilman by two votes.

"Two votes! Just two votes!" he whispered hoarsely as, grief-stricken and mortified, he roamed the house day after endless gray day, waiting for Mother to return from work, preferring her fits of hysteria to the emptiness. When, finally, he lost his voice, he scrawled the words on scraps of paper. For two weeks he flailed like that until he got his strength back and left again. Mother took the house apart, scrubbing and disinfecting everywhere as if a plague had blown through.

Then came the creditors. Wild Zion's mother would drop by in the morning on her way to work, demanding the few pennies she claimed Father had wheedled out of her son; toward evening it was the Antabis who waddled down the street. Mrs. Antabi was in the ninth month of her pregnancy, swollen and bloated. She and her husband would stop and stare at me for what seemed like ages as I made mud pies in the garden. "Is your father home?" Mr. Antabi would ask at long last in his throaty singsong.

"Don't know."

"And your mother?"

"Don't know. Maybe."

Mother chased them away with a broom, thwacking the ground with the brush, deafened by her own shrieks. Then, as they ran into the street clinging to each other, she tore her hair out clump by bloody clump. At night the police came looking for Father. The beam of their flashlight ranged over the dark wall, the folds of the curtains, the doorway, the kitchen table, my face. "There's a child asleep in here," Mother said.

In the mornings she polished the silver and brass chandelier at Rabbi Levin's house with a slice of lemon. Finally, she told the rabbi everything: he had connections to people in the courts. He could get them to leave her alone. Once he had tried to persuade her to send me to a boarding school but Mother had refused. "I didn't have a child so that strangers could bring her up," she said.

"With all your work you're not really raising her," Rabbi Levin persisted.

"It's not the same," she said.

"You're very stubborn, Inès, very stubborn," Rabbi Levin concluded in his gentle voice.

A grateful smile spread across her face. "Shall we see about the trees, Rabbi Levin?" she asked. Every morning the two of them would look at the trees. He had planted some twenty fruit trees—apple, pear, plum, and pomegranate—"for the generations to come," he said.

"What generations?" he wondered aloud as he gazed at the trees from his table on the porch, sipping the tea with lemon that Mother had made him. "I plant and plant, Inès, but who's going to eat?" the rabbi said.

"Someone will," Mother reassured him. "Don't you worry, there'll always be someone around to eat."

The rabbi and his wife were childless; Mother thought it had something to do with the war in Europe. Their large two-story house was elegant and immaculate. The sofa was trimmed with gold tassels that tickled and there was always a faint smell in the air of herring, mint, and little pellets of dogfood.

"Don't you dare touch them, they're from abroad," Mother warned me when I went to work with her. I had chewed one of them: it didn't taste half bad.

"Sit and wait for me here until I'm done," she would say, grabbing my arm and dragging me behind the kitchen door. Rabbi Levin always took an interest in me though. "What do you think about while you're sitting there, Esther?" he asked once.

I looked at the large black yarmulke that seemed ready to slide down the side of his head. "About God," I said. Pleased with the answer, he rewarded me with a chocolate. "You should bring the little one here more often," he told Mother. "Bring her with you. She shouldn't be left at home alone."

After Father left, the rabbi wanted Mother and me to move into his house; there was a nice room for us on the ground floor, next to the garage. "What do you say?" She had to think about it.

"I have to think about it, Rabbi. I can't make such a decision lightly," Mother said.

I led a group of children there to show them my new house. The rabbi let them shake and climb his fruit trees, following after them with a rake and dustpan to gather the pits.

"I don't like the idea, Inès. This whole business doesn't seem right to me," said Uncle Moise, who had been summoned from the Galilee for a consultation. Between them on the kitchen table lay a mound of chickens, eggs, onions, jars of honey, and bags of sugar that Moise had brought from his village.

"Why?" Mother asked. "Why don't you like the idea?"

"First of all, he's a rabbi," the uncle said solemnly. "A rabbi. Don't forget that, Inès."

"He's a sort of rabbi, not a real rabbi, not one of those holy ones," Mother tried to explain. "He drives his car to synagogue on Shabbat."

"Even so, he's still a rabbi, *et nous n'avons rien à faire avec ces rabbins*. We have no truck with those people."

"He's a good man," Mother said softly.

Moise sank his large, magnificent head into his ruddy double chin, which was covered with hard gray stubble. He leaned against the wall behind him, rubbing his cheek against a brightly colored calendar of snowy mountain peaks and glassy lakes. "He may be a good man, Inès, I'm not saying . . ." Moise began after a silence. "Maybe he is. But think about it. What do we know about these people—where they're from, what they did—" He stopped abruptly, gulping his coffee. "What they did during the war, for instance. There are rumors, Inès, all sorts of talk."

"What kind of talk?" Mother said curtly.

"I asked about him, Inès. I asked around."

"So what did you hear? Tell me."

"You don't want to know."

"Oh yes, I do."

"I spoke with someone whose uncle was over there, in the camp. There are rumors."

"What?" she cried impatiently. "Tell me already!"

"Well, it seems that he was on one of those Jewish councils that turned other Jews over to the Nazis. He had a different name then, apparently. He changed it when he went to America, before he came here."

Mother's lips drained white, as if they had shriveled. "I don't believe it. They love to drag one another in the dirt, those Ashkenazis. They spit on anyone who got out alive just like they spit on us. They can't stand seeing anyone else get on with their lives. Like that Greenspan woman on your kibbutz—you know who I mean."

"What about her?" Moise asked, exhausted.

"Whenever I come with Esther she looks at me like she wants to chew me up, just because I can have children and she can't. She makes my hair stand on end the way she looks at the child. *Tu te souviens?* You remember?"

"That's different, Inès. Who knows what she went through? Think for a minute, the things that happened there—I don't know. God preserve us from what human beings can do to one another."

"God preserve us indeed," Mother muttered. Dejected, she took Moise's bags and began unpacking them one by one. "What did you bring? We could feed the whole neighborhood with what you've brought!"

Once a month Uncle Moise came down with his assorted bundles and several large canvases wrapped in old packing paper. "*Nawartana, ya* Moise," Mother would murmur, beaming. "You have brought light to us." She would hurry to tear the wrapping off the paintings, and, eyeing the thick brush strokes, she would ask, "What's this? What have you painted here?"

"*Printemps,*" Moise answered one month with a shy smile, taking a step back and cocking his head to one side, studying his work. "Too much orange," he decided sadly.

"No, no, it's not too much," Mother said. "The orange gives it life. It's happy, that orange, Moise."

He pondered the painting for a moment, stroking his chin. At last he conceded, "If you say so."

They discussed where to hang it. "Somewhere that gets the light, Inès. This painting wants light," Moise recommended, trailing after her from room to room.

Wielding a hammer, three nails stuck in her mouth, Mother ignored him. "Who cares what *it* wants? It's what I want that counts," she mumbled through her pursed lips.

She hung the painting crookedly on the wall in the hallway.

"It's crooked, Inès," Uncle Moise protested.

"But if we hang it straight the door won't close," Mother explained. Later, on the sly, when she had vanished into the kitchen, he straightened it.

"Why don't you paint things that people actually see, like a flower or something, maybe a table?" she asked him as they sat at dinner, sopping up her red meatball sauce with hunks of bread.

"The days of flowers and tables and all that are over. No one paints like that anymore," he said.

"I'm not saying you should paint that way all the time," Mother said, defending herself. "But once, just once you could."

Moise sent a tentative, longing glance in the direction of the painting. "If you look hard you can see all the flowers you want in that painting, or something like flowers."

"I'll have to make a point of looking hard then," Mother allowed grudgingly.

"He spends all the money Jacquo sends him from Africa on canvases and brushes," Moise's wife always complained.

"So let him play with his paints. What do you care?" Mother would whisper, leaning toward her. "It helps him vent his anger."

"Not enough, it doesn't," Uncle Moise's wife would respond.

Moise's own kitchen was where he customarily set up his easel, smearing paint across the canvas while frying chicken parts or stuffing grape leaves and peppers. He painted with the same gravity and attention he devoted to every other task. He allowed no one to meddle in his kitchen, flaring up at the merest sign of frivolity or carelessness. "What are you doing to those cucumbers? Look at the way you're slicing them," he growled at Mother when she came to visit and attempted to help out.

"Great, all I need is you telling me how to slice a cucumber. What do you think? I don't know how to slice a cucumber?" she retorted, leaving in a huff.

Uncle Moise had sliced thousands of cucumbers on the kibbutz he'd helped found in the late 1940s. In the beginning he had swallowed all sorts of slop in the dining hall but one day he could stand it no longer. "How is it they manage to ruin everything?" he yelled. "Who could possibly eat these beans? They've had the living daylights cooked out of them! Who did this? Who?"

He was put in charge of the kitchen and over the next three years he became a genius at making something out of nothing. He drove the kitchen women crazy, poking a finger into the pots and declaring, "No, not done yet."

All along he dabbled in art, saving his meager allowance for paint, driving his wife crazy too, leaving the light glaring in their room half the night. "Turn the light out and go to sleep already," she would plead.

"Just a little longer. I'm nearly finished."

In the mid-1960s he took steps. He registered at an art institute in Tel Aviv and asked the kibbutz to let him study painting. The kibbutz refused. There was no money, they said. Moise did not argue; he hated antagonism. Besides, he still placed the ideals of the kibbutz above all else. But a month later another kibbutz member, an Ashkenazi, was sent to study in the city. Moise said nothing but secretly he made his plans: he found a post as an agricultural consultant in the lower Galilee, rented a house, and left overnight. Politely he rejected the kibbutz's offers of a review, rejected its promises. "That's that," he said. He never spoke of the matter again, locking his humiliation into a small, tight space, taking care to leave room for his soul; that was his way of protecting himself. His loyalty to the kibbutz movement and its ideology was undamaged but he had drawn a line, erected a wall between the personal and political. Never again would he mistake comrades for flesh-and-blood family. He now believed it was possible and necessary to separate his life from his politics, to select only the good and turn aside the bad.

"How do you separate them? With tweezers?" Father asked, savoring the story with a strange relish. "Your enlightened kibbutz friends, which ones are they—the good guys or the bad guys? How can you tell? By peeling off their skins? They're all rotten racists, that's what they are, sitting on Arab land."

Uncle Moise was furious. "You keep quiet, you hear? Don't you say a word."

Father shut up instantly, choking back the stream of rhetoric he had at the ready. He was in awe of Uncle Moise's integrity, determination, and brawn. In Father's eyes, the former kibbutznik was a kind of strongman. More than once Father had told how he had seen Moise crush a tin can with one powerful hand. With his own ears, he had heard the metal pop.

"I'd like to see *you* do that," Mother taunted him.

Father straightened his tie, passing his fingers through his greased hair. "Those macho games never much interested me, Inès. You know that."

In the neighborhood newsletter Father produced several years later—as editor, proofreader, writer, and publisher—he printed a story based on Uncle Moise's, which he called "The Expulsion."

"Read it. Read what he wrote," Mother urged Uncle Moise. He read it, a large, wicked smile of gratification spreading across his face. "For fifteen years Salomon had given his life and breath to the kibbutz; he had been among its founding fathers. But in the end?" Father had written. "Expulsion! Why? Because he was Sephardic. That was the thanks the Ashkenazi settlers gave their stepbrothers, their outcasts; that is the only way they know how to act toward the Sephardis, and toward our brethren, the Arabs: with might, might, and more might. Salomon tried to become one of them and failed—as have we all. They will never let us forget that we are not part of them."

"Salomon?" Mother had snorted in derision. "That's the only name you could think of? Salomon?"

It was Salomon who had accompanied Father to Africa. A short, mustachioed man with one eye lower than the other, he had the lopsided look of someone who has just been punched. He dressed in checked suits that were just a little too small. That was how he appeared in all the slides, always standing next to Father.

"He was one of those tagalongs who spend their whole lives waiting for someone to give them an order," Father said. Salomon ran errands for him, borrowed money, went wherever Father went, and cleaned up after him when he made a mess. They had met in Cairo and almost immediately begun to go about together. Father loathed his obsequiousness but found him *très serviable*—very obliging—as he was fond of saying.

Africa was a torment for Salomon: he feared the blacks, the beasts, the harsh weather, his own shadow. In the Belgian Congo he fell ill with malaria and lay near death in a stinking hospital in Kinshasa for two months. Meanwhile Father went on to Brazzaville.

Florence Goldman, the American student who had joined their group, came to visit Salomon. "How could he have left you here like this? You call him your best friend?" she cried, appalled.

Salomon affected his small, baleful smile. "Really, you must not speak that way, Mademoiselle Florence."

But she did speak that way. She was twenty-five and not very pretty but had a lovely ethereal air, an immense love of animals, the missionary zeal of an overstimulated soul, and the psoriasis of an overstimulated skin. She met Mother only once but wrote to her every few months for more than ten years, always sending four typewritten pages.

"She suffered a great deal, la petite Florence, poor thing," Mother said, digging through a heap of dusty slides covered with yellow spots of mildew.

One by one she lifted them to the light, holding them between her eyes and the round lamp. "Beasts, beasts, and more beasts," she sighed.

Photograph: Madame Sicourelle, Uncle Sicourelle, and Erouan, Brazzaville, 1955

Madame Sicourelle is reaching over, touching the boy's bare shoulder. "This child is mine," says the tensed arm that bisects the uncle just below his neck, taking possession of the boy, claiming her territory. How relaxed and nonchalant the uncle's hand is in contrast, cradling the boy just beneath the armpit.

The child is sitting on the uncle's knee leaning to the right, a bit unsteady, nearly sliding off the thigh that holds him up. "No, no, you won't fall," the uncle's reassuring hand says, supporting him casually, not intrusively, protecting him like a chaperone, like a watchful glance. "You won't fall."

The coffee shop they are sitting in is empty; perhaps it is early morning.

Uncle Sicourelle is an early riser. Madame is not. "What is there to do so early in the morning," she wonders sleepily, yawning, her sharp, tense features still veiled by a gauzy curtain of languor and docileness.

To this day Uncle Sicourelle adores the way she rises from sleep. "You are so very sweet when you wake, Marie," he says on Sunday mornings when he has time to linger. He fusses over a rich breakfast of many courses. "Don't you lift a finger, you just rest," he orders and Madame willingly complies, listening to the BBC World Service without understanding a word.

"Tell me what they're saying, Chouchou," she asks. She boasts about his knowledge of English. "That uncle of yours picks up languages from the air," she tells the niece. As for herself, she confesses, she has no talent for them. For two years they had a boy who spoke only English, not a word of French, and still she did not manage to learn. "Do you remember Chris, Chouchou?" she calls out to the uncle.

He brings a scalding frying pan to the table brimming with scrambled eggs and bacon. "What about Chris?" he asks.

"I was telling Esther that I never managed to learn a word of English from him," Madame says, taking a taste. "Mmm, that's good."

"You didn't learn because most of the time you were talking, not listening," Uncle Sicourelle comments.

"True," Madame agrees, giggling.

Erouan joins them, pouring three cups of black coffee into himself one after another and lighting a cigarette. "In another three weeks it will be Christmas," he says.

"We must think of something," says Madame.

Sated, heavy, the uncle pats his belly. "Let's invite everyone this year. Everyone. The de Karinis, and the de Vilalvilles, and

Sendrice, and Adnan, and the engineer—let's have them all. We'll do something big."

Madame Sicourelle beams. "You mean it, Chouchou?"

"I mean it. We haven't thrown a party in a long time and since Esther's here it's the perfect opportunity."

Erouan scratches at the tablecloth, scraping away some invisible dirt. "I thought it might be a good idea to send for the boy over the holiday."

The uncle and Madame Sicourelle say nothing for a long time. "He should be about five, if I'm not mistaken," Madame says at last.

"Five and a half," the uncle corrects her.

A dragonfly flits close above them and lands on the gleaming coffeepot, its translucent wings fluttering. Silence. From time to time a car passes on the road; the leaky faucet in the garden drips into the bowl that has been placed beneath it: drip, drop.

"What boy are you talking about?" the niece dares to ask.

Erouan lifts his glazed eyes with their swollen purplish bags. "My son," he says. "That is, mine and Dominique's."

"Will Dominique agree?" Madame speculates.

The uncle gets up. "The question is, will we agree?" he says in a quiet voice.

"He is our grandson after all, Chouchou," Madame says.

Erouan goes to pour himself some whiskey; though it's breakfast time, no one says anything. He comes back and sits with his legs outstretched, staring at the ice cubes floating in his glass. "I spoke to her a week ago. She agreed."

"How did you speak to her?" the uncle asks.

"By telephone from Jean-Luc's."

"So he's in on this, too, that shit?" the uncle says, furious, hurling his napkin on the table and striding into the house.

"You shouldn't have mentioned Jean-Luc, Fufu. He jumps whenever he hears that name. You should have said what we talked about. You've just gone and complicated things," Madame says. "The trick is to let him think it was all his idea." Madame nibbles on some melba toast. "Now we have to think how to turn the whole thing around."

Erouan lets his head fall against the back of the chair. "I'm tired of this, Maman, tired of thinking how to tell him and how to bring him around. I'm sick of these games."

Madame strikes her plate with her knife. Her face is lined in concentration. "*Courage*, Fufu, *courage*! We shall overcome this."

Madame Sicourelle has the mettle of her people, the hard-scrabble Brittany farmers who see the world in terms of struggle and counterstruggle, will against will. She has never forgotten where she came from. In fact, she has never adjusted to being wealthy. She scrimps and saves, petrified by the uncle's profligate spending, outwitting him bit by bit, penny by penny, item for item.

"*Il faut économiser*," she urges again and again. "We must save," she says, her narrow lips pursed. She cuts pieces of newspaper and leaves them in the bathroom for toilet tissue; she surveys the contents of the refrigerator twice a day, despairing of the extravagance and waste that she finds there. Old dresses she turns into skirts and old skirts into napkins. She keeps a close eye on the electricity, the water, the servants' wages; buys half-price damaged fruit and vegetables, only to watch them rot; and declares the spoiled yogurt she ate just fine.

Beneath her parsimony simmered a great craving for security—not for herself, she claimed, but for Erouan. Twenty years with Uncle Sicourelle had not changed the stubborn vow she made before she married him: to take care of herself and her son. Her core of miserly thrift was the toughest part of her; it tempered all else, even her love for her husband.

She remained hungry despite everything he gave her, according to Nona Fortuna, who knew this from rumors and from what her heart told her. Once, when the Sicourelles came to Israel for a visit, Nona had spent three hours with Madame. "We must hurry, *ma chérie,*" the uncle urged his wife, who went out of her way to show the old woman her respect. The two of them discussed the Catholic education they had in common. Nona Fortuna rambled nostalgically about her days at St. Anne's convent school; she talked of her old desire to enter the convent and of beloved Sister Thérèse, who had continued to offer a kind word and good counsel until Nona left Egypt. Madame Sicourelle did not understand. "But you are a Jewess, are you not?"

"Of course!" Nona Fortuna was appalled that there could have been any doubt about this fact. Her grandfather on her mother's side, after all, had been the ritual slaughterer for the entire Cairene Jewish community.

Madame Sicourelle was embarrassed: any ambiguity or deviation made her uncomfortable. She thought the old woman was no longer all there. "You have made a lovely home for yourself, Maman," she lied, holding a scented handkerchief to her nose to block out the stench from the open cesspool in the yard.

Nona Fortuna passed her fingers over Madame Sicourelle's flushed cheeks, pressing her palm to the soft flesh: "*Très jolie,*" she affirmed dryly. After Madame and the uncle left, Nona pronounced her "the Christian."

She had nothing against Christianity—the label was meant merely to indicate Madame Sicourelle's utter foreignness. Since the death of Jacquo, her husband, Nona Fortuna had adopted his perspective. It was her way of missing the man whose eyes, she liked to say, she had plucked out through the back of his head.

Grandpapa Jacquo forgave her. He forgave her everything simply because he was never conscious of insults, dismissing them before they could even reach him. He lacked whatever enzyme it is that might have allowed him to digest spite and malice the way other people do, to absorb it into his views, his feelings, his thoughts or deeds. Like a baby he would spit out the foreign object: for Grandpapa Jacquo, there was no evil. That was his great heresy.

He had only vague, superstitious notions about the customs, holidays, and prohibitions of the Jews. Of the many commandments he took to heart only the admonishments to charity and benevolence. His visits to Harat al-Yahud, Cairo's Jewish quarter, maddened him because of the poverty and destitution of its residents—not because of their Jewishness. "Ota, if you could see those poor people," he would sigh to Nona Fortuna when he returned from the quarter or whenever he encountered distress, privation, physical or spiritual anguish. He often negotiated with Allah, freely evoking his name. He stood in childlike awe of God, as if the Lord were a mighty boss, cruel and generous by turns. It was never clear—not to him nor to those around him—whether his Allah was Jewish, Christian, or Muslim, but the distinction seemed to be of no importance, the kind of silly hairsplitting that fools indulge in.

Although he was unsure what it was precisely, Grandpapa Jacquo sensed a connection between Nona Fortuna's hardheartedness and her fondness for Christianity, or what he took to be the spirit of Christianity. "Ota, how can you go to a place where people like to look at a man with nails in his hands hanging from a pole?" he puzzled.

She never explained. He could not be expected to grasp the beauty of such things, she believed: the silent steps of the nuns; the smell of rough soap that wafted from their habits and their skin, the distinctive scent of austere cleanliness; Sister Thérèse's wide, smooth, golden forehead under her white wimple, and her eyes, in which Nona thought she could detect only light; the chanting in the chapel; the way the nuns used to comb her long yellow hair and gather it in a bun; the innocent games of tag the girls played with the nuns; the songs they sang and the plays they put on. This confined, chaste universe of women and girls harbored a protest: in its cloistered halls they renounced the world of men, their mastery and authority. "They ruin everything," Nona Fortuna would say. "They dirty everything they touch."

For years she dreamed of turning her back on the world. To shun it, she thought, would be to achieve absolute victory, perfect and immaculate, beyond struggle, beyond petty losses and gains. But perfection was hard-won. The driving force in her life, the measure by which everyone and everything was judged, it exacted every last drop of spontaneity, warmth, candor, and joy from those around her. She was ever in the grip of renunciation, denying herself, denying others so as to feel the power of control.

Tearing up her roots and coming to Israel had been *un cauchemar*, a nightmare. She hated everything in sight. Jews and Arabs, Ashkenazis and Sephardis, the religious and the secular, the wealthy and the poor—she saw them all as riffraff, the uneducated masses, rude and charmless, cruel and ridiculous in their endless war over a piece of land she didn't consider "worth spit." The pioneering Zionist spirit of struggle, struggle, and more struggle, of disdain for anything not achieved through struggle and the exertion of physical and mental force, was anathema to her. Her ideal was an aesthetic one, an elegant life lived gracefully, a life without sweat, scars, or swollen veins, like a wound with no pus.

Uncle Moise found her ways absurd. "Change, Maman, change, you must change how you think. You don't know what you're saying," he would tell her. But his ideological hammer made no impact: there was nothing for him to pound on; Nona had not so much a worldview as a set of tastes, an utterly foreign lexicon from an utterly different place. Still Uncle Moise did not give up, as his good nature, optimism, and faith in progress convinced him that all problems could be solved, all wrongs righted with words. He would talk to Nona for hours on end, often tangled up in his own convoluted polemics, laboring, though, not to hurt her feelings—God forbid—but to show her what she did not want to see: that her endless self-absorption kept her from recognizing that they had all—the Germans, the Poles, the Hungarians, the Romanians, everyone—left behind a world that had been obliterated, that was no more, that was now but wishful thinking, a dream, a memory.

"The Egypt of King Farouk and King Fouad is over, Maman. It's gone," he insisted.

She remained obstinate, cloaking her face in the blank look that was only partly a consequence of her blindness.

Unlike Moise, who would worry when Nona assumed her pose, Uncle Sicourelle had no patience with her. "Stop your playacting, Maman, I haven't got the strength," he would say.

Uncle Sicourelle read her well, and that filled her with satisfaction and pride. "He knows how to read people, the devil," she would say.

He had to. In Africa he had no family or social network to protect him, to soften the blows, to absorb the errors and the personal failures; his keen eye and swift powers of judgment were not a luxury but his means of survival. He had no choice but to look the world in the eye.

And he did. He would fix his stare on the camera that sought to expose him, exposing the camera in turn, an eye for an eye. Madame Sicourelle's tense, intrusive arm neither disturbs nor distracts him. With chilling calm he's nailed his prey, holding it in his unflinching gaze.

How strong his sharp dark features are beside those of Madame Sicourelle and her son in the light of that empty coffeehouse. The jumble of rattan chairs, the tablecloth, the fan-shaped linen napkins, the wall behind them with its carved ornamental stonework, the dim interior—nothing overshadows his presence, a presence that seems to be part of a family composition but is, in fact, isolated, a solo portrait instead.

"Who are you like, Chouchou, your father or your mother?" Madame Sicourelle asks, looking at the photograph.

He laughs. "Neither." He has returned to the terrace, his good humor restored.

"You do have something of your mother; your mouth is like hers," Madame says.

"You barely met my mother. How would you know?" the uncle says, dismissing her observation.

"I've seen pictures, Chouchou. I've seen plenty of pictures of her."

"Pictures don't show anything. Haven't you noticed you always come out thinner in photographs than in real life?"

"Chouchou!" Madame Sicourelle cries, insulted.

His gaze wanders, landing suddenly on Erouan, who stirs in the sunlight. "Sometimes Erouan looks a little like me in photographs, don't you think? Something about the forehead, the expression."

Erouan and his mother look down at the tablecloth. Madame is busy with an empty cigarette carton, tearing the cardboard into tiny pieces. "Will you let the boy come visit us, Chouchou? For me? I don't ask for much. Just this once, Chouchou," she says, her voice quavering.

The uncle lights a cigarette, holding the flaring match until it burns his fingertips. His narrow, gleaming eyes are moist behind the screen of smoke. "Just this once, Marie. Remember."

Missing Photograph: The One Facing Us

A man stands facing us at the edge of a pool, casting his shadow, trying, it seems, to emerge. It is as if he is being projected onto the pool, being forced into the scene. The scene is the pool. He is being screened onto it in fragments, as something other than his true self, vaporized into parts that will soon be transported to another place, another time, that will regroup and try to appear once more.

He is planted there, handless, suspended between extreme dark and extreme light. The light goes before him, ahead of him; a great beam of light falls on him and a corner of the pool, stealing his shadow, wrenching it from him. The shadow, now stolen, moves away. Liberated, it lands on the fence behind the man, destroying the familiar continuity of shadow and form.

He appears against two backdrops, one a curtain or a fence and the other something black, a dark screen that blankets the picture, closing in on the man and on the scene, eclipsing it. The photograph looks like an outdoor picture, but one without depth. The background, obscured as it is, makes the man's stance theatrical, makes the pool's edge—where the man is trying to appear, to assume the form of a man while thwarted by the enigma of his own appearance—look fake.

The enigma—of the setting, of the man who stands, wanting something, and of the apathetic brush strokes that erase his corporeality—does not help his case. The play of light and shadow atomizes the man's parts; the flickering dims him, depriving him of his mass. The brush strokes undermine his solidity, making him one with the place. It is impossible to distinguish between the two.

But the place is the water. At one with the place, the man standing out of the water is, at the same time, out of place. The water and the figures who seem to be splashing in the water, who seem to be able to move—what does he feel toward them? He cannot move, blocked as he is by the light, detached from his shadow, standing in place as if blinded. He is trying to take the form of a man, to be a man, but instead he is a situation. Situated in this pool scene, he himself is the pool scene: not a person but a place.

Photograph: Uncle Sicourelle and Workers on the Deck of the Victoria Star, *Douala, Cameroon*

One time he bought his workers uniforms: short-sleeved knee-length jackets in a noxious fluorescent chartreuse. "They won't wear these, Monsieur," Richard cautioned. "You'll see, they won't wear them."

"*B'abouhum!* They'll wear them, on their fathers' lives!" the uncle retorted. "They'd better. Anyone who doesn't will feel it in his wages."

He lined his men up in rows on the wharf, all 160 of them, chartreuse and brown, arms crossed behind their backs and legs spread. He reviewed each and every one of them, straightening collars, pointing out buttons that had not been done up, sending away the peacocks who had put on colored polo shirts over the jackets. "Enough of all this chaos. From now on everyone will look the same, like in a real factory," he thundered.

The workers were not entirely displeased. "They were actually *très contents,* Mademoiselle," Richard recalled. *Très contents,* too, when Monsieur Sicourelle gave them tags with their names and positions to wear on the large pocket at the front of the jacket.

From time to time Uncle Sicourelle is overcome with an urge to impose order and discipline, to raze his work to the ground and start from the beginning, with everything as it should be.

"Don't fret, Chouchou. Sooner or later someone will do that for you," Madame Sicourelle notes coolly, amused. The preparations for the upcoming Christmas event have given her an ironic detachment, a sense of perspective about her husband and her own usual nagging worries and even a certain magnanimity.

Uncle Sicourelle drinks whiskey, smokes fancy cigars, shuffles about, dozes off, and fusses over the volatile household whose sole purpose is to divert him, to lock him in the moment and keep him from thinking of his uncertain existence, of his dispensable and all too prominent presence at the factory, a lone white man among 160 blacks.

"I've given my life to this place! What would they do without me? All these people I give bread and a living, what would they do?" he exclaims.

"Don't shout, Chouchou, don't shout. We'll understand you even if you don't shout. So you give them bread and wages—so what?" says Madame Sicourelle.

A few days ago something strange happened, he relates. He was leaving his office late, at eight or nine, walking to the car as usual. By the large steel doors of the warehouse, from behind the old refrigerator, two people suddenly appeared, at first motionless in the darkness, but then rolling an immense barrel across the floor toward him. He had moved aside quickly, miraculously unharmed.

"Who were they, Chouchou? Did you see who they were?" Madame asks, growing pale.

"Petty thieves. They fled before I could get a good look at them." He dismisses the incident with a shrug of his shoulders. Two stinking thieves.

"Thieves don't go rolling barrels around like that for nothing; they must have wanted something, money or jewelry," Madame Sicourelle insists.

"They were thieves. *Mon Dieu!* Just thieves, I'm telling you," the uncle bellows.

In response to Richard's urging, he has purchased a gun, but Madame thinks a gun is not enough. "What will you do with a gun, Chouchou? You've never used one in your life. You need a bodyguard, not a gun," she says.

"A bodyguard," he mutters. "What would I do with a bodyguard?"

"I'm serious, Chouchou," Madame persists. "Find yourself a bodyguard. Get one of those Israelis. Write your brother Edouard to send you someone he knows."

"Maybe he'll send a platoon if the price is right," the uncle adds in jest.

"Chouchou, please!" Madame pleads. "Please think of us. If anything were to happen to you, think of me and Erouan. And of Esther," she adds, looking at the niece.

"I am thinking, Marie, just not panicking. Please, I'm begging you, don't panic."

"I would have died of fright if that had happened to me," the niece says.

"Nothing will happen to you. Why should anything happen to you? Nothing will ever happen to you, *ya* Esther," the uncle says with sudden tenderness.

"Something could happen to anyone," Madame says, putting on her glasses and reviewing the guest list. "That Cohen who was here a few months ago, shall I invite him?"

"Who is he?"

"How should I know? Some Israeli man. A doctor, I think. Madame de Vilalville met him. She said he was very nice."

"So invite him. One plate more or less, what difference will it make?" the uncle says, stretching his legs out on the sofa and closing his eyes. "My head is spinning. I haven't eaten a thing since this morning. Come sit by me, Esther," he says, patting the sofa. "Tell me something."

She does not move, instead curling into the rocking chair. "What should I tell you?"

"Something nice. What did you do today?"

"Not much. Nothing special."

"Nothing? You must have done something since this morning. I can see you've changed your hairstyle."

"I took her to Claudine's today to do something about her hair," Madame says.

Uncle Sicourelle studies the niece with interest. "I don't like women with short hair."

"It's not short, Chouchou, it's medium length, to the nape."

"To me that's short. The child looked better with long hair. You looked fine with long hair," he tells the niece.

"Maybe I should wear a veil, too," she mutters in Hebrew.

"What did you say? What was that you said?" He sits up.

"Nothing, nothing. I said I'm more comfortable with short hair. It's easier to swim with short hair."

"You haven't been swimming in a long time, Esther. I haven't seen you go swimming for about two weeks now," Madame Sicourelle observes, stuffing invitations into envelopes, licking the flaps, and closing them.

"I swim. I swim when you're not looking."

"You mean you wait until I'm not around to watch," Madame Sicourelle says good-humoredly. She goes over to the drawer of the buffet and takes out stamps. Behind her back, the niece sticks her tongue out at Madame, then suddenly catches the uncle looking at her, smiling broadly.

"*Laisse-la tranquille*, Marie, leave her alone. She can swim whenever she likes. For all I care she doesn't have to swim at all," he says, opening a large box of chocolates.

"She should get like you, is that what you want? Esther has already put on some weight. She needs exercise," Madame Sicourelle comments. The niece rocks her chair forcefully back and forth. "Be careful you don't break something, Esther," Madame warns her.

"Let her break it. We'll buy a new one," the uncle says, downing After Eight mints in quick succession.

"That's all your uncle knows how to do," Nona Fortuna had said. "Break things. When he was little he'd take bottles and hammers and heavy stones and bash his toys until they broke into bits." Grandpapa Jacquo hired the daughter of one of the cooks, a feeble-minded girl of about thirteen, to play with him. After an hour she came away trembling. "He wants me to break his toys," she cried. "So break them," Grandpapa Jacquo said. "If that's what he wants, then break them." She would come for two hours a day to smash things on the shaded patio. Uncle Sicourelle would spread out his toys and look up at her, his eyes gleaming.

When they went to the family summer home in Hilwan, in the hills, they took the girl with them. Bousiana was her name. The uncle used to taunt her incessantly. "How come you're so black, Bousiana?"

"*Walla, ya ustaz,* I don't know, by God, sir," the girl said, abashed, pulling her sleeves down to hide her hands.

The uncle had an idea. "You know, Bousiana, if you want to be white you could scrub your skin really hard until you bleed. Don't stop until you start to bleed. That's how you'll know you've gotten rid of all your blackness."

So she scrubbed. For days afterward Nona Fortuna had to place chamomile compresses on the girl's scratched, burning, reddened black skin. "Just you wait. It'll be your turn one day, you rascal, just you wait," she said to Uncle Sicourelle.

"The boy was only having fun, Fortuna. Don't blow things out of proportion," said the big lady, Grandpapa Jacquo's mother, the mistress of the house.

That afternoon a heavy, hot rain fell. "Let's play hide-and-seek," the big lady suggested. "We'll all play. Even you, Fortuna," she said, beckoning her daughter-in-law, who roused herself from her armchair. No one ever dared defy the big lady. She took up a comfortable position from which to watch the game and appointed herself referee. "You stand and count, Fortuna," she commanded.

Nona Fortuna counted, cheating a little, peeking out of her still-good eyes to see her son sneak away with one of the large pairs of long underwear that had been laid out to dry on the many armchairs and couches. From the next room she heard him snicker as he pulled them on. "Three, two, one!" Nona Fortuna counted aloud. "But Jacquo has taken the big lady's underpants!" Gratified, Nona Fortuna looked on as the boy got what was coming to him. The big lady knew no mercy; she pummeled him with her walking stick as he writhed on the ground, trying in vain to undo the top lace and wriggle out.

As for herself, Nona Fortuna insisted, she never laid a hand on her children; she used only her mouth.

"With one like yours you'd be kinder to give them a swat now and then, Ota," Grandpapa Jacquo said.

They quarreled over the children's upbringing. Grandpapa Jacquo had only to say the word *children* and he would melt, misty-eyed. "The children want it," he explained the time he dragged a donkey home to their third-floor apartment.

Nona Fortuna was stunned by what she saw and heard: turds everywhere, braying, throngs of visitors coming to see the animal tied to her dining table. For the first time in her married life she made an alliance with her fearsome mother-in-law. "He has brought home an ass," she reported flatly.

Before Nona could count to three, the big lady was climbing the stairs, dragging her ottoman and panting. She positioned herself in front of the apartment and sat down. She waited for six hours, until Grandpapa Jacquo returned from his carousing well after midnight. "Maman!" he cried, startled. "What are you doing here?"

"It's me or the ass," the big lady said.

"He's not bothering anyone," Grandpapa Jacquo protested weakly. "Come see how nice he is. He won't harm a soul. The children want him, Maman."

She looked straight through him and refused to budge until he coaxed the donkey back downstairs, gently prodding its behind.

Years after he still missed the animal. "Do you remember the donkey?" he asked his son on the eve of Uncle Sicourelle's departure for Africa.

The uncle remembered. He nodded his head but Grandpapa Jacquo did not see the nod. He grieved, thinking the uncle had forgotten everything. "Everything!" he announced to Nona Fortuna later that night when he returned from the train station.

She was unconvinced. "He only pretends to have forgotten," she said.

Nona Fortuna thought she had seen too much, "much more than a mother should see in her children," she said. This seeming omniscience had set up a permanent state of wariness between her and them, reserve bordering on outright rejection. Yet even across the distance of years and continents, even in the midst of all the changes in their lives and circumstances, she never once abandoned her firm, wordless convictions about her children. "I see far from the eye . . ." was how she accounted for her knowledge, even before her blindness, pondering her information, musing on the way it came to her, but never quite explaining her method. Later, when her sight was gone, she would repeat the phrase, gazing ahead at the large clay pots or the porch ledge whose presence she could confirm only by touch.

In amazement and in horror Grandpapa Jacquo had watched her sentence herself to the lonely desert of her intolerance and arrogance. "One day, Ota, you will suffocate from the stench of your own socks," he had said to her near the end, after Uncle Moise had left for Palestine, urging them to follow.

Grandpapa Jacquo, penniless, was himself confused and puzzled by a world gone mad. The British, whom he detested, were on the right side for once; the Italians had sided with the enemy; the Moslems had suddenly taken to the streets with shouts of "*Sahayouni, Sahayouni*—Zionist, Zionist"; and the Zionists whom he had fed and sheltered in his home had, in the end, stolen his son.

He was suspicious of Uncle Moise's letters, which told of "this good land, which is ours."

"What's so good about the land?" he said. "Are the people there good?" he wanted to know.

He did not hide his preference for Uncle Sicourelle and "that Africa" of his, which he felt suited the *esprit de la famille* better than the Zionist dream, a foreign, even traitorous, path.

He understood the great step that Uncle Sicourelle had taken; he knew, too, of the uncle's consuming fear of Europe and of Palestine as part of it. There was continuity in the twisting course the uncle had taken from Egypt to Africa, for in his world there was no place for national identity but ample room to carry out any conceivable human whim.

The more Grandpapa Jacquo foresaw his death, the more intransigent his beliefs and aversions became, like the stubborn eccentricities of the very old and the not so bright. He insisted on ending his days in a public hospital like everyone else, swallowed up once and for all in the bustle of the masses he loved so well.

Two weeks before the family was to join Uncle Moise in Palestine, Grandpapa Jacquo died. He had an unreasonable terror of travel and all modes of transportation: trolleys, trains, boats, and planes.

"My father was a great coward," Uncle Sicourelle was fond of saying when he was in a good mood and feeling nostalgic. "The greatest coward there ever was."

"And you?" Madame Sicourelle derides him now. "For twenty years you haven't moved, just because you're afraid to get on a plane." She turns to the niece. "Can you believe it? A big man like him and he's that frightened?"

"And boats, how does he feel about boats?" the niece asks with interest.

"He'll only get on one if it's tied to the pier and barely moving," Madame replies.

"*Merde alors,* can't you wait until I've gone before you start gossiping about me?" the uncle says, feigning anger.

He's not ashamed of his fears, he claims, he just doesn't like to think about them.

When one of his boats docks, he has to examine its catch. Holding on to Richard on one side and Nicola on the other, he clambers aboard and pokes through the large crates, a handkerchief pressed to his nose—not because of the smell of fish, to which he has become accustomed, but because of the rocking, which makes him queasy.

He looks around, dropping his gaze to the floor, forgetting his protective instincts. The worker all the way to the left, standing on the dock, the one who is half naked, his body arched forward as if balanced on tiptoe, his neck thrust out, his palms face up behind his back—he looks like a heron, the strange bend of his body making him seem part of another scene, another story, outside the frame of the photograph. He doesn't belong with the workers on deck unloading the fish in a tangle of masts, nets, ropes, and rusty pipes.

The gray light signals afternoon or perhaps just wintry skies. Between the mast ropes, patches of sea appear at a distance. The strip of land is a thick green line, a good green, dark and rich, not like the fluorescent chartreuse of the jackets worn by two of the workers. One of them is bending over a barrel, the knobs of his curved spine protruding beneath the jacket. He is checking something; maybe he is vomiting. Three others are nearby, helping him: one points a finger inside the barrel. The uncle does not turn toward them even once. He asks no questions. He is self-absorbed, dreamy, engrossed in something on deck that has caught his attention. He stands close to a worker wearing a blue hat and a blue shirt with an upturned collar. One of his arms is hidden behind the uncle's belly; the visible arm is slack. The workers look toward the dock, attentive, hesitating. Suddenly the man close to the uncle whirls around, rending the stillness of the photograph. With a sharp movement he makes a half turn toward the uncle, thrusting a knife wherever he can, under the uncle's arm, at the top of his chest. He jumps from the boat, flees. The uncle falls facedown to the deck, into the net that held his attention a moment earlier.

He is carried away unconscious, bleeding. Holding him straight and high, muscular brown arms sail up the stairs toward the office. They lay him on the large desk, sweeping away papers, coffee cups, and ashtrays, removing his shoes. Richard reaches out to him blindly, hitting the furniture, his glasses having been trampled in the hubbub. "Monsieur!" he cries. "Monsieur!"

A great, heavy moan rises from under the high office windows. A dark mass of workers in chartreuse jackets turn their eyes upward, droning inaudibly at first, then wailing louder and louder, in a rhythmic keening cry that rises and falls, distant one moment in the rain that has suddenly begun pelting down, then coming closer, moving toward the building, stubborn, swelling, relentless, even when the dark, dense mass is sliced by the white-coated ambulance crew that races upstairs.

Forcefully they extricate their hands from Richard's wet, kissing lips. They ignore his frantic darting about, his outpouring of emotion. "He will live, Monsieur. Live," he pleads or demands. "He will live."

Photograph: Left to right: *Mother, Esther, and Nona Fortuna*

She's not so petite, that Florence. Why do they call her petite?" Nona Fortuna wonders aloud, dragging a brush through her wispy silvery hair and smoothing the thin strands with her fingers, the shadow of a knowing smile on her face—perhaps because of what she has just said or because she is pleased with herself, with the stroke of the metallic bristles pulling through her hair.

"How do you know whether she's petite or not, Maman?" says Inès. "Did you ever see her?"

"I just know," she insists, her mouth now crammed with hairpins that she removes one by one and presses into the bun at the base of her head. "I know everything, Inès. Don't I know everything, *sit al-banaat*?" she says, turning to me.

Mother gives me one of those looks of hers that remind me of a net dropped from above, from a tree, to catch the unsuspecting prey. I evade the question. "How should I know?" I say. "Why are you asking me?"

"You're going to grow a long nose like Pinocchio from all your lying," Nona Fortuna warns, feeling the bone at the center of my nose, as if checking it. "It will grow very, very long, and birds will come and eat it, just like Pinocchio's," she says darkly.

"The birds didn't eat his nose," I tell her. "The fairy shortened it because he was good."

"Good," Nona Fortuna repeats with disdain. "He was never good. When was he ever good, tell me?"

"In the end, when he saved his father from the belly of the whale."

Nona Fortuna snorts. "The belly of the whale. Why do you listen to those stories?"

I bring her the book, opening it to the picture of the large whale. "Look," I say, pointing. "Here he is with his father inside the whale. Now do you believe me?"

"What color is it?" she asks.

"What color is what?"

"*La baleine,* the whale. What color?"

"Brown, brownish gray with a little red inside. The red is the fire that Pinocchio has lit to keep his father warm."

"Brown, brownish gray," she turns the words over, sorting through her memory for a vague sensation long since lost, an object to tie the words to.

"Brown like the closet?" she asks.

"Lighter. Almost like your carpet."

She rubs her feet on the carpet. "Like the carpet," she says, a smile of comprehension crossing her face. "It was your father who brought me this carpet. *Il m'a fait un cadeau.* It was a gift."

Father revered her. "*Ya sit,*" he would address her, "Madame."
It was an informal term of respect conveying the warmth of a mea-
sured intimacy.

Even at times when Mother had thrown him out, he would
visit Nona Fortuna and tell her what was happening in the
world. The two of them would sit together for hours, close to
the radio, smoking cigarettes and sipping cups of coffee, chat-
ting or idly staring into space. They were almost always of the
same mind, firm in their belief that it mattered not what people
said but how they said it.

"*El-lissan al-hilwa,*" Nona Fortuna would sigh from time to
time. "Tell me, Robert, whatever happened to it, whatever happened to poetry?" Father would shake his head in sympathy,
then suddenly drop his head, dozing off.

The sonorous voice of Israel Radio's Arabic announcer
would wake him. "Turn it off, turn off that pest," he would tell
Nona Fortuna.

"Let me just hear the beginning," she would plead, turning
her beaming face toward the radio and listening intently.
"*Ahwani, ya oulad Misr al-taibeen,* My brothers, O worthy sons
of Egypt," the broadcaster would begin daily, stretching out the
syllables before commenting on the matter of the day, the trans-
gressions of Israel's neighbors, the Arab states. Father loathed
the program. "Israeli propaganda! How can you listen to that
garbage?" he would rail at her, leaping out of his chair.

"Garbage?" Nona Fortuna would marvel. "But he speaks so
beautifully. It can't be."

"It can, *ya siti,* it can," Father would assure her, turning the
radio off.

For months after the Six Day War he walked around like
someone who had been doused with cold water, shivering in

humiliation, blinking his eyes in disbelief every time he heard how the Egyptian soldiers had fled barefoot, leaving their boots behind. "Barefoot," he would repeat sarcastically. "Barefoot. A likely story."

"What's wrong with you?" Mother fumed. "Where've you been living all this time?" The night before Jerusalem was taken he stopped by to see if everything was all right. He stood on the porch, not coming in.

"Everything's just fine," Mother said, her arms crossed tightly over her chest. "We've won, as you can hear."

He straightened his tie with trembling fingers. "Who's this 'we'? And what do you think 'we've' won? We'll eat shit from this victory. We'll have it coming out of our noses."

Mother's eyes searched for an object. She caught hold of a potted plant and hurled it at his feet. "Get out of here, you traitor!" she screamed. "Go back to where you came from."

He looked down at the cuff of his pants, now filled with dirt, then up at her with his small, watery eyes. "Inès," he pleaded, "Inès."

She went inside, slamming the door behind her. He leaned on the porch rail, hiding his face in his hands.

"Go see if he's still there," Mother said, pushing me.

"He's still there," I said.

Through the blinds we could see him hobbling up the path. "Gone," Mother said.

Several days later he sent Florence Goldman over to talk to her. She stood in our entrance wearing dark glasses. Mother stared at her, astonished. "You're not a bit like your picture," she said, "not one bit."

"Perhaps the photograph is not like me." Florence smiled. "May I come in?"

"Of course," Mother said, catching herself but still unable to stop staring at Florence. "I would never have recognized you in a million years."

Florence was strong, athletic, with long, straight hair parted in the middle and a square face exuding frankness and affability. In seconds, she drained the glass of lemonade Mother gave her, wiping her mouth with the back of her hand.

She had come to Israel for a few days, so moved by the swift victory, she explained, that she had boarded a plane the minute the war had ended. For the past few years she had been working raising money for UNICEF.

"That must be interesting," Mother said shyly.

"Very," Florence said. Momentarily she was silent. "You must know why I've come, Inès," she began.

"He sent you," Mother said, averting her eyes, hardening.

"Not only," said Florence. "I wanted to meet you. I've heard so much about you, mostly from him."

"Don't mix me up in your affairs," Mother said, her anger building. "If you've something to say, say it."

Florence fingered the strap of her bag. "There are no affairs, Inès. And there never were. Not of that kind."

Silence.

"There's a Chinese proverb that says if you save someone's life you remain responsible for it because you interfered with fate. You've taken on the role of destiny," Florence said dreamily, as if talking to herself.

Mother shifted in her chair. "So what about this Chinaman?"

"Nothing." Florence shrugged her broad shoulders. "Just a story I remember. Inès, do you know what happened in Geneva, after he left Africa? Do you know what went on there?"

"No," said Mother. "I know nothing."

"He completely fell apart after Africa. He spent all the money he'd earned from selling the stories and photographs. He spent it on gambling, women, drink—you do know."

"Yes," Mother said.

"I hated myself for loving him. I knew what kind of man he was."

"Yes," Mother said.

"I could get over the love; I have discipline. But not the pity."

"Yes," Mother said.

"I supported him for a while, until he got back on his feet. That was how I got over the love."

"Yes," Mother said.

"I wanted to die, or make him die."

"Yes," Mother said.

"One day I found him in his hotel room. He had taken some pills."

"I didn't know that," Mother said slowly.

"Aspirin."

"Ah," Mother said.

"It doesn't matter. His health was so bad they had an effect. He was in the hospital for a month."

"He never told me," Mother said.

"He never told himself, either. He claimed it was an ulcer attack."

"He really does have an ulcer," Mother said.

"But that wasn't it."

"That wasn't it," Mother repeated.

"I got over it all. But it took me years."

Mother glanced at Florence's neck, at her bare arms in the short-sleeved summer shirt. "Don't you have that skin disease anymore?"

"I didn't get over that," Florence said, laughing, pulling up her shirt to expose the red rash across her stomach. "I still have it."

She picked up some cake crumbs from the edge of the plate. "Robert loves you very much."

"Yes," Mother said.

"And you him, I think."

"Yes," Mother said.

"So what will you do?"

"Nothing," Mother said. "What's done is done."

We walked with Florence to the bus stop, barely keeping up with her long, energetic steps. "So this is the little one," Florence said, looking at me, suddenly melancholy.

"This is the little one," Mother confirmed.

Florence took both of Mother's hands, pressing her palms together. "I'm so happy to have met you, Inès, really." She threw her head back, breathing deep. "What a life." Then she rummaged in her bag and took out a small camera. "Do you know how to take a photograph?" she asked me.

"No."

"Come, I'll show you where to press."

She placed her arm around Mother's shoulder; she was two heads taller. Mother looked up at her in awe. "You're not at all petite. Why did they call you petite?"

"Who did?" Florence asked.

"Everyone, according to Robert."

"Robert," Florence echoes. "Robert." They look at each other and laugh.

"Laugh?" Nona Fortuna asks, amazed. "What do they have to laugh about?"

"I don't know," I say, "but they're laughing. Looking at each other and laughing."

Nona Fortuna is curious. "What's she wearing?"

I pore over the photograph. "Some kind of suit. A skirt, a jacket, and a white shirt."

"Haute couture?"

"How should I know? Just some suit."

"You should know, *ma chérie*," she rebukes me. "You'll never be *une vraie dame* if you don't know. Even if you don't wear these things yourself you must recognize them on someone else. You have to understand these things."

"I don't want to be *une vraie dame*. Leave me alone."

But she does not. She takes me to the Christian mission school in Jaffa. "Just to have a look around," she says.

There is a fountain in the inner courtyard. She listens to the water, turning her face so the slight puffs of wind bring her its spray. "See how lovely it is," she says.

"Do the parents consent?" the head nun asks gently, tucking a curl under her wimple as she examines me discreetly.

"They will," Nona Fortuna promises. "The father has left and the mother has it hard, *vous savez*," she says as if sharing a secret.

"Forget it, Maman," Mother says. "Absolutely not."

"Do you want her to grow up like everyone else around here?" Nona Fortuna protests.

"Why shouldn't she grow up just like everyone else? What's so terrible? What is she, *bint al-paschari*? The king's daughter?"

"We'll convince her, don't you worry, *sit al-banaat*," Nona Fortuna says once Mother has gone. "You'll see," she says, holding open her dry eyes, soothing them with drops from a tiny bottle, then drying her damp cheeks with a wad of cotton.

"*La vraie Inès*, I left her behind in Egypt," she sighs to herself. "*La vraie Inès.*"

Missing Photograph: The Cathedral of Saint John the Divine, New York, February 1989

Armando, the owner of a large apartment building on Seventh Avenue and an expert at locating missing persons, wants to know the story behind the photograph. After all, he has to do the work, and he has no patience for hints, euphemisms, and diffidence, especially when they have to be translated from a foreign language.

He has a pleasant office in his apartment building, grandly tiled in marble and hung with icons and large drawings of ships, of the *Niña*, the *Pinta*, and the *Santa Maria*. Yet for some reason he prefers to meet us on a bench in Central Park near the placid pond ringed with red stones, the one where children launch miniature boats on Sunday mornings.

From one ship to another, Father jokes, but Armando is ill at ease with frivolity. He thinks for a minute before stretching his thin lips in a wan smile that is more like the symbol of a smile, the hint of a smile on an otherwise immobile doll face.

He is wearing a long green wool coat in whose pockets metal objects clink: keys on chains, coins, safety pins, brass buttons. His stubby fingers fumble inside the pockets, burrowing like hard-working animals, making shapes in the cloth. They scrunch into fists, catching hold of coins or gathering clumps of lining and rolling it over and over.

For a long while Armando studies the picture and makes notes on a tiny pad. Row upon row of crowded letters cling to one another. He has a method: first he lists his questions, then he reads them, in order, in a flat, noncommittal tone.

Father paces restlessly around the bench, kicking the frozen earth and rubbing his arms against his chest to warm them. His narrow eyes, bright slits, tear from the wind. "What?" he asks in a thick, unnatural voice through the scarf wound twice around his neck and the lower part of his face. "What did you say, Mr. Armando?"

Patiently, with almost mocking calm, Armando rereads his question. "When did you last see her?"

"No, no," Father says.

Armando looks at him coldly, waiting. "He's asking when was the last time you saw her," I translate.

Father calculates in silence. "Forty-four years ago."

"The Holocaust." Armando nods in sympathy, scribbling in his little book.

Father watches the letters fill up the page like the black prints of birds' feet. He pauses before pulling the pen out of Armando's hand and hurling it to the ground. "No Holocaust, no camp, Mr. Armando, understand? Egypt, you know what is Egypt? Good life, good people, good country, no Holocaust. You visit Egypt, Mr. Armando?"

"Unfortunately not," Armando says curtly, bending toward the ground, carefully lifting the pen, and wiping the length of it twice with a tissue.

The three of us start walking. Armando has asked us to sign some forms in his office and to give him a copy of the photograph. On the way he explains his plan: Enrique and Maria, his two assistants—who happen also to be his children and business partners—will conduct a search of the hospitals, prisons, psychiatric wards, and shelters for the homeless in Manhattan while he, Armando, will poke around Nadine's old neighborhood in Queens.

"Nay-deen," Armando says, emphasizing the first syllable with his American accent. He waves jovially to some bicyclists in green helmets who are pedaling in a tight line on the road that circles the park. One squirrel and then another race across the path, skirting a speeding bike wheel and disappearing into a small hole at the bottom of a thick oak trunk. Father stops to take a picture, braying with affection and pleasure. "Look, look," he says, wiping the camera lens with his sleeve. Thick, heavy rain drops fall on us, on the diligent bikers, on the stone walls, on the winding road, and on the piles of withered orange leaves that lie mangled in the brownish, pasty mud.

Father picks up a plastic bag, puts it on top of his head, and blinks worriedly at the blank gray clouds overhead, punctured in the distance by the spires of tall buildings. Halos of yellow light gleam around the stolid streetlights.

He sticks a damp, bent cigarette between his lips and rolls it from side to side with his tongue. "The weather is terrible," he says, impatiently searching his pockets for a match.

Armando retrieves one of his many key chains, this one a fat metal all-purpose rectangle: it is a lighter, a ballpoint pen, and a miniature calculator. Father opens his coat to shield the tiny flame from the wind and rain and tilts his face down toward Armando's tawny hands as if about to kiss them. The hem of his pants trails in the mud. "You've picked a fine time to light a cigarette," I say, raising my voice, trembling with cold and shame.

At night, in the hotel room that stinks of disinfectant and musty bed linens, Father offers me a pill and some cognac. "Take it, take it, it's good for the nerves," he urges me. I place the pill on my tongue, swallow two gulps of water, cringe at the bitter taste, spit out a thin, whitish slime.

My father places another pill in a plastic spoon, crushing it in the bowl with a knife, then mixing it with a little water and sugar. "Here," he says. "This is for children."

On and off, I sleep for sixteen hours. The people above us drag furniture across the wooden floor and stamp their feet, the pipes rattle, and the sirens of fire trucks and ambulances go wailing past. During the night I open my eyes three times to see the same dingy greenish light, the same curtain with its green circle pattern. Once I hear a rustle of papers and the hum of an electric shaver. I restore silence by pulling the two rough blankets up to cover my face and ears. Before I fall back asleep, I sense strange movements in the room, large shadows that cross the mirror opposite the bed: a shirt on a hanger swaying gently from the window to the closet and back, vanishing for a moment in the corner of the room, then reappearing, no longer a shadow but a white spot in the dark. "Are you awake?" Father asks.

• • •

We gulp coffee from paper cups and eat doughnuts that Father has bought from the place on the corner. "Armando called," he says. "He wants five hundred dollars up front. He's also got a few ideas about where she might be."

"Where?" I ask.

"I didn't get what he was saying—he spoke too fast. I couldn't catch it. I said we'd meet him at four."

I take a long time in the shower, washing my hair twice and rinsing it slowly. Father talks to me from behind the closed door, his voice louder and softer, depending on where he is in his ceaseless movement about the room. "I sold the camera to a guy downstairs. He gave me a hundred dollars. We bargained for more than an hour but in the end we settled on a hundred."

The chipped enamel of the bathroom sink quickly becomes littered with tangled black hairs. I brush my hair hard to untangle the knots, then scrape it back tightly into a ponytail. It takes some sawing with the scissors to cut the ponytail off all the way down to the roots. I pick the wet clumps up off the floor, wrap them in toilet paper, and throw them in the wastebasket.

"What have you done to yourself?" Father asks when I finally emerge from the bathroom. "*Now* how are we going to find her?"

"I'll cover my head," I say, "with a hat or a scarf. The hair won't make a difference."

He is not listening. He is shaking his head from side to side, hands at his temples. "Look," he says, hurrying over to the dressing table. He takes a photograph out of a manila envelope and waves it at me. "Look at her hair. Of course there's a difference."

Nadine is there in black and white, leaning on the high porch railing. The long arc of her crossed thighs is visible beneath the thin dark cloth of her calf-length dress, which falls about her legs in soft asymmetrical folds. Her feet are bare. One large toe is flexed and the little one is extended to the side at a noticeable distance from the other toes. Nadine is staring straight at the camera, at the photographer, at us, clasping her long, thick hair in one hand to reveal the sharp curve of her cheek and her sunken temple. Her other hand is resting on her chest. If you look closely you can see she has grabbed a button of the dress as if to pull it off. The background is blurry, barely distinguishable from the sleeves of her dress, whose narrow white cuffs stand out in the dark, gently cradling her wrists. She is smiling, a broad, generous smile that spreads across the width of her face, baring two buck teeth and stretching the large brown birthmark in the space between upper lip and nostrils. Her smile fills the photograph, bursting with life, nearly leaping out of the frame, wonderful and ominous both. She is seventeen years old, with an insane mother whose fortune has been squandered, a dissolute father, and a brother who nightly waits for her on street corners, asking for money, for the money she makes giving private lessons, a brother decked out in a rakishly tipped hat and a fine three-piece suit: my father.

She had wanted a great deal from life, Nadine, but pride and unnatural sensitivity—mirrored in those brown eyes hooded by thin, capillary-laced lids—had consumed her . In other times she might have been blessed. I did not know much about her, really. Bits of her life were disclosed to me as part of the family history—a photograph or two, a footnote to a story, memories of a dress she had worn, a sentence she had spoken, a light under a

closed door at the end of a long corridor announcing that someone was always home.

Arms entwined, she and her mother walked the streets of
Cairo. She took in laundry, though the skin of her hands bled
from the rough soap. Kind neighbors sent over meat patties and
baked goods wrapped in greasy newspaper. She sang beautifully.
The big house, full of the remnants of a fading grandeur, was
home to the stray dogs and cats she gathered in; at night she
would search the street for her cats, tapping a tin of food for
them and calling, "*Viens, ma douce, viens, ma jolie.* Come my
sweet, my pretty." Three times she slit her wrists and survived.
She learned to kosher chicken and light Sabbath candles when
they married her off to a rich observant Jew twenty years her
senior, who bore her away to America.

She had children and worked as a librarian at a public library
in Jackson Heights, Queens. She wrote a dissertation on Emily
Dickinson. She liked to quote Emily Dickinson in the slim pale-
blue letters that pursued Father to his various addresses. "After
great pain," she wrote, "a formal feeling comes."

There were five such letters, one every seven years or so,
written in a mixture of French, Arabic, and English that had neither the spontaneity of spoken language nor its nuances of tone
and music. "*Ta'aban in kan yinzal min battan ummeinu, kan
ahsan minnac,*" she had written in broken Arabic to Father two
years ago. "Had a snake come forth from our mother's belly, it
would have been better to me than you have been," he reads to
me, stressing each word of this, her last letter. Father takes a pen
and corrects her spelling, his sulky lips twisted in effort or pain.

We are alone in this city, isolated even from each other, seeing things that are hard to describe. Father has brought me
along to search for his sister so that she can forgive him, so that

he might die in peace. "If those are the words in her heart, neither of us can die in peace," he says over and over.

"So what's your plan?" I ask him.

"Don't be cruel," he says, smearing his dry hands with cream. "Don't be cruel just for the hell of it—I've had my share."

I get dressed: two pairs of socks, two sweaters, pants, gloves, a scarf, a short jacket, an overcoat, and a kerchief around my head. "Stop feeling sorry for yourself," I say.

We leave. His back has gone out and the elevator is broken. We walk down the stairs slowly, one stair at a time. "Just as long as we don't miss him," Father says, sitting on a broad window ledge to rest for a moment. He crosses his thin legs in front of him as if for the first time in his life; one swings forward awkwardly, clumsily, slipping off the other and falling to the floor. His hand grasps his side. "My back is killing me." The boy at the reception desk blinks at us, a vague greeting. He hates us: we don't tip.

Outside, the cold is biting but the light strong, bright, exhilarating. We walk along Fifth Avenue to the park, swallowed up by the indifferent mass that swells toward us, gathering us up with neither an embrace nor a struggle. Father studies our reflection in a store window.

"You'd be better off without the kerchief. At least he could see your face," he says.

"My face is freezing," I say. "This cold is slicing through me."

"At least take it off when we meet Armando, so he'll recognize you," Father persists stubbornly.

"He's looking for *her*, not me," I say.

"He won't recognize her in a million years. Even I won't," says Father.

"Of course you won't," I say.

"Of course," he repeats, fascinated by the image reflected in the glass, by his face, etched by four crooked channels of tears that wend thickly, sluggishly toward his chin. A group of Japanese tourists with cameras pushes us right up to the edge of the window. Father wipes his face with his scarf.

"What are they taking pictures of, those people?" he asks.

"It's Versace, the designer. They copy his clothes," I explain.

"How do you know that?" he asks suspiciously.

• • •

We are late for the meeting but Armando waits, hidden by a large newspaper. He chews gum, then discards it, replacing it with a fresh piece. "We have some leads," Armando says, thumbing through his little notebook. "Let's go sit someplace," he suggests and we walk to a bar. Father drinks Armagnac, Armando and I tea with milk. Armando dumps two packets of sugar in his cup, stirring and stirring.

"One thing's for sure," Armando says. "She's not here."

Father blanches to his ears. "Then where is she?" he asks.

"Where?" Armando brings a steaming teaspoon of tea to his mouth and blows on it. "She was last seen leaving her building and walking down the street a year and a half ago. She was wearing a gray tweed suit and a hat and carrying a large shopping bag and an umbrella. Three people remember seeing her: the Korean who owns the grocery store, a neighbor in the building, looking out from her window on the fourth floor, and another neighbor from across the street. They watched her for a long time, it seems, fifteen minutes or more, because she was engaged in—how should I put it?—some unusual activities," Armando says, reading aloud from his notebook. "At the first corner she opened her shopping bag, took out two coats and a scarf, and hung them on a tree, one after the other. At the next corner she took out a small reading lamp and left it on the sidewalk, then dropped pages torn from the New York City phone book. The lady on the fourth floor went out and picked them up. At this point the witnesses' stories diverge, all of them leading nowhere, I'm afraid." Armando continues. "The lady across the street thinks she later saw her up by Saint John the Divine's rummaging through a garbage can for empty soda bottles like the homeless people up there. You know, you can get five cents a piece for them. But who knows what this lady actually saw? People get some funny ideas going. They think they're telling the truth but half the time they can't tell the difference."

"Of course," Father says uncertainly.

"The second version," Armando says, "is even weirder, and frankly, I wasn't sure whether to tell you about it. To be perfectly honest, I don't set much store by this stuff, this supernatural stuff. Such phenomena inflame the imagination, though in truth tales of the supernatural are always crude and unimaginative. I don't have any patience with them."

"What is he saying?" Father asks, tugging at my sleeve. "I don't understand what he said."

"Nothing," I answer, keeping my eyes on Armando. "He's just talking in general, not saying anything about Nadine. What do you mean?" I ask Armando. "Where is she?"

"Well, in plain English, she flew away. Mary Poppins, Peter Pan, that sort of thing," Armando says, his nose in his notes. "At the corner of Fifty-ninth and Sixth, on the twenty-third of November, 1987. That's what the police have a dozen sworn witnesses saying. A woman in her late fifties, wearing a gray suit, opened her umbrella at the corner of Sixth Avenue, kicked her feet twice, and began to fly west, toward the Hudson River."

"That's impossible," I say.

"That's what I thought," Armando agrees. "That's why I tracked down the witnesses. I showed them the photograph and they all identified her beyond a doubt."

I translate for Father. "Which photograph?" he asks.

"Well, this one," says Armando, pulling the copy from the large pocket of his coat.

Father crushes a cigarette under his foot. His voice is thick and choked. "Is not my sister. My daughter. Look."

"It doesn't matter, Father. Forget it," I say.

Armando closes his eyes and lets his head fall back against the back of the banquette. "You gave me this picture, sir," he says in a clipped tone.

"Yes," Father says, then turns to me. "But just so that he'd get a sense of what Nadine looked like when she was older."

"So this is not your sister, then?" Armando asks.

"No, it's me," I answer. "I look like her. Father explained it to you in the park."

Father interrupts. "This one my sister, more than forty years now. This," he says, placing the blurry photograph of Nadine in front of Armando and thumping it.

Armando looks at me, then studies the two photographs again. "There's no resemblance at all."

"Take the kerchief off," Father orders.

"No," I say.

"Take it off or I'll knock your head off." Now he is shouting. The people in the adjacent booths turn toward us, and the waiter approaches our table.

"Did you want something, sir?" he asks with acid civility.

Father grabs Armando by the sleeve, pleading. "She cuts her hair. Mr. Armando, she cuts her hair."

Armando breaks free of my father's grasp and stands to put on his coat. "I don't think I can help you, sir."

My father does not let up, following him to the door and then out to the street. "Why, Mr. Armando, why?" In broken English, my father begs the detective to stay. The waiter runs after them with the check; Armando takes a bill from his wallet and tosses it at him. Finally they come back in. "Armando will try something else," Father announces. I get up to leave, but Father catches hold of me. "Where do you think you're going?" he asks, shaking me until the kerchief slides down my neck. "Where do you think you're going? Just when I convince him to continue!" People at the bar stare at my cropped head with its jagged clumps of hair.

Armando tries to talk sense to me. "Please stay, miss. You're the only rational person here."

"How do you know?" I say. "What makes you say that?"

"I can tell," he says, patting my head. "I have become all things to all people, miss."

. . .

We are back in the hotel room. Very quietly, Armando asks us to begin all over again. "Where did you last see her?"

"At the train station in Alexandria forty-four years ago," Father says to me so I can translate. They are all standing with their backs to the grand entrance of the station—Nadine in the center, Father to one side, and a small elderly woman in bulky clothing to the other. Nadine is holding the two of them close, one hand resting on the shoulder of my father, who is half a head taller than she is, and the other tight around the waist of the old lady, who is leaning a thick head of hair studded with hairpins on Nadine's breast, clinging to her, one eye open wide for the camera and the other hidden in the lapel of Nadine's dress. Her pale broad-brimmed hat casts a shadow on Nadine's face, leaving only the slightly parted lips completely visible. Nadine is thin: the belt of her dress is wrapped around her waist twice and tied in front in a large, tight knot; the shoulder seams droop halfway down her arms. At some distance behind the group is a man in a pale suit and fez, balancing a walking stick on his forefinger. It's her husband, and they are leaving for America. The hands of the round clock above the entrance—directly above Nadine's head—read twelve-thirty.

"Will you take care of her?" Nadine asks, brushing cake crumbs from the old lady's chin. "Will you take care of her, Robert, for me?"

"Of course," Father says, lifting his eyes toward the clock. "I'm just going to buy some cigarettes," he says. "I'll be right back."

He does not come back. Two trains leave. The old lady soils herself. Nadine cleans her, pulling men's long underwear over her legs and wrapping her in a blanket. Still Robert does not come back, so they take the crazy mother to America. First there is the night train. She wanders the cars and fondles the faces of the sleeping passengers. Nadine gives her a silk handkerchief to stroke instead and keeps her busy sorting buttons, separating the red ones from the white and the black. She whispers poems in the old lady's ears. In the morning the train reaches its destination. Nadine sprinkles eau de cologne on the floor of the sleeping car to cover the stench. The old lady is curled in her chair, her face pale. "*Ta'aban in kan yinzal min battni, kan ahsan minno,*" she says in a clear voice over and over, slowly. "Had a snake come forth from my belly, it would have been better to me than he has been." The more she says it, the duller the sounds become, sounding a heavy, weary truth.

She died a year later. Two years after that Nadine wrote to her brother: the night train, the passengers, the eau de cologne, her husband's underwear. Had a snake come forth from our mother's belly, it would have been better to me than you have been.

"I wasn't a snake," Father protests. "I was a man with all the weaknesses of a man, a weak man." He admitted it to Nadine. "I was always weak," he wrote her. "Nadine," he wrote, "I am only human." She never forgave him and now she has vanished. "Somewhere in the world there is forgiveness for everyone, even for the likes of such a weak man, even for people who have done worse things than that," he wrote. "*Je t'en prie,* Robert," she replied, "I beg of you, do not torment me." "Can you understand that?" Father asks. "Can you explain it?"

I am lying on the hotel bed with the blanket over my head. What is there to understand? I think. There's nothing to understand. You were always in the wrong place, doing the wrong things, saying the wrong things, leaving some ugliness behind you, some little pool of tragedy, someone's face streaked with sorrow. Every word you say hurts, whether it's good or bad. And still, your words are the center of the world for me, Father.

"Say something," he pleads, bending over me abjectly, like a fawning waiter. I stay as I am, warm, drowsy, covered by the blanket. "At least eat a little something," I hear him say, but I am too exhausted to eat, too exhausted even to answer, unable to stop myself from drifting off.

An aluminum tray is sitting on a white bath towel spread at the end of the bed. Armando has ordered curried chicken, vegetables, rice, and thick coconut sauce. He hugs his tray to himself in a corner of the room near the dressing table, carefully cutting the meat with a plastic knife, one paper napkin stuffed in his collar and another spread across his knees. He does not disturb us and we do not bother him; to each his own. We wait. Armando throws the remains of his meal into the wastebasket in the bathroom and stays there for some time, coming out washed and shaven.

He surveys the room. "It doesn't make a good impression," he says. He tidies the bed, plumping pillows and tucking in the corners, working around me.

Father mops his brow with a damp towel. He's hot from the spicy food, the heating; maybe he has a temperature. "Why you are doing all this?" he asks Armando, sitting in the easy chair, legs splayed, eyes closed.

"I have a lot of respect for detail," Armando says. "Order, routine, facts, secrets, a wisp of a tune whistled absently. The little stuff. This is what sustains us, the secret ceremonies of the soul that steel us as we face death or the unknown."

Armando examines the drawers. He opens them one by one and lays their contents on the bed. He picks out a pressed white shirt. "Wear this," he tells my father. Father puts on the shirt and Armando buttons it. "Now a jacket," he orders. Armando gives my father pomade to comb into his thick hair, to tame it. "You should have got a haircut," he says. There is a knock on the door: Enrique, Armando's son and right-hand man, arrives. His small skull protrudes above his large coat and heavy backpack like the head of a tortoise from its shell. He unzips his coat to reveal a Polaroid camera hanging from a cord around his neck. "Quick," Armando tells him. Enrique photographs Father in the chair, Father leaning on the desk, Father peering from behind the shower curtain in the bathroom, and then me on the bed, under the blanket. Armando examines the photographs, chooses two, and pins them to our coats. Father pulls gently at his. "It's okay?" he asks, concerned.

A yellow cab is waiting for us downstairs. Enrique sits in front, the three of us in back.

"Why we have the photographs?" Father asks.

Armando says nothing, staring ahead. Father sighs. "Gum?" Armando hands him a stick of gum, removing the wrapper first. We are driving north along Amsterdam Avenue. There seem to be young men everywhere, some on the sidewalk, some in the street, boys in leather carrying children on their shoulders, kicking empty plastic bottles and cans of soda.

My father is sweating, fingering his photograph, chewing his lip vigorously. Enrique asks the driver to stop at Saint John the Divine. The great stairs leading to the cathedral are wide and dark. The driver points to the meter.

"It's still running," he warns.

"All right, all right," Enrique says as he leans his head out the open window and snaps photographs, pulling them from the camera one after the other and tossing them back at us. The pictures are all blotches of darkness with bands of pale color. Father holds up the fresh prints and whimpers softly.

"This is going to hurt," he says. "I know this is going to hurt."

"Shh," Armando silences him, pointing at the vast church doors, which open with a heavy metallic clatter. An old bald man in a priest's robes comes out with a hose and douses the homeless people sleeping on the stairs. They form a line, taking plastic cups and wrapped sandwiches from the old priest. Armando opens the cab doors and orders us out. Father refuses. He covers his head with his coat and huddles in the corner.

"Don't hurt him," I say.

Armando and Enrique grab his arms and gently pull him out to the sidewalk. They drag him up to the top of the stairs and walk him past the homeless people, who look closely at the photograph pinned to his coat and shake their heads no. "*Yitgadal, v'yitkadash,*" Father implores, reciting the first words of the mourner's kaddish, pressing his forehead to the back of their hands.

"You, too," Armando calls down to me.

"But I didn't do anything," I say. A strong wind blows from the Hudson River and rustles our clothes, stinging our exposed skin.

Father wraps his arms around Armando's neck. "Leave her alone," he pants. "She has nothing to do with this."

"I have nothing to do with this," I repeat, pulling my coat more tightly around me as I climb the stairs.

Armando is indifferent to the arm tugging at his neck, to Father's body hanging off him like a chimpanzee. "In that case it's much worse," Armando says. "But let's go in."

We enter the cathedral, mingling with the others, who pass before us, walking toward the altar and the preacher's lectern. They line up by height in three rows. The old priest has exchanged his brown robes for white ones with gold trim. He holds a conductor's baton. When he gives the sign, the ragtag choir starts singing: "Ol' MacDonald had a farm, ee-i, ee-i o." We sit in the first pew. Other than the homeless people, there is no one else in the vast reverberating chapel. "One, two, three, four," Father counts time aloud. Enrique photographs quickly, from three different vantage points: facing us, facing the choir, and lying on the floor at their feet. He holds the pictures out to us and we strain our eyes in the darkness.

"Where is she?" I ask.

Three large chandeliers light up all at once, igniting the cathedral, consuming the wooden pews and devouring the photographs. We drop them in fright, our fingers scorched. The burned image of Father stares up from the floor, his mouth large and black, his nostrils flared. "Well?" Armando asks. I wrap my father's blistered hands in a tissue and hold his thin brown wrists.

"I've never touched his hands before, Armando," I say in a foreign language, my mouth full of glue. "I am his little girl, I've always been his little girl. If three thousand nails were driven through my body and my tongue were torn from my mouth, I would still let the world know I'm his little girl. That's what I am, forever and always. He is my father and I am his child."

"Well," Armando says slowly, "what now?"

Missing Photograph: Left to right: *Uncle Sicourelle, Nadine, Father, Cairo, 1945*

In order to really see a photograph you have to avert your eyes or simply shut them," Zuza announces, shutting her eyes and thrusting her chin forward.

Embarrassed, Mother pulls her pearls out from under her white collar, shifts uneasily in her chair, and reluctantly glances at the photograph Zuza holds out to her. "Drink your tea, Zuza. You haven't drunk a thing," she says.

Zuza had called the night before, eloquent, fervent, shooting rapid-fire French in an American accent and English in a French accent.

Mother listens for several minutes. "Who did you say you were?" she asks, confused.

"Suzette. Suzette, Nadine's daughter. Zuza."

"Ah, Zuza." Mother's face clears. "You are Zuza. You sound all grown-up, Zuza."

She arranges to meet us in the lobby of the Tel Aviv Hilton the next afternoon, three-thirty on the dot. "She said 'on the dot,' " Mother notes with annoyance at four-ten, examining the polished lip of the coffeepot. "Do you think it's real silver?" she asks.

Crossing the lobby at a run, Zuza arrives at four-thirty, a trail of typed pages flying from her notebook. A bellhop picks them up after her, carefully straightening them. "Please, Madame."

She blinks, pausing a moment before taking them. "Ah, thank you," she says.

She is thin and boyish, but with pendulous breasts that swing in front of her, spilling from the neckline of her blouse, giving her small, slight body the look of a toothpaste tube that has been squeezed from the bottom. Her face is girlish but bears the traces of vague sensuality, like the face of a sickly youth.

Mother looks her over warily: how she brushes wisps of greasy, dandruff-speckled hair back from her small forehead, how she pushes up her sleeves, how she smooths the surface of a photograph that she lays on the table, how she fusses over a tape recorder that she pulls out of her bag, tapping its speakers, blowing into the microphone, mumbling something, and then beginning in the tone of a lecturer, enunciating the words deliberately and pausing between them: "Tel Aviv, Israel, November 1986, Hilton Hotel. Tante Inès and *ma cousine* Esther, conversation."

"What are you doing, Zuza?" Mother asks, astonished.

"My work," Zuza says, sitting up in her chair and fixing a clear, steady gaze at us both. "I'm a journalist for the *Washington*

Post, Tante, surely you know," she says, shrinking back modestly, appealing to us with a childlike gravity.

"Yes, of course, *ya habibti,* my dear," Mother answers, pushing away with the edge of her shoe a slice of cucumber she notices on the carpet. Her eyes rove around the table, resting on the photograph near Zuza. "Your mother was so very beautiful, Zuza," Mother says tenderly.

"Really, Tante?" Zuza smiles with a sweetness that rearranges the sharp, jittery lines of her face, smoothing them into a nondescript blandness, like apple slices coated with dough. She slides the photograph toward Mother, then liberates it from her stubby nicotine-stained fingers.

Nadine is in the middle, squeezed between two men. Broad-hipped, the upper part of her torso flat as a playing card, two thick shoulder pads pushing up the polka-dotted fabric of her dress, she is leaning forward, faceless.

Uncle Sicourelle is lighting a cigarette for her. She is bending toward his hands, which have cupped the tiny flame. With one hand she presses her hair to her cheek so that it bisects her face, obscuring one eye, her nose, and half her chin. The uncle is looking at her bent head, at his cupped hands shielding the flame. His dense lashes throw a shadow on the high bones of his smooth cheeks. Only his eyes are cast down. He is standing straight, his shoulders square, his neck a short brown stump framed by two white lapels. The intentness of his downward gaze, the strained firmness of his shoulders and his neck make him seem more rigid than alive, his body frozen even before the camera froze it.

"That's Uncle Robert, isn't it?" Zuza says, pointing her red pencil at Father.

"Uh-huh," Mother says, absently resting her hand on the photograph, covering the other two figures and leaving only

Father visible at the picture's edge, his arm cut off, outside the frame. He is closest to the camera, pushed slightly forward by the people in the street who press and fill the spaces between their shoulders. His face is turned away, but he is holding on to Nadine's elbow as if to pull her after him.

"How old is he here?" Zuza asks.

"In his twenties," Mother says. She has turned to look out the large window facing the sea—at the lifeguard's station, where a rag flaps in the wind, at a man and his dog, at an orange surfboard left by the pier.

"Waiter!" Zuza suddenly calls in a high, chirpy voice. "Waiter! A tequila sunrise, please."

She gulps from the glass as soon as it arrives, then launches into a stream of nervous chatter. She is writing a book, two books actually. One deals with the family, with her roots. Roots are a very hot topic in America at the moment. A lot of people are writing books about them, articles, screenplays, she explains.

"There was that program on television, *Roots,* about those slaves and—what was his name?—Kunta Kinte," Mother notes.

"Exactly, Tante," Zuza says, nodding vigorously, pressing on. From what little she heard from her parents—after all, they weren't very talkative—she's gathered there's a story with immense dramatic potential. Colorful characters, the disintegration of the family, the disintegration of the colonial world, the dispersal—it's all very exciting. And not just as a story, she has to admit, but as a clue to where she's come from, who she really is. "What am I, who am I, what am I—that's what it's all about, Tante, don't you think?" she says, bringing the empty glass to her lips and replacing it at once, disappointed.

Mother agrees cautiously, as she hikes one of her stockings up over her calf. "Really, Zuza, that's very interesting. I hope you find out about what you said, about roots and all that." Mother says nothing for a moment, then slowly speaks again. "Do you have a family of your own, Zuza? I mean, a friend?"

"You're asking if I am married, Tante? No, no, I'm not married. My lifestyle makes it impossible. One week I'm in New York, the next in Washington, two days in Chicago, and I've just now come from Paris. I couldn't tie myself down. Besides, I have *un mauvais caractère,* a bad disposition, don't you think, Tante?" She laughs, exposing two rows of crooked teeth and a wobbly lower lip, pink and moist, that makes the bottom half of her face look unexpectedly vulnerable.

Mother peeks covetously at the dessert tray that is slowly making its way across the lobby with a clatter of wheels. "Where do they get them, strawberries, at this time of year?" she wonders aloud.

"They're probably from a can," Zuza pronounces, solving the enigma impatiently. "I'd like you to answer a few questions for me, Tante."

"Ask, *ya habibti,* ask," Mother says firmly, straightening in her chair.

"Did you know the parents of your grandmothers and grandfathers on both sides?" she reads from her notebook.

"No, I didn't know them. I heard a little about them, but I didn't know them. They never lived in Egypt."

"Who were they? What did they do? Do you know?"

"I've no idea, Zuza. Merchants, I think. Some came from Aleppo, some from Italy, Lebanon. We didn't have any of this—this roots. In our family you can't go back generations. We don't have all that much—what do they call it?—lineage, like you want."

"Forget about going back generations, Tante," Zuza says, agitated. "Look at me." She leans toward Mother. "Look at me. Do I have the face of someone with lineage? I ask you."

"I really don't know, Zuza," Mother mumbles, moving back. Zuza furrows her small brow in consternation, fingers pressing her temples. "What I'm trying to say, Tante, is that what interests me is just what there is—not what could have been, not what should have been, but just what *was*. Okay?"

"Okay," Mother agrees, eyeing Zuza warily, expectantly.

Zuza chews the end of her pencil, staring into space and then suddenly snapping alert, spitting a chewed bit of wood into the ashtray. "Where were we?" she says, flipping through her notebook, throwing a pleading glance at Mother. "I want you to try to remember what you know, what life was like, the people— every detail is important to me. Details are really important if you want to convey a vibrant, realistic picture."

"What was life like?" Mother considers. "It was very happy. We were all very happy in Egypt, much happier than here. We ate a lot, played a lot, did silly things. We laughed over every stupid little thing, Zuza, like children. That's what our life was like."

"That's all?" Zuza asks despairingly.

"I don't know. What more do you want to hear?"

"Describe the family to me, Tante. The traditions, the holidays, your education, everything."

"There wasn't any—I don't know—tradition. We were always eating from morning to night—we never shut our mouths! To this day I don't know where we put it all. Every morning these pushcarts would pass below our window. One sold all types of pastries, with cheese and potatoes and spinach and cold yogurt, and one sold *ful,* those hot fava beans, and hummus and hard-boiled eggs, and one sold rice pudding that you put in the oven, and one sold pickles, and another had little dishes of milk with a thick *eshta*—do you know what *eshta* is? It's the thick layer of cream on top. My father of blessed memory—his name was Jacquo—would call the man upstairs. My brothers would take the whole tray and poke their fingers into each of the dishes to skim off the layer. Father would pay the man for every dish they touched—sometimes twenty or thirty of them—so we could eat the cream. And that was just the morning, Zuza—I haven't gotten to the afternoon."

"Naturally, the women cooked and cleaned and served," Zuza says dryly, taking notes.

"The women, the servants, however it worked out. We would all sit together around the table. My father wouldn't let a crumb pass his lips until all the servants were at the table with us. He would even call the one who watched the gate, him and his family and children; they all sat with us around the table."

"Of course they were Arabs, the servants."

"They were Muslims. What else could they have been, poor things? They didn't want to let us go when we left Egypt. They came with us to the train, crying and kissing and hugging us. 'Why are you leaving?' they cried. 'Did we do something bad to you to make you leave us?' "

"But there were others, Tante, anti-Semites," Zuza says.

"Sure there were, *ya habibti*. Where aren't there? Weeds like that grow everywhere. Don't you have any in your America? Even here in Israel we have some."

She follows the frenzied movement of Zuza's pencil as it conquers more and more white space. And then there is Zuza's tongue, darting out to wet her thumb as she turns pages rapidly. "But why does all this interest you, Zuza? I mean, what is so special about it?"

"What's so special?" Zuza asks, lifting her head from her notebook. "You really don't see what's so special, Tante?"

"No," Mother says, "I don't. People live, they love, they leave, they die—what's so special about it?"

Zuza smiles broadly. "When you put it that way, Tante, it even sounds kind of miserable. But it all depends on your perspective. You can always turn something special into something dull and vice versa. Take this photograph, for example. What do you see there, Tante? Tell me."

"Three people in the street, that's what I see," Mother says briskly.

"Of course," Zuza says, momentarily conciliatory. "Of course. But how do they look, what do you feel toward them? That's the question, Tante."

Mother pushes her hair back. A look of impatience flashes across her face. "Perhaps you're right, Zuza. I don't understand much about all this," she says with mock humility.

"But you do understand, Tante Inès," Zuza cries excitedly. "You understand everything. Don't believe for a minute that you don't. That's what they've tried to put into your head all these years, that you don't understand."

Mother looks to either side anxiously. "Shh, Zuza, calm down. *Eib, ma chérie, aish yehesbouna i-nas?* My dear, what will people think of us?"

But Zuza does not let up. "Look and tell me what you see."

Reluctantly Mother returns to the picture. She says in a near whisper, "There's Jacquo, my brother, lighting a cigarette for your mother. That's before your mother got married. There at the end is Robert, Esther's father."

"Look again and tell me what you feel about them. Look hard and tell me off the top of your head. Pretend it's a game, Tante."

"A game?" Mother asks, studying Zuza closely, from her small, flushed forehead down to her crossed legs and her boot-clad foot, swinging nervously. "A game," she repeats slowly, knitting her brow as if in contemplation, then suddenly, decisively assenting and looking again at the photograph. "This one I love more than I love myself: my brother. Her—I never knew what to make of her. And as for him," she falls silent, dabbing her right eye. "Him—*Allah y'alam biha*. God only knows about him."

"What kind of man was Uncle Robert, Tante?" Zuza asks.

Mother turns toward the pianist at the end of the lobby, who had begun playing a familiar tune, then stopped and began something else. The tall waitresses in their black-and-white uniforms crowd around the door to the kitchen, their long necks revealed under their upswept hair; the impeccable maître d', in a red jacket and black shoes, tap-taps across the marble floor.

Mother speaks at last. "What did you say, Zuza?"

"I asked what kind of man Robert—your husband, Mother's brother—was."

"Why was, Zuza? Why do you say 'was'? He's still alive."

Zuza's cheeks, sucked in around the end of the pencil as if it were a lollipop, fall slack, flushing a bright, almost unnatural red.

"I didn't know, Tante. Forgive me. I thought he was no longer alive. My mother talked about him as if he were dead. Forgive me."

Mother gets up, smoothing her skirt. "We must be going or we'll miss our bus, Zuza."

Zuza extends a limp hand from where she is, still seated. "You're not leaving because of my nonsense, are you, Tante? Promise me," she pleads weakly, her fingernails absently peeling the blue paint off the pencil.

Hurriedly she collects her crumpled papers, stuffing them into the large notebook. "I'll go with you."

Her other book, she explains on the way out, is about Dr. Mengele. For a year and a half she has been researching it, delving into everything about him. Two weeks ago she made a startling discovery. She managed to get Mengele's wife to talk on the telephone. "She lives in France, Tante, did you know that?"

Mother did not know. She is not sure what doctor Zuza is talking about. "Which Mengele is that, Zuza?" she asks.

"The one from Auschwitz, Tante."

"Ah, that one," Mother says.

"That one," Zuza confirms. "Just imagine, Tante, I talked to her like a friend. She's a very outgoing woman. It's hard to believe that I actually got it out of her. My editor nearly fainted when he heard."

Mother is pleased at Zuza's happiness; she nods. A moment later she remembers to ask, "What was it you got out of her, Zuza?"

"The fact that we both love Marcel Proust. Can you believe it, Tante? Mengele's wife loves Proust! We talked for an hour and a half on the telephone about Proust!"

The doorman is shrouded in a black hooded coat. It has begun to rain.

"I'll get you a cab," Zuza says.

"No need, *ya habibti,* no need, the bus is right around the corner," Mother assures her.

"Absolutely not, Tante. I dragged you out here. Doorman," she says, "could you call us a cab, please?"

We wait inside behind the revolving glass door, watching the doorman out in the rain.

"I'd like to ask one more thing," Zuza says. "Are you sorry you left Egypt, Tante?"

"Sorry?" Mother is surprised at the question. "No, I'm not sorry. Sure, I miss it—I miss it like crazy. But I'm not sorry. Our life there was over, Zuza."

"But your roots are there, Tante Inès. What is there for you here?"

"Roots, roots, roots. A person doesn't need roots, Zuza, a person needs a home."

The doorman signals us to come, then holds a large umbrella over our heads as we hurry to the cab. Zuza hugs her narrow shoulders, squashing her large breasts.

"Don't forget me, Tante," she begs. "Write me."

Mother presses Zuza's narrow, wet head to her neck, kissing the deep part in Zuza's hair. "*Hali b'alec, ma chérie, ala nafsec.* Take care of yourself, my dear."

The back windshield wiper briskly flips streams of water from side to side, alternately revealing and obscuring Zuza, who stands just beyond the hotel's large canopy, wet, hugging her shoulders, indifferent to the black umbrella that the doorman holds above her.

"Tell the driver to stop here," Mother whispers to me, looking back apprehensively. "This ride could put us in the poor house."

Missing photograph: The Pool, Douala, Cameroon

For a week now the uncle has been padding about the house like an animal, driving everyone crazy. "You just don't know how to be sick, Chouchou," Madame scolded him this morning as I sat over my coffee, waiting for the explosion that, to my astonishment, did not happen.

Luckily the wound itself was not serious, a deep gash by the left armpit. But it was very close to the heart, and the doctor said another inch or two and matters would have been completely different. "What do you mean, 'completely different'?" the uncle bellowed.

Everything annoys him, every movement, every word, good or bad. He's always looking for a fight. Jean-Luc, who came to see him two days ago, claims that he's petrified. "Your uncle is scared to death," he said.

"So why doesn't he leave?" I said. "What's keeping him here?"

Jean-Luc thinks it's precisely the fear that's keeping him in Africa. "Monsieur Sicourelle loves danger," he said.

"And you?" I asked.

"I like it, but not the way he does. My life doesn't depend on it," he said.

We were sitting by the pool drinking Campari and sodas. We were talking quietly, almost whispering; it was nice. I was glad he had come. During the last few days life in the house had become more and more like a nightmare. It wasn't really clear what made things so nightmarish, but it felt as though a nightmare had just happened—or was about to.

Then one night I really did have a nightmare. I was wandering in a garden with a million paths and benches when I came to a low, arched doorway. I opened the door easily and found myself at the entrance to a cave. At my feet was a long row of stairs leading down. It was dark and hard to see. From the top of the stairs, I could make out a long chamber with a row of yellow lights on either side and all sorts of glass display cases. It reminded me of some sort of museum. Suddenly I felt an intense desire to pee like a boy. I couldn't stop the urge, much as I tried. I stood at the top of the stairs and peed down into the chamber in a large arc. Someone, a man in a white coat, moved inside the chamber. He, or someone else, said, "You've defiled the hygiene of the crematorium." It was awful the way he said it, just his disembodied voice. Especially the word "crematorium," which woke me up.

I told Jean-Luc about the dream, mainly because I wanted to forget it. "That's very interesting," he said when I finished. I hated him instantly. I got up and jumped in the pool. He jumped in, too, and started splashing me like a child. My eyes were stinging from the chlorine so I couldn't even open them. I yelled at him to stop but he just kept splashing me until I began to cough from all the water I was swallowing.

"What's the matter? Are you bored, Monsieur Jean-Luc?" I suddenly heard the uncle say from the edge of the pool, where he was watching. He was wearing a bathing suit. I had never seen him in a bathing suit or in any other clothes that revealed his body. I was astonished. His face and neck were tanned and dark to the chest and so were his arms, up to the line of his shirt sleeves. The rest of him was totally white—especially his huge belly above the black bathing suit. He had taken off the bandage and his wound was exposed. "You should bandage your wound," I said. "The doctor said you should leave it covered for a few days."

"Are you concerned about me, *ya* Esther?" he asked.

"Somebody has to take care of you, Monsieur Sicourelle, if you don't take care of yourself," Jean-Luc joked, getting out of the water and drying off.

The uncle joined him, pouring himself a whiskey. "It's nice of you to find time to think about me, what with all of your affairs, Jean-Luc," the uncle said.

I shrank at his mockery. I prayed he would leave and not make a scene.

"I don't have so many affairs, Monsieur. Work in an office has its routine, you know."

"Of course, of course," the uncle said, pretending to be jovial.

I saw he was watching me as I swam. He wanted to know if it wasn't a little chilly to be in the pool.

"It's thirty-seven degrees in the shade today," Jean-Luc told him.

The uncle took a deep breath. "I've been hearing things about your project," he said to Jean-Luc. "Things aren't going so well, I hear."

Jean-Luc seemed to blush. He said there were some problems but he thought things would straighten out. They were working on it.

"Yes, I'm sure you are," the uncle said. "It's important to remain optimistic. So what if it costs another billion? What difference does it make? The main thing is that the machine keeps going."

Jean-Luc sat frozen, not moving a muscle. "I think, Monsieur, that you've decided to insult me today," he finally said.

"Insult you? Why should I want to insult a guest in my house? I look at you, young man, and see only good intentions. Only good intentions."

"What are you saying? I think you should explain yourself, sir," Jean-Luc said, putting on his shirt.

I got out of the water. The uncle quickly held out a towel for me. I asked what was going on, what they were arguing about.

"We are not arguing, *ya* Esther. What have we to argue about? Sit here, dry yourself," the uncle said, lighting one of his stinking cigars. Suddenly I was shivering with cold.

Jean-Luc began to speak very quietly, obviously forcing himself to control his anger. "The fact that we're having problems with the project doesn't mean the whole business has gone bust, Monsieur. There are problems, and we will overcome them. We made some mistakes with the planning. We thought the bridge would hold up at that site. It doesn't mean that all is lost. Mistakes happen—it's only human. Surely you know this, Monsieur."

I didn't understand. "What happened to your bridge?" I asked Jean-Luc.

"Nothing so terrible," the uncle answered for him. "A few million down the drain, followed by a few million more. And all because mistakes are human. You see, *ya* Esther, they can't build a bridge in north Cameroon, where they wanted to. It's impossible to put a bridge there—the topography doesn't allow it. Any five-year-old could have told you that. But the big experts, they like to play games, sitting in their air-conditioned offices in Douala and Yaoundé. They thought they could build a bridge. And why not? They were paid good money to think that way. After all, this isn't France or America, where you go to jail for issuing fake permits. This is only Africa, the backside of the world. Isn't that right, Monsieur Jean-Luc?"

"Is it true?" I asked Jean-Luc. "Did you know that the bridge wouldn't hold up? Did you just keep quiet?"

He started playing with the ice cubes in his glass. "What could *I* have done? I'm just an insignificant cog, Esther. No one would have listened to me. From the start I thought we should have checked out the terrain more carefully. But they kept reassuring me that everything was all right. What was I supposed to do?"

"You could have resigned," I said to him. "You could have slammed the door in their faces. You could have quit."

Jean-Luc smiled sadly. "You're very young, Esther. Things don't work that way."

I felt disgusted—with him, with the uncle, with all of rotten Africa, with everything.

"At least tell me you filled your pockets," I said to Jean-Luc. "Why are you trying to make it look better than it is?"

"I did all right," he said, taking his keys and leaving.

We sat there by the pool for about another hour after he left. The uncle kept feeling his shoulder, as if it hurt. "Does it hurt?" I asked.

"It's nothing," he said. "It's much better today." Suddenly he took something out of the pocket of his robe. "Here, you keep it."

It was my passport. Inside I found a plane ticket and some bills—I didn't count how many.

I began to cry. "I don't want to leave you like this."

"Like what, *ya* Esther?" he asked. "What are you talking about?"

"Like this," I said. "In this situation."

"There is no situation. It's all in your head. Life is a situation—there's nothing special about this."

"So do you want me to go?" I asked him.

"I want you to do whatever you want. Go conquer the world, *ya* Esther. You show them."

I didn't understand. Show whom? "Why are you letting me go now, when you wouldn't before?"

"Before was before and now is now," the uncle said, getting up and starting toward the house, dragging his feet. "Before was before and now is now."

I felt not a shred of happiness, not one. I didn't really want to leave, but I didn't want to stay, either. I felt a pain in my chest and a weakness in my legs, pins and needles, as if they had fallen asleep. I opened the passport: there was a note pinned to the bills. I could barely decipher the handwriting. The note said that the money was meant to cover my first few months of studying in France and that the rest should be put in the bank. There was a huge amount of money there, several thousand francs. I began to count but kept losing track and having to start over. Meanwhile, it got dark.

Madame came to call me to dinner and found me with the money on my knees.

"Are you still out here?" she asked, looking at the bills.

She sank into the chair beside me, staring at the water. "You did it, Esther. *Mille compliments, ma fille*—you won."

"What do you mean?" I asked.

"Don't play innocent with me now, Esther, after I've watched you for months, wrapping him around your little finger."

I wanted to throw something at her. "Do you think he should have given it to you? Would that have been better? At least I'll do something with the money!" I screamed.

"You really have some nerve, Esther, do you know that?" she said.

I don't know what got into me, but I stood up and threw the bills in the pool. "Go ahead, Madame, jump in," I said to her.

She couldn't believe her eyes. "Have you lost your mind? Have you gone completely mad like the rest of your family?"

I walked away. From my window I could see her bending over the pool, trying to fish out the bills. Madame doesn't know how to swim.

I stayed in my room the entire evening, starting to get my things together.

The uncle must have gone to sleep. I heard nothing from the living room. From time to time I peeked out at the pool. Some bills were still floating there, among the yellow leaves.

I wanted to tell Jean-Luc what had happened, to laugh with him about it. All of a sudden I missed him. I remembered how his face looked as he was leaving and the way he kept toying with his watchband with those lovely long fingers of his. I forgot why I'd been so angry with him. Suddenly I felt ridiculous and pompous, pouncing on him like I did. I got dressed and went out to the street, looking for a cab. Augustin had fallen asleep on the table in his shack. He didn't notice me leaving.

The driver drove around for at least twenty minutes, through parts of Douala I'd never seen, neighborhoods full of high-rises. I was sure he was trying to cheat me, but then he stopped in front of one of the apartment buildings. I checked the names on the mailboxes. I had never been to Jean-Luc's apartment although he had invited me over several times to see his photographs. He lived on the eighth floor. I rang three or four times but nobody answered. I was about to give up and leave when the door opened. Jean-Luc stood there in a robe, his hair all messy, as if he'd just gotten up. I apologized for waking him.

I hadn't, he said, peering behind me into the hallway. He looked a bit confused but invited me in. I sat down on a white leather couch. He lit the side lamp and sat opposite me.

"So?" he asked.

"Nothing," I said, looking around the room. "It's clean here."

"That's because it's cleaned," he said impatiently, picking a crumb up off the carpet.

I heard water flush in the bathroom. "Is someone here?" I asked.

"Not really," he stammered but I could make out a tall figure standing in the corridor in his underwear. Jean-Luc looked at me and then at the figure. "Come, Julien, come sit with us," he said quietly. Julien sat down in a far chair, crossing his legs.

Suddenly I burst out laughing and couldn't stop. I was practically in pain. Every time I tried to stop and say I was sorry, I started up again, giggling, hiccuping, even stamping my feet, which I couldn't seem to control. Part of me was thinking that something was wrong with me and wondering what it was.

Through my tears of laughter I saw Julien's face become hard, severe. Once or twice he moved toward me, but Jean-Luc said, "Leave her. She'll calm down in a minute."

He brought me a glass of juice. "Drink," he said. I drank, but spit everything on the pale carpet. Julien brought a cloth and kneeled by my side to mop up. Jean-Luc and I watched him, down on all fours, half naked, rubbing.

"I think you should go now, Julien," Jean-Luc said.

I was finally almost completely calm, except for an occasional giggle. By the time Julien came back fully clothed, I was quiet. "See you tomorrow, Mademoiselle Esther," Julien said, leaving.

Jean-Luc and I sat without speaking for a while. He leaned his head back on one of the pillows. I thought he had fallen asleep.

"I'll go now too," I said.

"How?" he said in a heavy, sleepy voice. "Wait, I'll drive you." But he didn't move, and neither did I.

"I'm going home," I said. "The uncle gave me my passport."

"Good," Jean-Luc said in the same voice. "I wish you every success."

"What about you?" I asked.

"What do you mean?"

"What will you do? I mean with your project and all that."

"The same. Just go on the same." He was quiet a moment. "You must be wondering about what you just saw."

"I think I know."

"What do you know, Esther? What do you know?" he asked gently, looking at me with affection and sadness.

"Well, that you and Julien are—together." I barely got the words out of my mouth.

"We're not 'together.' This is the second or third time he's been here."

"But there were others before him," I said.

"There were others," he said, holding out a cigarette. "Want one?"

We smoked, going out onto the balcony and looking down at the dark city. "You can hardly see where the city ends and the sea begins," I said, just to say something.

"So, you're leaving?" Jean-Luc said, suddenly reaching out and stroking my head. "What stiff hair you have, Esther," he said, taking my hands between his and rubbing, as if to warm them. "Stiff hair and soft hands," he said, resting his warm lips on my hands.

We hugged. Beneath his robe, which had fallen open, I placed my hands on his protruding ribs, on his slim, narrow boy's waist.

We lay down on one of the couches, chilled by the cool leather, wrapping ourselves in his robe. We lay in an embrace until morning, not moving so as not to fall off. I dozed every so often, waking in tears or in alarm. Every time I opened my eyes Jean-Luc's were wide open, gleaming in the darkness, waiting.

At six he got up and went to the kitchen to prepare breakfast. I heard the water run, the refrigerator door open and shut. I went and stood in the doorway, watching him. He changed the filter in the coffee machine, not letting on that he sensed my presence.

"It's strange what you have to go through before you realize that you love someone," he said with his back to me.

"Who are you talking about?" I asked.

"You know," he said.

Missing Photograph: Uncle Sicourelle, Christmas Eve, 1976

Thirty-two wooden crates packed with escargot in shredded curlicues of straw, twenty-five kilos of Norwegian smoked salmon, jars of caviar, cheeses, chocolate, wine, and champagne were flown in from France with the boy. They sat him atop one of the crates in the overloaded car, his little legs swinging under the blue wool coat buttoned to his neck.

"I'll sit next to him," Madame announces, clearing her way through the crates and packages in the backseat, landing on mountains of sweating salmon.

Richard and the niece press into the front seat beside Erouan, who stares into the rearview mirror for several moments, nailing the boy in his gaze. "Are you all right, *mon petit jeune homme?*"

he asks. The boy is preoccupied, carefully sticking chewing gum to the hem of his coat.

"Drive, drive on," Madame insists. "The little one is exhausted. Can't you see he's exhausted?"

Uncle Sicourelle is waiting on the terrace, pacing its length and width, his arms clasped behind his back, like a ship's captain surveying the sea, a smoldering pipe between his lips.

"Go say hello to Grandpapa," Madame Sicourelle instructs, pushing the boy. "Say 'Hello. How are you, Grandpapa?' "

The boy straightens up inside his coat, an insulted expression on his face. "I know what to say all by myself," he answers, going up to Uncle Sicourelle and shaking his hand. "Hello, Monsieur."

Uncle Sicourelle looks down over his belly, incredulous. "I can't believe it," he says, spreading his arms in astonishment or helplessness, then turning to go indoors.

Madame Sicourelle and Erouan look at each other. "He'll get over it, Fufu, you'll see," Madame says, unbuckling her spike-heeled shoes. "You can go now, Richard. I don't think we'll be needing you anymore today," she says.

Richard cracks his knuckles, looking at the child. "Yes, Madame," he says, not moving. He goes up to the child, taking something out of his pocket. "This is for you," he says, removing the wrapper, placing the long whistle in his mouth, and blowing. "It makes the sound of a canary. Do you know what a canary is, Cédric?"

Gravely the child examines the plastic yellow bird that is stuck on the end of the whistle. "I'm afraid to say I've never seen one," he says.

Snorting with laughter, Madame slumps over her shoes, still undoing the buckle. "Did you hear that, Fufu? He's afraid to say he's never seen one!"

"Don't worry, you will," Richard solemnly promises, shaking the little hand, then nodding toward the others as he leaves.

Uncle Sicourelle watches from the doorway, munching on a radish. "Take that coat off him. The boy will die of the heat," he says.

Erouan kneels opposite the boy, undoing the loops of the coat, fumbling with the buttons. "How the hell do you undo this?" he curses softly.

"Let me." The uncle pushes him aside. "Here, like this," he says, redoing the buttons Erouan has succeeded with, then unbuttoning them all. "You can take off your sweater too," he suggests. "Just keep your shirt on, like me."

The child studies the uncle's big white shirt. "I don't have such a shirt," he says.

"Just say the word and you will," says the niece. "Just say the word."

The uncle turns to her. "Are you making fun of me, *ya* Esther?"

Julien brings glass dishes with three globes of ice cream each, brown, white, and pink.

"I don't like vanilla," the boy says. "At home I never eat vanilla."

"*Trop gâté,*" Madame whispers to her son. "He's spoiled."

Erouan watches the boy through his whiskey glass with reddened eyes, sliding his silver key ring onto his finger and twirling it. "Stop that with those keys," the uncle bellows. "You'll drive us all crazy."

The stench of chlorine rises from the pool, spreading through the dense, humid air. The languid afternoon has turned to night without the respite of twilight.

The flies are being hit by the metal blades of the ceiling fan, to Madame Sicourelle's delight. "If it doesn't bring in any air, at least it kills off some of those flies," she says, fanning her face with her hand.

Spoons clink in the glass dishes; a distant siren wails; a sprinkler hums as sprays of water splash against the house and dribble in a thin stream to the edge of the tiles around the pool. In the dark foliage at the edge of the garden, dried leaves crush underfoot as Julien turns the sprinkler off before leaving. Silence falls briefly.

"Leave it on a little longer, Julien," Madame calls out. "It'll freshen things a bit." The boy falls forward onto the table, his straight hair dipping in a pool of ice cream. "The little one's fallen asleep," Madame Sicourelle says, wiping the sticky liquid from his hair with her fingers, then licking them. "So sweet," she says, her eyes welling. The four of them look at him, hostages to the scene and the ennervating humidity. The telephone rings. "I'll get it," Erouan says, suddenly alert.

The uncle picks the boy up, wrapping the tiny arms around his neck, carefully carrying him in and placing him on a couch.

The niece splashes her feet in the pool, her head bent toward the water and the yellow leaves that float there in sticky clumps.

"Another three days and you'll be gone, *ya* Esther," the uncle says from behind her.

"Yes."

"Have you got everything ready?"

"More or less."

"Good."

He sits down beside her heavily, sticking a hand in the water and then pulling back. "He's nice, the boy," he says slowly. "He's got his own personality."

"How long will he stay with you?" the niece asks.

Uncle Sicourelle looks straight ahead, beyond the pool, beyond the tiled wall and the green garbage cans by the gate. "We'll see."

For two days he watches the boy from a distance, taking note of his movements, the life he brings to the large house, to the high, somber rooms that seem to lighten because of him.

"We ought to change the furniture," the uncle says to Madame Sicourelle. "We haven't redecorated in ages."

She looks up from her shopping list in surprise. "You never noticed the furniture before, Chouchou."

"I did, of course I did," he says. "I just didn't say anything. But I noticed. It's all junk."

"Junk," he says with a wave of his arm to the arriving guests the next day, dismissing their compliments, opening and slamming doors for them before they've even had a chance to look inside the rooms.

The Cohens are the first to arrive. Madame peeks out from behind a curtain. Seeing them striding toward the house, she leaves her post in alarm and rushes up to her room.

"What's happened now?" the uncle asks.

"It's those new people, the doctor and his wife," Madame pants, taking off her dress and putting on another. "His wife is wearing something plain—I can't be too dressed up next to her. Go, go keep them occupied," she says.

"Esther will keep them busy," he says, shrugging his shoulders. "They're her people, these ones. *Ma nièce!*" he calls, dragging his floppy slippers. *"Où elle est, ma nièce?"*

"What a character," Dr. Cohen whispers in Esther's ear, watching the uncle examine the knives in the light, disgustedly discarding the ones with dried soap stains.

"What are you a doctor of?" the uncle calls to him from the other end of the room.

"Veterinary medicine," the guest replies. "I'm a veterinarian."

The uncle sits down beside him, staring at the man's large, protruding earlobes. "Where have you been?" he asks.

"A year in Zambia and two in Malawi with a delegation of doctors from various countries."

"Who were your patients—the animals?"

"Among others," the doctor says, chuckling. "The situation was so bad that sometimes I had to take care of people too. In Malawi I worked with an Israeli ophthalmologist who did cataract operations on children. I assisted him."

Gradually the large room fills—with scent, with glitter, with the delicate swish of one expensive cloth against another, the buzz of conversation and laughter, the tinkle of crystal champagne glasses and Christmas tree ornaments.

"It's strange to meet an Israeli here," the doctor says.

"Why strange?"

"I don't know, it's just odd. I barely belong here myself."

"He's my uncle."

Madame Sicourelle flutters in her silver dress like a giant moth. She seats the doctor and his wife to Esther's right, Jean-Luc to her left. "Take care of them, Esther," she says, pointing a bejeweled finger.

Jean-Luc catches Esther's hand under the table. "Is everything all right, *la nièce?*"

"Yes, everything's fine," she says, surveying the pristine tablecloth, the immaculate china trimmed in gold, the red roses scattered across the surface of the immense table, as if haphazardly.

"In Malawi," the doctor is saying as he piles pieces of cold salmon in lemon sauce on his plate, "a strange thing happened, one of those things that perhaps could happen only in Africa."

"What was that?" Jean-Luc asks with interest, leaning toward the doctor, his shoulder brushing Esther's.

"I was working there with this Israeli ophthalmologist, performing cataract surgery on some two hundred Malawian children who lived in a mission boarding school. They were totally blind."

Uncle Sicourelle gets up at the head of the table, waving a glass of champagne, tapping his fork against his glass. "*Mesdames et Messieurs,* let us raise our glasses in honor of the New Year!"

All at once white napkins are stained with red lipstick as crumbs of food are quickly wiped away. Full glasses are held aloft, and the toast is echoed. "To the New Year!"

"The operations were quite straightforward. Cataract surgery is really very simple, so it was upsetting to think that, just because of the terrible conditions there, these children—"

"And another glass," Uncle Sicourelle says, raising his voice and hoisting the boy onto the table, one arm around the child's waist. "Another glass in honor of my grandson, Cédric!" He brings the glass to the boy's lips, beaming. "Drink, drink," he says. "It's good."

"How long is the boy here for?" Monsieur Sendrice asks, filling Uncle Sicourelle's empty glass.

Uncle Sicourelle blinks. "For ever," he announces aloud, majestically looking over the diners. "For ever."

The niece chokes, coughing and spitting into her napkin, red-faced. "Are you all right?" Jean-Luc asks, patting her back. "Drink some water." She waves her arm no, forcing herself to swallow her saliva.

"In any case," the doctor continues, "the operations went well and the children were able to see. And then something really strange happened—"

"And one last toast, *Mesdames et Messieurs,* in honor of Esther, *ma nièce!*" the uncle calls out, resting his belly on the table and watching with satisfaction the glances and nods that ripple her way.

The doctor clinks his glass against hers. "There's no chance that I'll finish this story tonight."

"Go ahead," Jean-Luc encourages him. "It sounds fascinating."

"Well, when the operations were over, the children didn't want to see."

"What do you mean?" Jean-Luc asks in astonishment.

"As soon as they'd regained their sight, they began to go at their eyes with glass, nails, sticks—anything to make themselves blind again."

"That's incredible," Jean-Luc says.

"It really is. I don't quite understand it myself."

"What don't you understand, Doctor?" Madame Sicourelle asks, leaning toward him coquettishly. "Tell me what you don't understand."

Thick, flushed, a lone stringy lock of hair across his smooth bald pate, Monsieur Sicourelle pounds at the head of the table. One hand holds the boy sitting on his lap and the other bangs the table. The deep wrinkles around his mouth extend into his cheeks. He presents one profile to the camera and the other to Monsieur Sendrice, who sits at his right. "*À nous les Orientaux!* To us sons of the East!" he says fiercely into the other man's ear. "*À nous les Orientaux!*"